Skewered

After what seemed an eternity, a man with skin drawn tightly over the contours of his face flashed a badge at me and said he was Detective Kenner. I told him the whole story.

When I finished, he said, "You know the store has cameras. We'll be able to verify what you've said."

Of course. Why hadn't I thought of that? "So you'll be able to see who killed that guy and put him in the Dumpster."

"How do you know he was murdered?"

"Most people don't bleed spontaneously from the chest."

His cold eyes narrowed. "You're in a lot of trouble, Mrs. Winston. Being a wiseacre isn't going to help any."

Was he trying to scare me? "I didn't do anything. The store videos will back that up."

"Then how do you explain the blood on your sweater?"

The Diva Runs Out of Thyme

KRISTA DAVIS

BERKLEY PRIME CRIME, NEW YORK

THE BERKLEY PUBLISHING GROUP
Published by the Penguin Group
Penguin Group (USA) Inc.
375 Hudson Street, New York, New York 10014, USA
Penguin Group (Canada), 90 Eglinton Avenue East, Suite 700, Toronto, Ontario M4P 2Y3, Canada
(a division of Pearson Penguin Canada Inc.)
Penguin Books Ltd., 80 Strand, London WC2R 0RL, England
Penguin Group Ireland, 25 St. Stephen's Green, Dublin 2, Ireland (a division of Penguin Books Ltd.)
Penguin Group (Australia), 250 Camberwell Road, Camberwell, Victoria 3124, Australia
(a division of Pearson Australia Group Pty. Ltd.)
Penguin Books India Pvt. Ltd., 11 Community Centre, Panchsheel Park, New Delhi—110 017, India
Penguin Group (NZ), 67 Apollo Drive, Rosedale, North Shore 0632, New Zealand
(a division of Pearson New Zealand Ltd.)
Penguin Books (South Africa) (Pty.) Ltd., 24 Sturdee Avenue, Rosebank, Johannesburg 2196,
South Africa

Penguin Books Ltd., Registered Offices: 80 Strand, London WC2R 0RL, England

This is a work of fiction. Names, characters, places, and incidents either are the product of the author's imagination or are used fictitiously, and any resemblance to actual persons, living or dead, business establishments, events, or locales is entirely coincidental. The publisher does not have any control over and does not assume any responsibility for author or third-party websites or their content.

PUBLISHER'S NOTE: The recipes contained in this book are to be followed exactly as written. The publisher is not responsible for your specific health or allergy needs that may require medical supervision. The publisher is not responsible for any adverse reactions to the recipes contained in this book.

THE DIVA RUNS OUT OF THYME

A Berkley Prime Crime Book / published by arrangement with the author

PRINTING HISTORY
Berkley Prime Crime mass-market edition / October 2008

Copyright © 2008 by Cristina Ryplansky.
Cover illustration by Teresa Fasolino.
Cover design by Diana Kolsky.
Interior text design by Laura K. Corless.

ISBN: 978-0-425-22426-7

BERKLEY® PRIME CRIME
Berkley Prime Crime Books are published by The Berkley Publishing Group,
a division of Penguin Group (USA) Inc.,
375 Hudson Street, New York, New York 10014.
BERKLEY PRIME CRIME and the BERKLEY PRIME CRIME design are trademarks belonging to
Penguin Group (USA) Inc.

PRINTED IN THE UNITED STATES OF AMERICA

10 9 8 7 6 5 4 3 2

For my mom, Marianne,
my friend and my biggest fan,
who has always encouraged me,
even when I decided to become a writer.

ACKNOWLEDGMENTS

Many thanks to my agent, Jacky Sach, and my editor, Sandra Harding, without whom the divas would not exist. Special thanks to Janet Bolin, Daryl Wood Gerber, and Sandra Parshall, who read, critiqued, and offered insights with humor and patience. Thanks also to my valuable first reader, Betsy Strickland, as well as Susan Erba and Amy Wheeler, who showed me true friendship by enduring the ups and downs of my life over the past few years. And special appreciation to Trudy Wheeler, who knew just how a Frenchman might express disdain.

Finally, endless thanks to the Guppies for cheering me on and urging me to persevere. You are far too many to mention but you are undoubtedly the best friends I've never met.

To the residents of Old Town, I apologize for taking liberties with your beautiful city. Sophie's home and several other locations are blends of various places and are not based on any particular existing structure.

ONE

Live on *Good Morning Washington*!
Special guest in the Washington, DC,
television studio: Natasha

"*My very favorite holiday is Thanksgiving. No other day is so much about family and friends and fabulous food. By now, I hope everyone has sent out their invitations. We crafted these darling ones by ripping recycled natural-colored paper into the shapes of maple leaves. Don't cut them or you won't get this lovely soft frayed effect. Glue each leaf to a square of darker linen. Ours has a slight golden cast to it that says autumn. Then, with a calligraphy pen, handwrite a special note to each guest. Don't forget to make matching envelopes out of the recycled paper.*"

Natasha's velvety voice drifted up the stairs. I clenched my teeth at the sound. In sixth grade she started a rumor that I wet the bed at her slumber party. That scandalous lie had followed me to graduation.

I didn't actually hate her but found her annoying in the

way perfect people so often are. Even though I felt fairly content with my life, Natasha had a tendency to pop up and make me feel inadequate, like an embarrassed sixth-grader again.

We'd competed against each other for almost everything when we were in school—sports, grades, honors. Competition became the norm for us. I fought it but Natasha loved to act superior, which brought out the worst in me. I never entered her world of beauty pageants, though. She did quite well, but I took some satisfaction in the knowledge that she never won a Miss Congeniality title.

Who'd have imagined that Natasha would have her own lifestyle TV show on a local cable channel in Washington, DC, not to mention a lifestyle advice column? And now that my ex-husband, Mars, had set up housekeeping with her, the sound of her voice made me boil. It seemed like she was turning up everywhere lately. But not in my house!

I pounded down to the family room off my kitchen. My mother immediately changed the channel.

My sister, Hannah, reached for the remote. "Mom! I was watching that!"

Dad leaned against the doorway to the sunroom, a mug of coffee in his hand. "I warned them. You shouldn't be subjected to that woman in your own home."

"It's been two years since Mars and Sophie split. She told me she's moved on. Besides, it's not like Natasha had anything to do with their divorce." Hannah tugged the remote from Mom and switched the TV back to Natasha's show.

The baby in the family, Hannah wore her blonde hair long and loose like a teenager and still thought the world revolved around her even though she was about to turn forty.

My brother and I headed for Northern Virginia, just outside of Washington, DC, after college. But Hannah married two losers in a row and remained in Berrysville,

Virginia. Fortunately, she turned out to have an uncanny knack for computers, but I wondered if living in the same small town as my parents had sheltered her too much.

I stifled a sigh of frustration and headed for coffee. Less than twenty-four hours with my parents and sister and I already felt like a child again. I was forty-four, a competent, self-sufficient woman. How did they do that to me?

A fire crackled in the stone fireplace in the kitchen, dispelling the November chill. My dad must have lit it. Just being in my kitchen made me feel better.

Antiqued cream-colored Old World cabinets with plenty of glass doors had replaced drab brown ones. The new hardwood floor still gleamed, as did the Madura Gold granite countertops. But the very best part was the stone wall we uncovered when we renovated. Most likely part of the original house, the rough stones were thought to be ballast stones, used to weigh down ships crossing the Atlantic, then discarded in the streets in colonial times. A four-foot-tall fireplace with hooks for kettles made the wall the best feature in the room.

Built in 1825, my house retained its original Federal-style exterior with red brick walls and tall windows. But when Mars and I inherited it from his aunt Faye, the interior had been authentic 1960s flower power. Twiggy would have been at home in the kitchen with orange countertops and faded mod daisy wallpaper.

The heavenly aroma of fresh coffee and sizzling bacon wafted to me, and Mom joined me. I flashed her a grateful smile as I poured coffee into a Spode mug. I couldn't remember the last time someone else had fixed breakfast.

"Well, anyone can see you're single again," she said. "Married women don't wear flannel pajamas."

Ah. I'd been married long enough to have forgotten her rules for catching men. I leaned against the kitchen counter and dumped an extra spoonful of sugar into my coffee along with nonfat milk.

Mom, petite and trim, moved the sugar bowl away from me. "Now that you're single again, you can't afford to keep eating this way. That sugar will settle right on your hips."

How many times was she going to say "now that you're single again"? Would that be her constant refrain?

She handed me a plate with bacon and pancakes. A chunk of butter melted on the top pancake. I could eat *this* but wasn't supposed to take sugar in my coffee?

As though she could read my mind, she said, "They're pumpkin spice pancakes." Was the bacon made out of pumpkin, too?

"Your aunt Melly made the boysenberry syrup that's on the table. She was sorry she couldn't drive up for Thanksgiving, but she and Uncle Fred will join us for Christmas."

I straightened the picture of Mars's Aunt Faye that hung over the fireplace, poured syrup on the pancakes, and settled into my favorite armchair by the fire.

Mom busied herself at the sink like the Energizer Bunny. "I didn't get an invitation to Thanksgiving."

She was here, wasn't she? "You're the one who told me it would be at my house this year. I didn't think an invitation was necessary."

"Do you have an extra one? I'd love to see them."

I didn't want to spark an argument by telling her I hadn't sent invitations. It was just family; it wasn't like they didn't know where I lived.

"What kind of soup are you serving?"

"Soup?"

"Sophie! Haven't you worked out a menu yet? You know everyone has high expectations because you throw parties."

"I don't throw parties, I plan events."

"Natasha's serving squab and leek consommé in hollowed-out acorn squashes."

"Squab? She's serving pigeon broth?"

"Not pigeon, squab. Don't you watch her show? I think

it's very appropriate for Thanksgiving. Where does a person buy squab?"

I had no idea and I didn't care. The thought of cooking pigeons was revolting. Besides, could anyone really tell the difference between squab broth and chicken broth?

"Natasha smokes her turkey. She did an entire episode on smoking meats."

Wonderful. Natasha probably had an entire kitchen staff on hand to do it all, too.

"Her mother tells me that Natasha is dying to get her show on a national network. I'm sure it won't be long before people in California love her as much as we do. That girl perseveres until she gets what she wants." Mom frowned at me. "Do you always eat in that chair? Just because you're alone doesn't mean you should be sloppy."

I stuffed my mouth with pancake so I wouldn't be tempted to snarl at her.

"Hannah," she called into the family room, "are you dressed yet?" She turned back to me. "We're swinging by Saks because Hannah says they have gorgeous wedding gowns. We're having lunch in Georgetown and in the afternoon we'll pick up her fiancé at the airport." She walked over to me and kissed my forehead. "I'm so glad to see you, sweetie. I know you're busy with that stuffing contest coming up, but don't you think you could find time to squeeze in a haircut?"

My mother, the micromanager who'd have had Thanksgiving dinner planned a month in advance, didn't wait for an answer. I watched her flounce from the kitchen and told myself not to be upset. She lived in a different world.

Dad's timing, as he settled in the other chair by the fire, made me suspect that he'd been waiting for her to leave. "Are you really over Mars or is that a line you gave your sister to shut her up?" His square brow furrowed in concern.

Dad looked young for a retiree. His dark hair hadn't thinned much and he'd kept himself in good shape.

"It's true." I took a deep breath and mustered up a strong voice and a big grin. "I've moved on."

"You two finally come to a decision about the house?"

"Thank goodness that's over. It's all mine now." I wasn't about to mention that my savings had dwindled and I'd given up my rights to Mars's retirement funds. No point in worrying Dad. "I think Natasha still wants to buy it from me . . ."

The picture of Aunt Faye that hung over the fireplace slid to a slant.

Dad looked around. "That's odd."

I swallowed the last bite of pancake. "Happens sometimes. Something about the draft from the fireplace, I think. Anyway, it's not for sale and especially not to Natasha." My home was the one thing she couldn't have. I loved the creaky old place with odd drafts that made pictures move and original peg-and-groove floors that canted so anything dropped on the floor in the living or dining room rolled toward the outer wall. And I adored life in Old Town Alexandria, just across the river from Washington, DC. The historic houses and brick sidewalks made it feel like a village instead of a suburb.

I would replenish my savings soon if I could resist the temptation to add a bathroom or renovate the existing one and a half baths. Who was the idiot that started the green-and-black-tile craze? It never was attractive.

It wasn't as though I didn't have a decent income as an event planner for A Capital Affair, but I'd taken a hefty mortgage to buy out Mars's interest in the house.

In a flurry of questions about the best routes to Saks and the airport, Mom reappeared with Hannah, collected Dad, and hurried them out the front door. I watched them from the stoop. A chilly fall wind blew colorful leaves up around them like an image in a snow globe.

Dad's blue Buick pulled away from the curb and Nina Reid Norwood, who lived across the street and one house over, jogged across to me.

On the day Mars and I moved in, before the movers managed to bring in one piece of furniture, our new neighbor, Nina, barged in carrying a wriggling black-and-tan hound puppy. Mars and I immediately adored the puppy with one freckle on her nose who happily followed us up and down the stairs. We adopted sweet Daisy the next day. Nina later confessed that adoption had been her goal but she wanted to check us out first.

Nina's husband, a renowned forensic pathologist, traveled constantly, leaving her plenty of time to help homeless animals. The daughter of a professor of pathology, Nina met her husband at a backyard barbecue hosted by her parents. She claimed the serious young doctor was just the antidote for her first marriage to a man who never met a woman he didn't like.

She must have been right. I'd never heard her utter one negative word about her current husband, although she had plenty to say about his mother.

On the sidewalk, Colonel Hampstead sang "Walkies, walkies!" and waved as he walked his bulldog, MacArthur. His ever present walking stick tapped along the brick walk.

I whispered to Nina, "Do you think he has anyplace to go for Thanksgiving?"

She gave me a sad puppy-dog look.

"Colonel!" I sprang after him. "Would you care to join us for Thanksgiving dinner?"

The grateful look in his eyes told me everything.

"You can bring MacArthur if you like." I bent to pet him. "You like turkey, don't you, fella?"

"MacArthur and I would be delighted to accept your kind invitation."

Shivering, I told him I'd call about the time and raced back to the house.

In her North Carolina drawl, Nina said, "My mama would die of a conniption right here and now if she could see me standin' on the neighbors' lawn talking in my bathrobe."

I had no doubt that she would. Nina had a voluptuous figure, and even in the November cold, she didn't mind showing a little cleavage. Maybe Mom was right about married women and flannel. Nina's quilted silk bathrobe was certainly more seductive than my jammies.

We dashed inside and Nina warmed her hands by the fire while I poured more coffee. I made a point of putting extra sugar in mine.

"So how's it goin'?" she asked.

"They're making me crazy already."

"They're supposed to. That way you don't miss them so much when they leave."

"I just wish the stuffing contest wasn't the day before Thanksgiving. It's putting a big crimp in my preparations for the grand feast."

Nina accepted a cup of coffee from me. "My mother-in-law has informed me that she expects place cards à la Natasha. Now, assuming I had the time, which I don't, or the inclination, which I don't, why on earth would I make place cards out of moldy old moss and dirty leaves?" She straightened Aunt Faye's picture. "At least you don't have to put up with your in-laws anymore." Still standing, Nina asked, "When is Daisy coming back?"

A peculiar question. Neither Mars nor I could stand giving her up, so we shared custody. "After Thanksgiving."

Nina stared into her coffee. "Last night while you and your family were out at the charity dinner, Francie called the police about a Peeping Tom."

"What?" Francie, the elderly woman next door, was prone to unusual behavior.

"I'm afraid so. They found some evidence of an intruder behind her house and she swears she saw him in your yard, too."

I hadn't noticed anything disturbed. Then again, I hadn't looked. "I'm sure it was a fluke. He probably won't be back."

"I hope not. I'd just feel better if Daisy were around when your family leaves."

She turned as though she was going to sit. Instead she craned her neck and walked around the table to the bench in the bay window. "I swear I just saw someone sneaking around the colonel's house."

TWO

From *"Ask Natasha"*:

Dear Natasha,

I have no idea how to decorate my home for Thanksgiving. Pumpkins and gourds seem tired. Any suggestions?

—Lost in Louisa

Dear Lost,

Create a nut garland to add that special touch.

Using an electric drill, make holes in assorted nuts. You may need a vise to hold the nuts. String them on rough twine to make your own harvest garland. Mix the nuts for a variety of textures and colors.

—Natasha

I joined Nina at the window. "I don't see anything."

"He disappeared behind the colonel's house." Nina downed the rest of her coffee. "I'm outta here. I've got enough problems of my own with my mother-in-law arriving tonight. My house will never be clean enough for that woman. I have to go by the shelter, too. We're fostering a golden retriever until they can place it."

"And you want to be sure that person you saw isn't lurking behind your house now?"

She laughed. "You know me too well."

I tamped down the fire while she let herself out. She might have tried to laugh it off, but I could tell she was worried about the man she'd seen.

That prompted me to have a look at my own backyard from the glass-enclosed sunroom on the back of the house. Sure enough, a few flowerpots lay on their sides as though they'd been knocked over. I consoled myself with the notion that the police knew about it and the guy probably wouldn't return.

After a quick shower, I pulled on a long-sleeved amber sweater. Checking to see if my roots needed a blonde boost yet, I popped hot rollers in my hair. Jeans seemed like a good idea for my grocery run. Except I couldn't find a pair of jeans that I could button at the waist. I hated to acknowledge that Mom was right, but I was developing curves where I shouldn't have any. I caved to comfort and put on khaki trousers with elastic around the back.

The car Mars called Nike on Wheels was still packed with votive candleholders and tablecloths from a charity dinner the night before. I never knew what kind of cakes, plants, flower arrangements, and odd decorations I might have to cart around in a pinch, so I'd insisted on a hybrid SUV. Mars had hated it. At least the car was one thing we didn't squabble over.

Too lazy to unload it, I shoved all the supplies together to make room for groceries.

The drive to my favorite natural food grocery store didn't take long, but the parking lot was jammed and I had to park around the side of the store. When I stepped out, a short, stocky man approached with a banana box in his hands. I braced myself and prepared to say no to whatever he was selling.

"Could I interest you in a kitten, ma'am?"

I didn't look. I didn't dare see it. "No, thanks."

"He's awful cute. Purebred ocicat."

"Aussie-what?" *No. Say no, Sophie. Walk away now.*

"Ocicat. My wife breeds 'em, and this little guy got stripes instead of spots so nobody wants to buy him." He held up an adorable kitten with huge green eyes.

Say no, Sophie, I chanted to myself. *Think of Daisy.* She had a sweet disposition, but I had no idea how she'd react to a kitten. The wind kicked up again and assorted bits of paper trash swirled past. I smiled at the man, said, "Good luck," and ran for the store entrance to extract myself while I could.

I grabbed a cart and headed straight for the turkeys. I selected a twenty-five-pounder, far larger than we needed, but I rationalized that everyone loves turkey sandwiches. Cranberries, organic gold Yukon potatoes, fresh green beans, almonds, butter, but no matter where I shopped in the store, I couldn't get the bright eyes of the poor little kitten out of my mind. That man was willing to give it away to anyone. What would happen to it? I placed canned pumpkin in my cart for the soup my mother thought was so important and decided that if the man was still there when I left, I would take the kitten to Nina. At the very least, she'd make sure it got a decent home.

With that off my mind I was able to concentrate and checked my lists—one for the stuffing contest and the other for Thanksgiving dinner. I was picking out a chicken for stock when Tamera Turner, a local news anchor, cornered me.

"Sophie, they don't have squab and they're out of acorn squashes. Where are you going to get yours?"

A well-fed, bespectacled man leaned over the poultry selection as though he was trying to listen in. A fan of Tamera's?

"I'm not doing Natasha's dinner."

"You're not?" Tamera placed her hand on my arm. "What are you making? My Thanksgiving is already a disaster. I have to work. I don't have time for this."

"Mostly family, right? Are you having a formal sit-down dinner or will the guys be watching football?"

"My husband made a deal with me. As long as he can watch all the football he wants, he'll smoke the turkey. I thought I'd set up a buffet."

"Then why are you serving broth? You know all they want is turkey, stuffing, and potatoes. Maybe a little pie for later. Besides, it wouldn't be practical for your guests to carry around acorn squashes with soup in them."

Tamera smacked her forehead. "You're so right. What was I thinking?" She thanked me and bustled off, relief evident on her face.

The pudgy man smiled at me. "Are you Sophie Winston?"

I assumed the gentleman had an event in mind and handed him one of my business cards.

He reached out to shake my hand. "Dean Coswell. How very fortunate that I ran into you. I was going to give you a call this afternoon. Your ex-husband, Mars, thought you might be the right person for a project I have in mind." He adjusted his glasses with his thumb and middle finger. "My wife wasted yesterday looking for squab and acorn squash. This morning I had to take her to the emergency room because she mangled her finger with the electric drill trying to make a nut garland. Can you imagine—she was their seventh nut garland victim this morning. Anyway, it occurs to me that despite Natasha's popularity, a lot of people dislike her. My newspaper is planning a column called "The Good Life." Think you could bring back some good sense to the good life?"

"Me? Write a column?" It was like a dream come true. I didn't even care if they paid me. The opportunity to vie with Natasha would be cathartic. "Yes!"

Coswell raised his arms and cheered, "I've found my anti-Natasha! Could you have something ready for the Thanksgiving edition?"

Why was it always like this in life? I'd taken time off work so I could prepare for my family's visit. One day would be eaten up by the Stupendous Stuffing Shakedown and now, already pressed for time, I was committing to another project. But this was important to me. I agreed to write something to ease his overstressed wife and he handed me a card with his e-mail address scribbled on the back.

I waited in line for fresh loaves of crusty country bread for my stuffing, amazed by my good fortune. Mars had recommended me? We might be divorced but no matter how I looked at it, he was still a good guy.

When I left the store, I searched the parking lot for any sign of the man with the kitten. I didn't see him anywhere and guessed he'd moved on. A kitten was the last thing I needed, but I still felt a tiny twinge of disappointment. I just hoped the kitten would be okay.

I loaded the groceries and backed the car out but was blocked by an elderly woman who could barely see over the steering wheel of her ancient boat-sized Cadillac. She was having trouble maneuvering and somehow managed to stop traffic in the parking lot. There weren't a lot of choices. To give her room, I eased backward toward the rear of the store.

A dark blue pickup truck idled next to a Dumpster, a banana box on the hood. My stomach churned. Surely that man hadn't tossed the poor kitten? Driving too fast, I slid alongside the truck.

The insistent wind blew mercilessly and the box threatened to tumble. I hopped out, raced for it, and caught it before the wind could sweep it away. Inside, the tiny kitten stretched toward me. I couldn't mistake the huge curious eyes. I scooped it up and held it close, immediately rewarded by baby purrs.

I could feel my face turning scarlet with anger. What kind of person would throw out a kitten? Where was that jerk?

Outraged, I assured the little guy I would take care of him. He mewed and I realized I would have to go back for kitten food. He was probably starved.

I didn't want to put him back in the box. It seemed like a symbol of the horrible man's callous treatment. Steaming mad, I picked up the box, stepped over to the Dumpster, and threw it in.

And then I saw it. A trail of glistening blood on the asphalt. A crimson smudge on the rim of the Dumpster. I stepped on a concrete block and peered over the edge.

THREE

From *"Ask Natasha"*:

Dear Natasha,

My mother-in-law loves to drop by for inspection. If I want to stay married, I can't tell her not to visit. What can I do?

—Constantly Cleaning in Clarksville

Dear Constantly Cleaning,

Treat your mother-in-law as a treasured guest by entertaining her. I always have a delicious homemade treat on hand. If you bake a cake every Saturday morning, you'll have a delicious dessert for dinner and extra to serve unexpected guests during the week. You never know who might drop by.

—Natasha

The kitten's owner was sprawled faceup on heaps of discarded produce. A stain the color of pomegranate seeped across his white sweatshirt.

I jerked back, my heart pounding.

The kitten let out a shocked yowl and I realized that I was holding it too tight. I ran back to my car, jumped in, slammed the door shut, and hit the locks. Only when I released the kitten did I realize that my hands were shaking.

I fumbled in my purse for the cell phone. Whoever that man was, he needed help. I wasn't tall enough to hoist myself into the Dumpster. Maybe he was just unconscious. But deep inside I suspected something worse.

Seconds after my call, sirens sounded behind me. A squad car must have been in the area. My heart still hammering in my chest, I opened the door, careful not to let the kitten out. Pouncing on prey that only he could see, he scrambled happily over grocery bags in the back of the car.

A young officer, surely fresh from training, greeted me with a serious face. My knees weak, I led him to the man. The pink flush drained from his cheeks and his voice broke when he called in on his radio. He jammed it back into its holster and tried to climb into the Dumpster. After a couple of unsuccessful attempts, he turned to me and asked, "Could you give me a boost?"

I formed a cradle with my hands and tried to help him over the edge. The Dumpster wasn't impossibly high, just tall enough for most people to have trouble jumping in. He stepped on my shoulder and pushed off, crashing inside with a loud groan.

Peeking over the edge, I saw that he'd landed facedown on the bleeding man. I swallowed hard and a tremor ran through me. Was he lying across a corpse?

The paramedics arrived and I stood aside to make room for them. A slender red-haired woman stepped on the concrete block and hoisted herself into the Dumpster with the ease of a gymnast.

Her male counterpart watched.

"Is he alive?" I asked. It came out in a whisper.

A tall, lanky man with oddly large hands pushed past me. "What the devil is going on?"

The male paramedic stopped him from touching the Dumpster.

"I'm the manager of this store. I have a right to know what you're doing here." He stretched up and looked over into the green Dumpster.

We all observed him in silence.

He rubbed his forehead with a nervous hand. "What happened?"

At that precise moment, cars careened toward us on both sides of the narrow strip behind the store, blocking us in. Seconds later, police swarmed the area and the manager and I were pushed back, away from the Dumpster. When everyone was otherwise occupied and not paying me any attention, I snuck to my car and fetched the kitten. I didn't want him overheating. Even though a cold wind blew, the sun would surely raise the temperature inside the car.

The turkey!

I felt guilty for thinking about my groceries when someone had probably died, but they would spoil if we were detained for a long period. I scanned the officials milling around.

A man in a tweed sport coat impressed me as calmer than the others. Not emotionless, just more experienced perhaps. The sun glinted off silver hair on his temples. Most important, he wasn't a skinny runner type; this guy liked to eat. I sidled toward him.

After introducing myself, I explained that my Thanksgiving groceries were in my car. "And I'm in a stuffing competition tomorrow and I'd rather not poison the judges with tainted ingredients."

"Farley!" he barked. "Get the groceries out of the SUV and put them in a cooler in the store." In a pleasant but unmistakably authoritative tone, he said, "We'll take care of it. Please stand back. Someone will be over to take your statement soon."

I waited, holding the restless kitten and watching the store manager pace from officer to officer trying to get information. Press crews arrived, adding to the confusion.

After what seemed an eternity, a man with skin drawn tightly over the contours of his face flashed a badge at me and said he was Detective Kenner. I told him the whole story.

When I finished, he said, "You know the store has cameras. We'll be able to verify what you've said."

Of course. Why hadn't I thought of that? "So you'll be able to see who killed that guy and put him in the Dumpster."

"How do you know he was murdered?"

"Most people don't bleed spontaneously from the chest."

His cold eyes narrowed. "You're in a lot of trouble, Mrs. Winston. Being a wiseacre isn't going to help any."

Was he trying to scare me? "I didn't do anything. The store videos will back that up."

"Then how do you explain the blood on your sweater?"

Huh? I looked down. Sure enough, thin streaks of dried blood ran underneath my right arm. At least it sure looked like blood. Above it, toward my shoulder, was an enormous dusty dirty spot. Instinctively I brushed at it.

He caught my wrist midair. "We'll be taking your sweater as evidence. I don't appreciate your sassiness. A man is dead and it looks like you were the last person to see him alive."

Was that supposed to be some kind of absurd warning? "The store cameras will back up my story."

"Believe me, we'll be taking a very close look at those tapes."

I was losing my patience with him. "Oh, this is absurd."

"Not in my line of business. People don't just pull over to Dumpsters and happen to find corpses. I consider that extremely odd behavior on your part."

Moments later I was seated in the back of a squad car and being driven to police headquarters. Once there I was surprised that no one objected to the presence of the kitten. While I was fingerprinted, surrendered my sweater, and put on the T-shirt they gave me, a female officer played with him.

It was late afternoon by the time they drove me home. The warmth and familiarity of my kitchen had never felt so reassuring. I placed the kitten on the floor and let him explore. Luckily I found a piece of leftover chicken breast in the refrigerator. He wolfed the diced meat but ignored the water I set out.

The discovery of the dead man shook me more than I wanted to admit. I put the kettle on and plopped a bag of organic English Breakfast tea into my favorite mug. What had happened to that guy while I was in the store? Granted, it must have taken me about an hour to do all the shopping, but who would kill someone in a grocery store parking lot when there were so many people around? His truck had been parked by the Dumpster. Had that been his fatal mistake? The back of the store was eerily quiet and unobserved. Trees and brush separated it from the lot behind it.

The kettle whistled. I poured boiling water into my mug and looked for the kitten. He was valiantly trying to climb the chair next to the fireplace. I lifted him to the seat and after adding sugar and milk to my tea, sank into the other chair. He was already curled up in a fat little ball.

As I watched the kitten sleep, I couldn't help wondering if the man had been killed because of the kitten. But if that was the case, wouldn't the person have taken the kitten with him?

The brass acorn knocker on my front door banged briskly. Reluctantly I pried myself from my comfy chair, shuffled through the kitchen to the front door, and peered through the peephole. The policeman with the silver temples stood on my stoop.

I opened the door with dread. Wasn't I through with this yet? I hadn't even had a chance to change out of my police-issued T-shirt.

He smiled at me and offered a bag of groceries. "I thought you'd be needing these."

I'd forgotten all about the groceries. I took the bag from him. "Thank you so much!"

He nodded. "I'll get the rest."

I unloaded them almost as fast as he brought them in. Everything appeared to be in good shape. And, as if by magic, six cans of kitten food and a bag of kitten kibble appeared among the groceries.

"Did you add the kitten food?" I asked, staring at him in wonder.

He set two carryout cups on the kitchen counter. "Yeah, figured you might be in a bind without a car."

I offered to pay for it but he waved me off. "I took the liberty of bringing some mocha lattes."

Uh-oh. He brought me my groceries, kitten food, *and* mocha lattes? Either he was too good to be true or this was some kind of good-cop, bad-cop routine. I poured the lattes into mugs and popped them in the microwave to warm them up. The refrigerator was getting a little bit crowded so I took out the leftover Bourbon Pecan Pie and cut two pieces for us.

He placed them on the kitchen table along with the mugs of latte.

This guy was no dummy. He intended to make me feel comfortable and relaxed so I would spill information. It had the opposite effect. Foreboding welled in my chest.

We sat down and he tasted the pie. "This is amazing." His gaze stopped at my untouched plate. "Your first body, huh? You never forget your first murder."

"How was he killed?"

The detective paused as though he was constructing a careful response. "Stabbed. The knife was in the Dumpster with him."

I swallowed hard. It all happened so fast. One minute he was trying to give away a kitten and the next he was gone. A question had been tugging at me and I finally decided to bring things out in the open. "Am I a suspect?"

I couldn't read his expression.

He studied me quietly. "Kenner thinks so. But he also thinks he's Clint Eastwood and that everyone is guilty."

"I don't even know your name," I blurted.

He grinned. "Detective Fleishman. Wolf, they call me Wolf."

"What about my sweater? The blood on it must belong to the dead guy."

His grin turned into a chuckle. "Mrs. Winston, I've seen a lot of murders in my day. There are a few things I know without having to make a big study of it like Kenner. One, it is possible for a woman to throw a dead guy into a Dumpster. When that adrenaline gets pumping, people can do incredible things. Two, killers go to the trouble of putting victims in Dumpsters because they want to hide them. Very few call the police and wait around for them. Three, that knife is going to come up clean, no fingerprints. I guarantee it. Somebody wanted that guy dead."

"So I'm not a suspect?"

He avoided my gaze and it didn't escape me that he failed to answer my question.

"How exactly did you know Otis?"

"Otis? Was that his name?"

He looked me straight in the eyes like he was trying to read me.

As much as I wanted to avert my gaze, instinct forced me to meet him dead on. Guilty people and liars looked away, didn't they? "I think I was very clear in the statement I gave earlier. The first time I ever saw him was when he offered me the kitten in the store parking lot."

"Otis Pulchinski. You sure that doesn't ring any bells?"

His smile had disappeared and while I didn't think he meant to intimidate me, the serious expression on his face told me I was in more trouble than I thought. I sipped the mocha latte. Could I have known the guy? Over the years I'd met thousands of people at events I planned. I nearly choked on the latte at the thought.

Pulling my shoulders up straight, I gave him the best answer I could. "The name isn't familiar and if I ever met him before, it could only have been in passing. I certainly didn't recognize him."

On the floor, the kitten wiggled his behind and sprang in two great leaps to a chair and onto the table. That stinker! He hadn't needed my help to get on the chair earlier. I reached out to remove him but Wolf stopped me.

"It's okay. What are you going to call him?"

"I don't even know if it's a boy or a girl."

Wolf picked up the kitten under its arms. "Congratulations, Mrs. Winston, it's a boy."

A smile crept to my face and eased the tension I'd felt. "Please call me Sophie."

Back on the table, the kitten promptly investigated Wolf's mocha latte.

Wolf stopped him. "Have a little milk? I don't think the mocha would be good for him."

At the word "mocha," the kitten turned his big eyes on Wolf.

I fetched a tiny bit of cream. While I was up, Wolf kept repeating the word "mocha."

"Hey, look at this."

Holding a saucer with a few drops of cream in my hand, I paused to watch.

Every time Wolf said "mocha" the kitten looked at him.

"He thinks his name is Mocha." Wolf picked him up and placed him on the chair by the fireplace. He walked away from the kitten and called, "Mochie!"

The kitten's head swiveled around.

"That's silly." It was cute but he probably responded that way to lots of words. "Ice cream!" I said as a test.

The kitten ignored me.

"Mochie!"

By golly, the little guy turned his head immediately.

Laughing, we settled at the table again. Mochie leaped onto the table and lapped cream while Wolf stroked him.

He didn't look like a Wolf. He didn't have that sly, hungry look like Kenner. Wolf struck me as being more like a Great Dane, calm and confident with friendly brown eyes. Maybe that made him more dangerous. Lurking behind the amiable facade was a detective noting my every move. It would be easy to relax, to enjoy his company—to fall into some sort of horrible trap that might make me seem guilty.

Wolf finished his slice of pie and settled back in the chair, too comfortably for my taste.

My hands had grown cold. Even the latte couldn't keep me warm.

The front door opened and chatter filled the air. My family barged in and stopped in a cluster at the sight of us.

A tall, fair man with a bad comb-over was with them. Hannah's fiancé, I presumed. I introduced everyone to Wolf. When I said he was a detective, I thought I noticed a slight twitch of apprehension on the fiancé's face.

My mother took great pride in introducing him as *Doctor* Craig Beacham. He was unfailingly polite but when I shook his hand, a chill ran through me.

Wolf distracted me by saying good-bye. I thanked him again for delivering my groceries, bringing kitten food, and for naming Mochie, too. At the front door, speaking softly, he said, "You seem like a decent person, Sophie, so I'm going to give you a little advice." He leaned toward me. "Cops don't like being lied to. It makes us very angry." He sucked in a deep breath and his eyes narrowed. "Isn't there something you'd like to come clean about?"

My pulse quickened. He obviously thought I'd lied. "There's nothing else to tell."

He shuffled his feet uncomfortably and crossed his arms over his chest. The nice cop of the latte and kitten food disappeared. "Really." He fixed me with an unfriendly glare. "Suppose you explain why the dead man had your name and photograph on the front seat of his truck?"

FOUR

From the *Live with Natasha* show:

Don't skip the all-important step of brining your turkey. It needs to sit in salt water for four to eight hours. Wash thoroughly, then let it rest on a roasting rack, uncovered, in your refrigerator for twenty-four hours before you roast it.

"He had my picture?" I shivered as though a cold fall wind had blown.

Wolf watched me from the stoop, his brown eyes narrowed.

"But that doesn't make any sense. Do you think he brought the kitten as a lure? Like people who want to kidnap children?"

Wolf's eyebrows shot up.

I clutched the door frame. "Do you think someone hired him to hurt me?"

"Does someone want to hurt you?"

"No!" It came out too loud. "Not that I know of."

Wolf gave up his bad-guy stance and patted my arm.

"Relax. It's probably nothing quite so sinister. Otis was a private detective. A little on the sleazy side, but I don't think he ever operated as a hit man."

"Hit man?" That was worse than I'd thought. "But what would a private investigator want with me? And why bring the kitten? And then get killed?"

"Precisely." He turned and walked toward his car. Looking back, he said, "Thanks for the pie. I'll be in touch."

It was the polite thing to say, yet I felt an ominous undercurrent, like this wasn't the end of my involvement with Wolf or Otis.

I closed the door behind me and leaned against it, wondering why Otis had been looking for me. Dr. Craig Beacham stood ten feet away. He quickly averted his eyes and disappeared into the kitchen. I could have sworn he'd been listening.

I trailed after him and found my parents making a fuss over Mochie. I kept my explanation about his presence brief, saying only that I'd found him in the grocery store parking lot. No point in worrying them about the murdered private investigator and his troubling interest in me.

To my immense relief, that evening Hannah and her fiancé walked down to King Street for a romantic dinner. I remained at home with my parents, listening to my mother talk at great length about wedding gowns and doctors. All the while, I went through the motions expected of me in a daze.

I measured flour and dumped it into the bread machine along with water, a knob of butter, salt, and yeast. Barely paying attention, I set the timer so we would have fresh bread for breakfast.

No wonder the police thought I had something to do with the murder. Would the videotapes of the parking lot help me? There wouldn't be any audio. The police might assume that Otis said something threatening to me. Had he meant to? Had he brought the kitten as a diversion in case anyone saw him talking to me?

"Sophie!" Mom practically shouted into my ear. "Did you hear me? You need to brine the turkey tonight."

I didn't have the energy. "It'll be just as good without brining." The scandalized look on Mom's face forced me to debate which would be worse—a lengthy argument about the benefits of brining or actually brining the turkey. I didn't think I had the strength for an argument.

I rearranged the contents of the refrigerator and removed a shelf to accommodate the brining tub. Once the turkey rested safely in salted water, I used the stuffing competition as an excuse to go to bed early.

Lying in bed that night, I heard Hannah and her beau let themselves in and walk up to their third-floor bedroom. They whispered and carried on like teenagers, and I was glad that Hannah had found someone to share her life with.

I drifted off into an uneasy slumber with Mochie nestled by my feet. At four in the morning I sat bolt upright in bed. How had Otis known I would be at the grocery store? He parked there before I did so he couldn't have followed me.

Finding the dead man had been bad enough, but knowing that he'd been looking for me scared me. Who would hire a private investigator to hunt me down? And why?

Mars and I had settled everything in our divorce with relative ease. We'd had a few squabbles but they were behind us.

Natasha and I had known each other for years. Surely she wouldn't hire a private investigator. Ours had always been a friendly rivalry. Had her relationship with Mars changed that? She coveted my house but I couldn't see how a private investigator would help her there. And though she was annoyingly perfect, Natasha wasn't an evil person at heart.

I was far too restless to sleep. Thinking back through names and faces of people I'd worked with, old friends, old not-so-friendly acquaintances, I picked my way down the ancient stairs, treading carefully to lessen creaks that might wake the others. Mochie scampered along ahead of me. I padded silently into the glass-roofed sunroom that overlooked the backyard, retrieved a throw, and curled up in a chair, tucking my feet underneath me. The moon illuminated the yard but the fence and plants cast eerie shadows. I still hadn't righted the pots overturned by the Peeping Tom.

Could the Peeping Tom have been Otis, the dead man? Why would he prowl around my house? What did he want from me? Who would have hired him to nose around?

A stair groaned behind me. In the still house, the noise seemed amplified. Holding the throw around my shoulders, I ventured into the foyer.

"Mom? Dad?" I whispered.

The only response came from Mochie, who rubbed against my ankles. Could the kitten have caused that loud sound? Surely not. I stood still, listening.

Was Craig sneaking around the house at night? I'd spent a whopping twenty minutes with Dr. Craig Beacham and it wasn't fair of me to jump to conclusions, but there was something about him that I didn't like. I couldn't put my finger on it, but he gave me the willies.

I was being ridiculous. Finding Otis's body had me on edge and now I was inventing things. I picked up Mochie and walked into the kitchen. Before I switched on the light, I could have sworn I heard a door close somewhere in the house. But in the stillness that followed I wasn't sure.

Berating myself for imagining things, I concluded that someone might have been using the bathroom. There was certainly nothing wrong with that.

I collected the items I needed for the stuffing competition and placed them in boxes. Mochie roamed around sniffing everything. Crouching low inside a box, he wiggled his tiny bottom and jumped up at me when I neared.

I rearranged the contents of the refrigerator again, replaced the shelf and set the brined turkey inside on a rack to dry off so the skin would crisp up nicely.

At six o'clock, I put on a pot of coffee, poured organic orange juice, and set the table for breakfast. The heavenly scent of baking bread soon filled the kitchen.

I had to put Otis out of my mind. I hadn't done anything wrong. If I let his murder get to me, I wouldn't be able to focus on the competition today.

Since no one was up yet, I took advantage of the quiet to draft Thanksgiving Day advice for "The Good Life." Satisfied with my scribbles, I e-mailed the column to Mr. Coswell.

The ancient hardwood floors upstairs creaked and I heard water running. I made a quick list of things I needed to do after the contest in preparation for Thanksgiving. I should have baked the pies and made the stuffing yesterday, but a dead man got in the way. I'd have to catch up tonight.

Keeping an eye on Nina's house, I rinsed serving dishes that I would need for Thanksgiving but hadn't been used since last year. With my car, Nike on Wheels, impounded by the police, I needed a ride to the contest. The hotel where it was being held was walking distance from my house but I had too many ingredients to carry. Nina had planned to go anyway, so I didn't think I'd be imposing on her if I asked for a ride. That way, Hannah or my parents would be free to come to the contest late or leave early if they wanted.

When Nina stepped out to fetch the morning paper, I dashed across the street, spilled the entire story about Otis, and asked if she would mind giving me a lift to the contest.

At eight o'clock, Nina's low-slung Jaguar purred in front of my house. Almost before I buckled my seat belt, Nina started in on me. "Sophie, sugar, first thing you do is throw Natasha off her stride. I bet you a latte and a chocolate croissant that she says something ugly to you while you're cookin'. You better be ready to laugh in her face."

I took a deep breath and released it. Nina was right. I needed to be prepared to let Natasha's barbs float past me.

"You go right in there and say somethin' that'll get her goat."

That wasn't my style. "I'm not playing dirty. Besides, the results will hinge on whose stuffing is best."

"Honey, I wasn't the college tennis champ for four years without knowing a thing or two about psyching out the competition. Trust me on this.".

Nina pulled her Jaguar up to the entrance of a fancy hotel on North Fairfax Street. My pulse quickened with anticipation.

The Stupendous Stuffing Shakedown began in the summer with a staggering two hundred contestants. They were whittled down to one hundred amateur cooks, like me, who prepared our stuffings for a panel of judges. My Crusty Country Bread, Bacon, and Herb Stuffing had made the final three. Then the sponsors invited three local celebrities to compete in the finals, Natasha among them.

The contest was the brainstorm of media mogul Simon Greer, a self-confessed stuffing addict. Never one to overlook an opportunity to make money, his TV crew was already set up and filming when we entered the ballroom.

Each contestant was provided a small workspace equipped with a stovetop and two ovens. The bellman in tow with my boxes, I passed Emma Moosbacher and Wendy Schultz, the other two amateurs. Emma entered Chesapeake Cornbread Stuffing, and Wendy was a serious contender with her Cranberry Mushroom Wild Rice Stuffing.

The bellman led me to the workspace between Natasha and Wendy.

Natasha posed in front of her work counter, smiling and signing autographs. Her ebony hair gleamed under the harsh lights, every strand flowing perfectly onto her shoulders. Although she wore a simple robin's-egg blue shirt tucked into matching trousers, they draped on her like they would on a model. She still maintained the beauty queen figure of her youth. Just seeing her made my own shirt and khakis feel tighter.

I tipped the bellman and unpacked my boxes, clustering ingredients on my work counter. I couldn't help noticing that while I'd brought my ingredients in cardboard boxes rescued from the grocery store, Natasha's items rested on her counter in baskets beautifully decorated with harvest ribbons and turkeys constructed of pine cones.

"Sophie!" Natasha elegantly picked her way past her fans to give me a hug. "Who'd have thought you would make it to the finals? The two gals from Berrysville all grown up and competing again."

Fans clustered behind her, waiting patiently for autographs. Fans who aspired to the perfection she represented and served up to them each day on her show. No one could meet the expectations she created.

She waved vigorously at someone. "Mars will be here; I hope that won't be too emotional for you." She clutched her hands to her chest. "Oh, poor Sophie. The holidays are always so difficult when you're alone, aren't they?"

Two parents, my sister, and her fiancé didn't qualify as being alone in my book. "I'm not exactly alone."

"You have a boyfriend? How wonderful. What a relief to know that love handles don't deter all men. You're an inspiration to us all."

Was Natasha trying to psyche me out exactly as Nina predicted? I recalled Nina's advice and tried to serve Natasha a little of her own medicine. "I see you're making Oyster Stuffing. Mars detests oysters and mussels, you know."

For one long second, I thought I had her. But she came back fast. "Not the way I make it."

She turned quickly and resumed her pose in front of her counter. I couldn't help gloating a little bit. Obviously, she didn't know about Mars's aversion to oysters.

Simon Greer ambled toward us, a sly grin on his face. A crowd gathered behind him.

Wendy, the amateur contender on my other side, ran her fingers through her short, curly hair, and mock whispered, "He's so gorgeous. Wish he were the prize."

Simon wasn't tall but he cut an imposing figure anyway. Sharply creased khaki trousers and a cashmere hunter-green sweater showed off a well-toned physique. Wavy hair in a controlled tumble only emphasized his boyish charm. No wonder women fawned over him. He had looks and gobs of money. Every step seemed to ooze the confidence of wealth. He prided himself on being a self-made man, though Nina, who kept up with celebrity doings, told me his wealth originated with early cell phone technology deals that had since been made illegal. He parlayed those millions into a national cable network and a magazine publishing empire.

I'd met him in passing at some of the bigger charity events I'd handled but this was the first time I could ever remember seeing Simon without a tuxedo. And today the women drooling over him were a little older and chubbier than the usual line of gold diggers that trailed him.

He kissed Natasha on the cheek and thanked her for participating. She flushed despite her flawless makeup. Clearly used to publicity, he put his arm around Natasha and offered a practiced grin for photographs.

A chestnut-haired man slightly taller than Simon, fit but not brawny, moved with him. At first I thought he might be a friend of Simon's but he appeared to be scanning the people around Simon. He wore a bored Secret Service agent expression. A bodyguard? If so, he didn't seem to sense any urgency.

Natasha was still talking to Simon when he broke away and swung easily into my work space.

I held out my hand but he ignored it and leaned in to kiss me. If I hadn't turned my head fast, he'd have planted one right on my lips.

Up close, tiny laugh crinkles around his eyes made him even more enchanting. Loud enough for everyone to hear, he said, "So good to see you again. Good luck today, Sophie." And then he lowered his voice. "I have tickets to *The Nutcracker* at the Kennedy Center for Saturday. My driver, Clyde, will pick you up at seven."

Did he just ask me out? His bored shadow gave me a curt nod so I assumed he must be Clyde.

Simon winked at me and strode away to welcome Wendy.

She drifted over to me when he moved on. "I can't believe that just happened. I couldn't be more excited if he'd asked me for a date. It's . . . it's like going out with a movie star, only better."

"Better?"

"Are you kidding? Do you know what he's worth? I'd dump my sweet, fat old Marvin any day for Simon." She paused, waved, and called out, "Hi, honey!"

A portly guy sitting in the front row of spectator chairs waved back.

Maybe she had a point, but the whole thing left a sour taste in my mouth. It wasn't an invitation, it was . . . a command. As though he assumed I'd love to go with him. Was he so used to women agreeing that he didn't bother asking?

Wendy watched me with a dreamy expression. "What I wouldn't give to have Simon Greer interested in me."

Stupid Simon. He was a judge. What had he done? Didn't he realize the position he put me in by asking me out? He couldn't wait a few hours until after they announced the winner?

Natasha rushed over, the color drained from her face.

"Did I hear that right?" She reprimanded me like an angry schoolteacher. "I never expected this from you. Sleeping with a judge to win? It can't be easy for you to continually be an also-ran, but, Sophie, this is practically prostitution. What will your new boyfriend think?" She emitted a small gasping sound like something terrible had occurred to her. "Simon's your new beau. You've rigged the contest!"

FIVE

From *Natasha Online*:

Don't let your herbs die with summer. Start new plants in colorful window boxes in August. A sunny kitchen window is the perfect place for your indoor herb garden. They bring gorgeous greens and interesting textures to your kitchen, and your holiday dishes will burst with fresh herb flavor.

Like winning a stuffing contest was so important that I'd sleep with a judge. The winner would get a one-hour television special on one of Simon's networks, as well as the cover of one of his trendy magazines. That prize could propel the winner to diva stardom, or at least put her on the right road. But I'd never been the type to sleep my way to success.

For one brief moment I considered bowing out, but I didn't want to give Natasha the satisfaction. I'd have to find Simon and set him straight. Holding my chin high to show I had nothing to be ashamed of, I faced Natasha. "If you're so sure you're going to win, then why are you concerned about Simon and me?"

Her lower lip pulled into a bitter line. "It's not fair to the other contestants."

She was right about that. It wouldn't be fair to anyone. But I'd set things right before the competition started.

"Sophie! Sophie!" Hannah rushed at us, wearing an uncharacteristically subdued baby-blue turtleneck. Mom and Craig followed close behind and Dad stood back to snap pictures on his fancy digital camera.

"Is it true?" Hannah said. "Simon asked you out?"

News traveled fast in the ballroom. "Where did you hear that?"

"Everyone's buzzing about it. I can't believe it. My sister's going to be rich. Filthy rich!"

Great. The first date I'd had since my divorce could have been with a rich and charming guy and I was going to ruin it all by telling him I couldn't go.

Mom beamed. "I knew you wouldn't be wearing flannel pajamas for long. That cute cop from yesterday is here, too. I believe he's sweet on you."

Wolf? Here? I'd zeroed in on him because he looked like the kind of guy who liked food, but I didn't imagine he'd be interested in the stuffing contest.

Mars's sister-in-law, Vicki, joined us and I could hear her husband, Andrew, talking too loudly nearby. Although Andrew looked a good deal like Mars, he'd never found contentment in any of his business undertakings. He drifted from idea to job to disaster on a regular basis. Thankfully, the svelte, very together Vicki sustained them by being one of Washington's most-sought-after marriage counselors. She exuded self-confidence in a way I never could.

Vicki gave me a big hug. "What's this I hear? A new man in your life?"

Hannah practically swooned. "Simon Greer asked her out. Can you believe it?"

"Simon! Aren't you the lucky one."

I excused myself to look for the rascal but could hear my mother asking Vicki, "Exactly how much is this Simon worth?"

I plowed through the crowd searching for him but found Mars's mother, June, instead. She waylaid me with a hug and kisses. I'd always enjoyed June and was genuinely pleased to see her. Mars's entire family was present. Which made me wonder why Natasha's mother hadn't made the trip to cheer her daughter on. Or maybe she was there and I simply hadn't seen her yet. With a twinkle in her lively eyes, June said, "I have to sit over by Natasha, but I'll be cheering for you."

I was parched from all the chatting. Besides, I needed a fortifying cup of coffee to face Simon. I stopped by the refreshment table and was filling a cup with steaming coffee that smelled like hazelnuts when an arm curled around my shoulders. My ex-husband, Mars, short for Marshall. I'd known he would be there and steeled myself for a little shock of awkwardness that didn't come. Seeing him again was like eating a bowl of lobster bisque. Warm, cozy, familiar, even a little exciting, but I didn't want more. We would always be friends but I realized with joy at that moment that I truly had moved on.

Mars's magnetic personality earned him the nickname Teflon Mars among friends. No matter how dire his actions, everything slid off of him. A handy attribute for a political advisor.

He kissed my cheek. "Good luck, Soph. Don't tell Nat but your country bread stuffing was always my favorite."

"Gnat? You call her Gnat, like a bug?"

He shook hands with someone and we moved away from the coffee setup. "Yeah, she hates it. So undignified."

He jammed his hands into his pockets, a gesture I knew well. Something was wrong.

"I hear Simon is taking you out."

This was my lucky day. I couldn't resist a chance to tweak Mars a little bit. "The ballet."

"Steer clear of him, Soph. You'll end up getting hurt."

"Why, Mars," I said in my best imitation of Scarlett O'Hara, "I do believe you might be a tad jealous."

I'd always liked Mars's eyes. They twinkled with humor like his mother's. He stared at me with those kind eyes.

"He's trouble. On the outside Simon comes across as a great guy, but he's crafty and conniving beneath that facade. Trust me on this, Soph. Don't get involved with him. He's ruthless. He didn't get to be rich by being nice."

I didn't resist the grin that came to my lips. "You don't get to tell me what to do anymore."

The loudspeakers crackled and a woman's voice announced, "All contestants report to the check-in desk immediately."

I should have skipped the coffee and found Simon. With a quick wave to Mars I made a beeline to the desk in the ballroom foyer.

Enormous arrangements of orange and gold mums flanked the desk. The contestants clustered together and Wendy shrieked, "It's sabotage. Someone's cheating!"

Her lips drawn so tightly they almost disappeared, Natasha focused on the contest coordinator. "I hate to see her go but I have to agree. It's simply not right for a contestant to have a relationship with a judge."

They were talking about me. "Hey! I was looking for Simon to tell him off. We don't have a relationship of any kind."

The contest coordinator blinked slowly. "Simon? What's he got to do with thyme?"

Wendy shoved a small herb bottle under my nose. "My thyme. It's gone. Someone has been tampering with my ingredients."

Each contestant searched the faces of the others—except Natasha, who held her chin high and acted as though she were above the fray.

"I brought extra. You're welcome to have some of my thyme," I offered.

Tears welled in Wendy's eyes. "Thank you so much."

I hated to leave Natasha there to bring up the subject of Simon again but I had no choice. I sprinted through the ballroom doors and toward my work station as fast as the crowd would allow. Leaning over the work counter, I snatched my bottle of dried thyme and hustled back to the lobby.

Wendy grabbed it and unscrewed the top. "I can't thank you enough . . ." She shook some out and sniffed it. "What's the big idea? This isn't thyme. It's"—she dabbed the tip of her finger into it and tasted it—"cilantro."

I seized the bottle from her, smelled it, and tried some. "It *is* dried cilantro." The saboteur had erred in a big way. Cilantro might be a popular herb but it wasn't one of my personal favorites. I didn't keep it on hand in my kitchen so there was no way I'd goofed and brought cilantro instead of thyme.

The contest organizer grumbled. "I'll get thyme from the hotel kitchen. Everyone will use the same thing, even those of you who have thyme."

Natasha groaned. "Hotel restaurant herbs. You know they're not fresh. My stuffing depends on the quality of the herbs."

"If you brought your own fresh herbs, then you may use them. If you brought dried herbs, you must use what I give you. That's my ruling."

"What about the contestant who is dating Simon?" asked Emma.

"I am *not* dating him." My voice was a bit louder than I meant it to be. I sucked in air and willed myself to speak in a calm tone. "I have never dated Simon. Never had lunch with him, never had a phone conversation. To be sure this is fair to all of you, I was on my way to find him and tell him that I will not go to the ballet with him. Is that okay with everyone?"

"He'll still be biased," said Wendy. "Maybe he should withdraw from judging."

Natasha acted horrified. "It's *his* contest! We can't ask him to bow out of his own contest."

Local celebrity chef Pierre LaPlumme focused on the ceiling and muttered in a French accent, "Zees is why I don't work wiz zee amateurs."

The organizer rubbed her temples. "All the stuffing will be judged without names or other identification. I know your recipes but Simon doesn't. Is that satisfactory?"

Everyone except Natasha nodded.

She smiled sweetly at the organizer and said, "You are aware that the contest is misnamed. Stuffing goes into something, like a bird. Dressing is baked separately."

Emma whined, "Who cares about that? No one stuffs a bird anymore. Stuffing and dressing are interchangeable these days. What's crucial is that Sophie breaks her date like Natasha said she should."

"Fine." I practically spat it. Even though I'd meant to do it anyway, it was irritating to have to do it on Natasha's demand. I could feel the fire burning in my face. Where did that devil Simon go?

Clyde, who'd been by Simon's side earlier, walked through the lobby. I jogged up to him and asked if he knew where his boss was.

Clyde assessed me with amusement. Did he think I intended to fawn over his boss like countless other women?

"They gave him a conference room so he could work during the contest. The George Washington Room, right down the hall."

It figured that a big shot like Simon wouldn't want to mingle with the rest of us all day. I made a quick pit stop in the ladies' room to catch my breath and regain my composure. Holding a wet paper towel against my flaming face I wondered why he had put me in this position.

I stormed down the hall to face Simon, rapped on the door, but didn't wait for permission to enter.

"Simon!" I charged into an empty room.

Almost empty.

SIX

From *Natasha Online*:

Salt isn't one size fits all anymore. Today's home kitchen should contain at least five different kinds of salt. Kosher for brining, coarse grinder salt for the salt mill, fine French sea salt for cooking, marvelous fleur de sel for salt shakers, and sel gris, also known as gray salt, my personal favorite.

Simon was sprawled on the floor facedown. Blood seeped from the back of his head onto the carpet.

A scream caught in my throat as the implications sank in. I ran toward him to help him, stopped abruptly, and backed up, scanning the room. Whoever injured him was gone. I darted at him again, knelt next to him, and felt his neck for a pulse.

There was none—but my own blood hammered in my head.

The door behind me opened and I shrieked, anticipating a bat-wielding killer.

Natasha's willowy shape filled the doorway. "Sophie. What have you done?"

I leapt to my feet. "I found him this way. He . . . he's dead."

Natasha pointed a well-manicured finger at me. "You killed him?" She swallowed hard and edged toward Simon's corpse. "You have to remain calm. I'm sure it must have been an accident. Don't worry. I'll stand by you. So will Mars."

"I didn't kill him!"

The muscles in Natasha's neck looked like taut rubber bands. She backed toward the door—fast. "I'm going to get Mars. He'll know what to do. You stay here and try to be calm." As she reached behind her for the handle, the door burst open.

Clyde stopped dead just inside the room. "What happened?" His normally calm demeanor dissolved. He dove at his boss and felt for a pulse. Natasha fled into the hallway. I could hear her shouting for Mars. I watched Clyde's face, hoping he'd find some sign of life that had eluded me. He rolled Simon onto his back and started CPR.

I felt my pockets for my cell phone. Rats. I'd left it in my work station. Running out of the room, I caught up to Natasha in the hallway.

"Do you have your cell? Call nine-one-one."

With her face as frozen as if she'd just had a BOTOX treatment, she stared at me for long seconds. "Yes, of course."

I ran back to the conference room to see if I could help.

The room was filling with hotel employees and contest participants. Mars and his brother wedged in, as did my dad. So many people were crowding into the room, I couldn't see Simon. Finally I managed to break through the crowd and cross the small space around Simon.

Clyde and a couple of guys from hotel security were still trying CPR. I backed away from the body to give them ample room, stepped on something hard, and lost my balance. Flailing my arms in a vain effort to break my fall, I landed, rather painfully, on top of the thing that tripped me. It was the stuffing trophy, a finely detailed turkey of heavy golden metal, the tail smeared with Simon's blood. Stunned, I threw it down and watched as it tumbled toward Simon until one of the security guys kicked it out of his way.

Like a sudden thunderbolt, Wolf stormed in and the atmosphere changed. He took over for the guy who'd been giving Simon heart compressions. While he worked, he growled, "Everyone out! Right now." The onlookers filtered out and I crossed the room to join them.

Wolf didn't raise his head or stop compressing but he said, "Everyone out except those with blood on their hands."

I looked at my fingers. A sticky red mess covered them.

"That means you, Sophie."

I stopped and looked down, shocked to realize that I had wiped Simon's blood on my pants. Even my shoes bore traces of red.

When the rescue squad arrived and took over tending Simon, Wolf seized my arm and propelled me to the service corridor behind the room. Thrusting my back to the wall, he assumed his police stance, feet apart, fists on his hips.

"Two murders in two days and only one constant—you."

"I had nothing to do with either of them."

"Give it up, Sophie. Your photograph wasn't in Otis's truck by accident. There's no way you're not tied to these murders. This doesn't look good for you."

"Oh, please." I said lightly. "I barely knew Simon."

"Rumor had it you knew him so well you were about to be disqualified."

"You're going to rely on a rumor?"

"You'd be surprised how often rumors can lead to

something useful. Did Simon and Otis threaten you? What did they have on you?"

"Nothing! I told you, I didn't know the PI at all and contrary to what some people seem to think, I wasn't involved with Simon."

Wolf turned his head to the side in a gesture of disbelief. "Then what were you doing here with Simon? You were supposed to be getting ready to cook."

"He put me in an awkward position by asking me out. I was looking for him to turn down the invitation. I admit I was upset, but you don't kill somebody because of that."

"People have been murdered for less."

Sarcasm got the better of me. "Oh, right. Let's see, either be disqualified or kill the judge. I don't know . . . seems like I wouldn't win the contest either way."

His mouth hardened. "So what's your story this time, wise guy?"

"There's no story. I walked in and found him dead."

"You seem to be doing that a lot." After glaring at me until I was uncomfortable, he said, "Don't take any trips."

He left me in the back corridor, reeling from the events of the last two days. He was right. Normal people didn't find two corpses in two days. Why should he believe me? It seemed like men were dropping all around me. And it didn't help that I'd picked up the murder weapon and handled it.

When I returned to the conference room, the rescue squad was loading Simon onto a gurney. A blanket covered him, including his face.

"Wolf?" I said. "You're going to find my fingerprints on the murder weapon."

He ran a hand across his forehead. "I'm going to end up arresting you, aren't I?"

"No. No!" I hastened to explain. "I fell over it and picked it up. There were lots of people in the room; someone must have seen me."

"Where is it then?"

I looked around. Assorted pieces of medical packaging littered the carpet but I didn't see the trophy. "It's the contest trophy. A heavy golden turkey, bronze or brass, I guess. I threw it on the floor."

Wolf stopped the rescue squad. "Any of you guys see a turkey?"

They shook their heads and kept going.

Wolf glared at me. "Why do you think it was the murder weapon?"

"There was blood on the tail."

He groaned. "Sometimes I look at you and I think you're a nice woman who happened to be in the wrong place at the wrong time. And other times I have to wonder if you're devious enough to pick up the murder weapon in front of people so there will be a good reason for your fingerprints to be on it. Now get out of here. This is a crime scene."

I walked out of the room a few yards behind the rescue squad. People lined the hallway, watching and whispering. Natasha wept in Mars's arms as though she'd lost her dearest friend.

Mom flew at me. "Oh, honey."

My family clustered around me.

"Simon's dead," I said.

"Heart attack?" Dad asked, ever logical.

"Someone killed him," I whispered.

Natasha must have overheard. Sniffing, she pulled out a dainty handkerchief trimmed in robin's-egg blue. "Are they going to arrest you?"

Mars's British friend, Bernie, appeared out of nowhere. "Arrest Sophie? Are you mad? It's a wonder no one did the man in sooner. And how about you, Natasha? You came on the scene suspiciously fast."

Her mouth dropped open.

In spite of the horrible situation, I flashed Bernie a

grateful smile for defending me. Bernie had been Mars's best man at our wedding and dropped in on us occasionally during our marriage. He was always the perfect houseguest, loads of fun, pitched in, and was easy to have around the house. The last I'd heard, he was tending bar at a pub in England. Had the situation been different, I'd have cornered him for an update on his life.

Dad's hand gripped my shoulder. His eyes met mine and I knew what he was thinking. I was in deep trouble.

Hannah clung to Craig. "I can't believe this is happening. Do you think we'll be on the news?"

Craig eyed me like a hawk, his face grim. His scrutiny made me want to squirm.

"Inga," Dad said to my mom, "I suspect we'll be a while. Wasn't there a wedding store in Georgetown that you didn't get to yesterday? And didn't you want to show Craig the tux we saw?"

Dad knew exactly what to say to sell the trip to the wedding enthusiasts.

Mars's brother, Andrew, chimed in, "No such luck, Mr. Bauer. We're corralled in this hotel like a bunch of cattle. It's stupid, if you ask me. If I'd wanted to kill Simon, I'd have done it two years ago." He snorted. "I got my satisfaction, though. The money he stole from me won't do him any good now."

Vicki looked aghast. "Andrew! Don't even joke about that. They're likely to take you seriously." She elbowed me and glanced around. "Do you think anyone heard that?"

"Only your family and mine."

I'd spent a lot of time with Andrew and Vicki when I was married to Mars. Vicki had a rough childhood. She'd lost her parents quite young and been raised by a brother who had lived abroad as long as I'd known her.

Sometimes I wondered how Vicki and Andrew felt when Aunt Faye left her fancy house to Mars and me. I imagined quite a bit of tooth-gnashing went on privately when we divorced and I ended up with the house. Vicki and Andrew had bought a nice townhome in Old Town, an easy walk from my house, but it couldn't compare in size or architectural charm.

I chalked up Andrew's ill-conceived remark to his desperate desire to be important. It didn't take a shrink to realize that Andrew longed for the kind of success and respect his brother, Mars, had achieved. Although Mars's connections to the rich and powerful opened a lot of doors for Andrew, I'd seen more than one person with a panicked expression try to dodge him at parties. His reputation for financial disaster surrounded him like a barnyard stench.

"What is wrong with you people?" Natasha dabbed at her eyes. "A wonderful man has been murdered and you're all just thinking about yourselves. I'm devastated."

Andrew smirked. "Knock it off, Miss Prim and Proper. If I were Mars, right about now I'd be wondering why you're blubbering about the death of a virtual stranger."

My dad intervened. "Let's settle down. We're all upset, Natasha. Let's stop this pettiness before people say things they'll regret."

The loudspeaker squawked and came to life with a piercing squeal. "Ladies and gentlemen, this is Detective Fleishman of the Alexandria Police Department. I'm sorry to have to ask you to return to the ballroom for the time being. We'll process everyone and get you out of here as quickly as we possibly can. Please relax. We've asked the hotel to serve additional refreshments."

Emma shouted, "What about the contest?"

I wished I could see Wolf's face.

"Uh, it's up to the organizers to determine what to do about that but I can assure you that it will not take place today in any event. Thank you."

After the requisite moans and groans, everyone headed back to the ballroom. Gossip ran rampant, though, and I could tell people were looking my way. They stared first but turned their heads quickly when I noticed them. I made a detour to the ladies' room.

I felt as though my entire body was quivering. Water ran over my trembling hands, washing off blood. I splashed cold water on my face, heedless of the small amount of makeup I wore. The trauma of finding Otis still haunted me, and discovering Simon's corpse shook me to the core.

For the sake of my family, I tried to pull myself together, patted my face dry, and took several deep breaths before returning to the ballroom. Mom and Nina brought coffee and bagels for Dad and me and we hunkered down behind my work counter. The hazelnut aroma had lost its appeal, though, and the dry bagel was nothing more than something to do. Dad wisely clamped down on us and forbade us to discuss the incident.

Hannah sulked while Craig went for refreshments. She slouched in her chair, her arms wrapped across her chest. "I had everything perfectly planned for Craig this weekend. Now my sister is a murder suspect and Craig is going to have to be interrogated by the police. Can you even imagine what he must think of us? I'll be lucky if he doesn't break off the engagement."

Mom patted her arm. "Darling, this is a good time to see how he acts in the face of adversity. He's an intelligent man. I'm sure he understands that this isn't typical for us."

"What's with the pale sweater, Hannah?" I asked. She'd always preferred fuchsia and periwinkle to soft shades.

"Craig likes me in muted colors."

I'd done my share of silly things for boyfriends, so I couldn't fault her for trying to please him. Wondering what could be taking him so long, I stood to look for him. If he was in the ballroom, I didn't see him. I did, however, see Natasha being escorted by a police officer, probably for her turn at being questioned. I wouldn't be far behind.

Hannah pasted a smile on her face and sat up straight and I realized Craig must be on his way back.

Obviously pleased with himself, he handed out foam

boxes containing French fries and roast beef sandwiches. He dug in his pocket and pulled out packets of ketchup. "Hope I got enough for all of us."

Hannah and Mom gushed appreciation but I wondered where he'd bought the food. No one else in the ballroom held foam boxes.

A pink flush crept up the sides of his face and culminated in red cheeks reminiscent of someone who'd been out in the cold. He wore a black, long-sleeved polo and jeans, not enough to keep warm outside. I spotted the sleeve of his bomber jacket hanging from the pile of coats we'd left on a chair.

Hannah dug into the French fries. "Yum—they need salt, though. Sophie, do you have any salt in your cooking ingredients?"

Of course I did. I found the salt and offered it to her.

She sprinkled a heavy dose on her fries and took a bite. "Ugh. Are you trying to kill me, too?"

Dad's face looked like it did when we were kids and didn't know when to stop pushing his buttons. "Hannah, your sister didn't kill anyone. You cannot say things like that. I don't think you understand how serious this situation is for Sophie."

"It's always about Sophie. This weekend was supposed to be about me and Craig. Besides, taste this."

Dad took one of her fries and bit into it. "Sugar."

I shook out a pinch of salt and tasted it. Definitely sugar.

"Hey, Wendy," I called, "do me a favor and taste your salt."

"Oh, my gosh," she cried, "it's sugar. Someone was doing everything possible to sabotage the contest."

Thinking that the saboteur wouldn't have tampered with his or her own ingredients, I was tempted to demand a check of everyone's ingredients. But a young police officer arrived to escort me to be questioned.

Not quite sure what would happen, I bent over my

father's shoulder and said, "Don't worry about me. You go shopping and I'll meet you at home."

I hated the fear etched on his face and as I walked away, I heard my mother say, "For heaven's sake, Paul, they're just going to ask her questions."

Detective Kenner met me in the ballroom lobby and took me aside to grill me. Across the room, I could see Wolf questioning Natasha.

Kenner asked me the same questions in different ways. When I stuck to my boring story about finding Simon's body and picking up the turkey with blood on it, Kenner's nostrils flared.

I worked at remaining calm as his rage rose. His voice grew louder but I didn't allow him to intimidate me.

Wolf, busy across the lobby, watched us periodically.

Kenner's face turned a shade of purple that suggested high-blood-pressure issues. He squinted at me and hovered too close for my comfort. "You may think that you've suckered Wolf into believing your lies, but you don't fool me for a second."

His face inches from mine, he snapped his fingers and yelled, "Take her to the station."

SEVEN

From *"Ask Natasha"*:

Dear Natasha,

My in-laws are arriving in droves and they expect to stay with us. I have to work and don't have time for all the extra meals and laundry. What to do?

—Crowded in Cranston

Dear Crowded,

Everyone deserves fresh 1,000-count Egyptian cotton sheets and fluffy down pillows. A gracious hostess pampers her guests. Get up a few hours early to make breakfast and clean. The extra effort will be worth it. If you have to be gone during the day, hire a limousine to show them around in style.

—Natasha

Was I being arrested? I looked over at Wolf. He made no effort to help me. The young officer didn't handcuff me, though, he merely showed me out the side door of the hotel to the backseat of a police cruiser.

When he climbed into the front seat, I asked, "Am I under arrest?"

In a polite southern accent, he said, "Why, no, ma'am. You just need to give your bloody clothes as evidence."

<hr/>

By the time a cop drove me home, all I wanted was a nap. I unlocked the front door of my house and listened. The others must still be out. But something wasn't right. Where was Mochie?

I slid off the jacket that hadn't been warm enough for the November chill and called Mochie's name repeatedly. When I hung the jacket in the hall closet, I heard pathetic mewing. I found Mochie in the living room, looking down at me from the top of the grandfather clock.

"You managed to get up there, you little rascal; are you sure you need help getting down?"

He continued meowing and watched me with those big eyes. I fetched a ladder from the basement and set it next to the clock. I hadn't even climbed to the midpoint of the ladder when the scamp leapt onto my shoulder and clung to my police-issued T-shirt. I patted him to reassure him. He crawled next to my ear and thanked me with heavy purring. But when my feet hit the floor, he sprang from my shoulder and raced through the house like a wildcat. He flew over furniture and in and out of rooms so fast that his paws barely touched the floor.

I couldn't help laughing at his joyous antics. He tore through the kitchen while I put away the ladder and raced ahead of me when I headed up the stairs for a much-needed shower.

My hopes for a nap were dashed when I stepped out of the shower and heard voices and footsteps on the stairs. I dreaded the evening. I was dog tired and still had to make chicken broth for the soup and stuffing, not to mention two pies and a batch of my famous brownies. I thanked my lucky stars it would just be six of us for Thanksgiving dinner the next day and that, except for the colonel and Craig, it was really all just family. They'd understand if things weren't perfect.

I'd anticipated being too tired to cook after the contest and had prepared a vegetable lasagna on Monday, before my parents arrived. When I joined everyone in the kitchen, the heady scents of oregano and garlic already mingled in the air as the lasagna heated. The others set the table for dinner while I quartered an onion, peeled six carrots, and washed celery. I popped them all into a stockpot along with a whole chicken, a large bay leaf, and four cloves of garlic. Dad built a fire while Mom cooked sweet potatoes for a dish she'd promised Craig. Except for my exhaustion and the fact that I'd found two dead men, everything seemed almost normal.

After dinner, I brewed a pot of strong French vanilla coffee to drink with the leftover Bourbon Pecan Pie. In spite of the caffeine, I felt myself relaxing. The fire crackled and bathed the kitchen in a warm light. My family bantered in a friendly way, evoking laughter and sly grins. Maybe the worst was behind me.

Craig and Hannah insisted on cleaning up, although I couldn't recall the last time Hannah washed dishes without complaining. They were playful and sweet, teasing each other gently. Maybe I hadn't given Craig a fair chance. After all, he seemed far different from the drop-dead gorgeous, girl-in-every-port types she usually lusted after.

But there was still something about Craig that made me keep my distance. It wasn't the bad comb-over. That was unfortunate but not off-putting. And it wasn't his looks. Tall and broad-shouldered, he'd been blessed with good bone structure, high, defined cheekbones, and a strong jawline. I was baffled, and returned to my Thanksgiving meal prep.

I chopped carrots and celery for the stuffing and asked, "So where did you lovebirds meet?"

Hannah giggled. "Don't tell Mom and Dad, okay? On the internet."

I swung around and stared at Hannah. She was serious.

"You should try it." Craig handed Hannah a goblet to dry. "We could help you fill out the questionnaire."

I wanted to snap at Hannah. Did she know anything about him? I'd spent part of the day with him and I knew nothing. "What's your specialty?"

"I'm an internist."

Hannah beamed.

It sounded impressive. But wouldn't an internist have come to Simon's aid today? Had Craig crowded into the room with the others?

He nuzzled Hannah's hair and I knew I couldn't just come out and ask a question like that without starting a sibling squabble.

"At Berrysville Community Hospital?" I asked.

"In West Virginia. Where do these go?" He held up serving spoons.

I pointed to a drawer. "Where in West Virginia?"

He shut the drawer. "Morgantown."

Had his voice grown tense? "Where did you go to med school?"

Hannah tugged at him. "Let's watch a movie. I'll make some popcorn but would you be a sweetheart and get my pale pink sweater from the bedroom?"

As soon as he left, she turned on me. "Stop it. You're jealous because you don't have Mars anymore. It's your own fault for letting Natasha steal him. I'm finally happy and you're being mean because Craig is wealthy and successful and handsome and you can't stand it. This time it's me who landed the great guy. Get used to it. You're so obvious. He knows you don't like him."

I longed to hug her to me, to protect her, but instead I twisted a dish towel in my hands. I knew she must be right. Craig hadn't done anything to deserve my suspicion. "I'm sorry, Hannah. I'm on edge because of the murders." I wanted to bite my own tongue off as soon as I said "murders."

But she didn't notice. She shut the microwave door and set the timer.

"Just try to be nice and stop grilling him. Is that too much to ask of you? After all, he's going to be family." The popping accelerated. She pushed the stop button, poured steaming popcorn into a bowl, and disappeared into the family room.

"And Natasha didn't steal Mars," I muttered in her direction.

<hr />

By midnight, everyone except Mochie and me had gone to bed. A pecan pie cooled on a rack on the counter. The brownies rested in the fridge, next to the stuffing that was ready to be baked the next day. I'd cleaned and cut the green beans and toasted the almonds. I'd even found a few minutes to make a double recipe of cranberry sauce.

I was taking a pumpkin pie out of the oven when I heard the purr of an engine and a knock at the front door.

A lump formed in my throat. It could only be the police. They didn't arrive at midnight with good news. They'd come to arrest me. Standing on my tiptoes, I peered through the peephole but couldn't see anything. The knock came again, louder this time. Leaving the chain on the door, I pulled it open a hair. Mars's mother stood on the stoop with a suitcase. I closed the door and unchained it as fast as I could.

"June! What on earth are you doing here?"

She picked up her bag and walked in.

"Sophie? What's going on?" I turned to see my mom and dad standing on the stairs.

I shut the door against the cold night. June took off her coat, revealing a fuzzy lilac bathrobe. She hung her coat in the hall closet. "You don't mind, do you, dear?" She looked up at my parents. "Hello, Inga, Paul."

The kettle whistled and I ran to silence it before it woke anyone else.

June and my parents followed me into the kitchen.

"Perfect! It's as though you knew I was coming," June said. "Have any of your fresh chocolate chip cookies?"

"Of course." I hauled some out of the freezer, cut the dough into chunks, and popped them into the warm oven.

Mom found china mugs and brewed a holiday tea scented with orange and cloves while Dad threw another log on the fire.

June nestled into one of the fireside chairs and Mochie jumped into her lap. My parents watched her curiously.

"You must think me audacious," she said, "but I couldn't stand another minute with that woman. Can you imagine, all I wanted was to put the kettle on for tea and she flew into a rage."

"Natasha?" asked my dad.

"Every night I pray that Mars won't marry her. Acted like I was an old coot who couldn't do anything right. That kitchen of hers belongs in a restaurant. Cold. I think everything in it came from Italy. So many buttons and gauges you can't tell what's what. Not like this kitchen where you can settle in and get cozy. Everything about her is cold. Do you know she put plastic under my sheets because she thought I would wet the bed?"

"That doesn't sound like her at all. Natasha puts a lot of stock in being a gracious hostess," said Mom.

"You're welcome to stay with us, June," I assured her.

"I told her I was going to a hotel, but I didn't think

you'd mind. I'm so much more comfortable in my sister's home."

Her words stung even though I didn't think that was her intent. It *was* her sister's house. Maybe Mars should have bought me out and kept it in his family. Just because I liked it didn't give me special rights to it.

The cookies and tea calmed June. It was creeping up on one in the morning and we were all bushed. Everyone said good night and I carried June's luggage up to a second-floor guest room with an antique canopy bed that was too big for it. As she sat on the bed, June ran her hands over the coverlet. "Faye always let me sleep in here. There's something special about this room. Reminds me of a fancy bed-and-breakfast."

Bidding her good night, I tiptoed downstairs in the dark, trying to avoid squeaky spots on the stairs. With all the commotion, I thought I'd better check to be sure the fire had died down and that I had locked up. After hooking the chain securely on the front door, I shuffled into the kitchen.

Golden embers glowed against the ashes like demonic eyes. In their fading light I made out a horrifying, misshapen face pressed against the window of the kitchen door.

EIGHT

From "THE GOOD LIFE":

Dear Sophie,

Every year my wife is a basket case trying to make everything perfect for the holidays. Do you have any advice to help her?

—Anxious in Alexandria

Dear Anxious,

Thanksgiving is one of those holidays when people want traditional fare. Your wife doesn't have to knock herself out coming up with new gourmet twists. Turkey, cranberries, stuffing, and pie. The basics are what most people yearn for. And a lot of those can be prepared in advance.

Besides, no one will remember the perfect Thanksgiving anyway. Five and ten years from now, family and friends will be laughing over the time the turkey burned and you had to order in Chinese food. Or the impossibly hard biscuits Aunt Beth insisted on making every year. All the perfect food will be long forgotten.

Your wife should relax and enjoy herself. It's the mishaps and the funny incidents that create the best memories.

—Sophie

It clawed at the door and released a mournful wail. I shrank from the sounds before I realized there was something familiar about them. Daisy. But whose face was pressed against the glass?

"Daisy?" I whispered.

More scratching.

Had I been alone I would have been more cowardly about opening the door. All sorts of dire thoughts ran through my head. Maybe Mars had grabbed Daisy and run away from Natasha, too. Maybe the Peeping Tom was back. Or maybe someone had kidnapped Daisy and wanted a ransom. None seemed likely.

I opened the door a crack and Daisy barged in with hound-style enthusiasm, wagging her tail, which in turn wagged her entire back end. She rushed at me, pawing the air.

I grabbed her wriggling body in a big dog hug. To my complete surprise, Mars's old college chum, Bernie, stood in the doorway.

"Is everything okay?" I asked. "It's the middle of the night."

In his delightful British accent he replied, "Natasha was trying to impress some stuffed shirts tonight, and I believe she was trying to hide me. So I snagged the other mongrel without the right pedigree and here we are."

I'd always liked Bernie, but he was a bit of a wild card. Bawdy, likely to blurt the thing everyone was thinking but was too polite to say, and generally unemployed. His sandy hair was always tousled and he usually looked as though he'd just rolled out of bed or left a pub after a rowdy night of drinking.

I grinned. Bernie probably didn't realize that Natasha didn't have much of a snazzy pedigree herself. Her father abandoned the family when Natasha was only seven, leaving her mother to support them by working long days at the local diner in our hometown.

"Daisy offered to share her dog bed with me if I'd bring her home to you." He tilted his head like a questioning puppy.

"No need to share. That tiny bedroom on the third floor is still available or you can bunk on the pullout sofa in Mars's old den."

"The den by all means. Mars didn't happen to leave any good Scotch in there, did he?"

Mochie scampered into the kitchen.

"Good gods. A kitten!"

It was too late to lunge for Daisy. Bernie and I froze, waiting for hissing, barking, and the inevitable chase that would wake everyone.

Mochie lifted his tiny head to sniff Daisy's saggy hound jowls. Daisy stepped back, unsure what to think of the little interloper.

When Daisy didn't pose a threat, Mochie jumped up onto the table to investigate Bernie.

"What a scamp. I've only known one cat who wasn't afraid of dogs. My mother's fourth husband owned a farm in England and there was a yellow barn cat who bossed the dogs around. Amazing to watch, really." He scratched Mochie under the chin. "I bet you wouldn't even be afraid of Natasha."

I brought Bernie towels and linens and he took to Mars's old den as though he planned to stay awhile.

Mochie and Daisy followed me to my second-floor bedroom and curled up on the bed, albeit on opposite ends.

On Thanksgiving morning, I slept later than I should have for a person with a house full of guests. Neither Daisy nor Mochie was in the bedroom when I woke. I showered in a rush and pulled on a pumpkin-colored sleeveless turtleneck, beige trousers, and a sweater embroidered with fall leaves. The kitchen would be hot today with both ovens going. I figured I could shed the leafy sweater to keep cool.

I found my guests in the sunroom, which had heated nicely in spite of the crisp weather. The brick floor warmed my feet.

Daisy stretched out next to Bernie, whose bare calves jutted out from under a flannel bathrobe. Daisy didn't bother to get up but her tail flapped on the floor when she saw me. I bent to tickle her tummy.

Mom was relaxing with a mug of coffee, her feet on a footstool. "There's a ham and asparagus frittata keeping warm in the oven, sleepyhead. Bernie's been regaling us with tales of his mother's many marriages."

Hannah blushed and I wondered if that was an intentional jab by Mom. Craig would be Hannah's third husband, but if I recalled correctly, Bernie's mom had made the trip down the aisle seven or eight times.

I headed to the kitchen for coffee but paused when I heard voices. One voice, actually.

June was talking in the kitchen. I paused for a moment, wondering who wasn't in the sunroom.

"I couldn't agree more," she said. "You made the right decision. And I love what they did with the kitchen."

I peeked in. June sat by the fire, knitting. Only Mochie kept her company.

"Good morning." Had she been speaking to the kitten? I slid the frittata out of the oven and offered June a piece.

"I've eaten, thanks. It was quite good. And your mother

was so cute pretending Hannah cooked it." She giggled. "Your sister doesn't share your culinary skills."

Food had never been one of Hannah's interests. "She has very impressive computer abilities, though. It's a good thing she's honest because she'd make a heck of a hacker."

"I was just telling Faye how glad I am that you own the house. It's so cozy and inviting."

Faye? Faye was dead.

I glanced up at the photo of Faye over the fireplace. It hung straight. No odd drafts today.

June reached out to stroke Mochie.

Maybe I'd heard her wrong. "Could I get you some more coffee?"

"No, dear. I'm fine as I am. Just having a lovely chat."

"With the kitten?" I held my breath, hoping I'd misunderstood about Faye.

"With my sister. She adores Mochie. Faye always had a cat and she's so pleased that there's a little one in residence now."

Was June losing her mind? Suddenly I had new appreciation for Natasha's need to protect her mattress. Maybe June wasn't well.

Dad joined us from the foyer. I hadn't seen him so worried since my brother, at the age of sixteen, bought a motorcycle from a friend for fifty dollars. He waved the newspaper at me. "Why didn't you tell me this?"

Dad slid his reading glasses on and opened the paper. "According to reliable police sources, the person of interest in the slaying of Simon Greer is also a person of interest in the murder of Otis Pulchinski, a private investigator killed one day earlier." He lowered his glasses and took a deep breath while fixing his eyes on me.

"I didn't want to worry you."

"Good job, Sophie. I'm worried now."

"It's all coincidence. Being in the wrong places at the

wrong times. If I hadn't beat her there by seconds, Natasha would have found Simon's body."

"Honey, you need a lawyer. Simon was a rich and influential man. They're going to be under a lot of pressure to find his killer."

"But I didn't do anything. There can't be any witnesses or anything tying me to either murder because I didn't kill anyone."

"Oh, Sophie!" June interjected. "Don't be naive. Mars's father always said most killers are convicted on circumstantial evidence."

June didn't sound delusional now. Mars's father had been a judge. June probably knew a thing or two about trials.

Dad massaged his jaw. "Let's not mention anything to your mother or Hannah yet. They're in vacation mode and will be oblivious to the news for a few days. Tomorrow I want you to call a lawyer."

June studied her knitting, a soft cream sweater with a thin thread of bronze Lurex shot through the wool. "Could Natasha have had time to kill Simon and wait for you to enter the room before raising the alarm?"

Given the way she'd been treated, I couldn't blame June for disliking Natasha, but I honestly couldn't imagine Natasha murdering Simon and trying to pin it on me. She prided herself on her own perfection and expected nothing less from others. While that made her seem starchy sometimes—okay, a lot of the time—I'd known her long enough to think it unlikely that she could be the killer.

On the other hand, June made a good point. Natasha knew I was looking for Simon. "I'm sure she could have. There were two back doors to a service corridor. Anyone could have slipped away quickly."

I checked the time. If we were going to eat turkey, I would have to get moving.

Dad and June joined the others in the sunroom. As soon as they left the kitchen, I phoned an attorney I'd met in passing several times. I knew he wouldn't answer since it was Thanksgiving but I left a detailed message anyway in the hope that he would be working on Friday.

I hung up, picked up the coffeepot, and realized that Craig was lurking in the kitchen behind me, listening. He wore running shoes, a Georgetown University sweatshirt, and shorts that showed off long muscular legs.

I hated that he'd overheard my call. And his habit of sneaking around and eavesdropping didn't do anything to engender warm feelings for him. Mindful of Hannah's outburst the night before, I asked politely, "Coffee?"

He reached back with his left arm, grabbed his left foot, and stood one-legged while he stretched. "No, thanks. I'm going for a run."

An awkward moment passed between us.

"If you're half the cook Hannah says you are, I'm certain I'll be overeating later." He flashed me a grin of perfect teeth. "Better work off some calories ahead of time."

It was a transparent effort to be nice but I gave him credit for trying. I followed him to the front door, opened it, and said, "Enjoy your run."

Laughter filtered in from the sunroom. I returned to the kitchen, set the oven to preheat and slid off my sweater, then took the coffeepot into the sunroom to see if anyone needed refills.

Bernie had stepped outside to use the phone. Through the glass, I could see his worried expression. Daisy roamed near him and sniffed at the overturned pots I'd forgotten to set straight.

While I poured coffee, Bernie returned, shivering.

"That was Mars. Bad news, I'm afraid," said Bernie. "They had a rather nasty fire in Natasha's kitchen last night."

June paled. "Was Mars hurt?"

Everyone asked questions at once.

Bernie motioned for quiet. "Mars and Natasha are fine but the house is uninhabitable. They've moved into a hotel and, of course, there will be no grand feast at Natasha's place today."

"You're welcome to join us," I offered. "We have plenty. I bought way too much anyway."

Mom rewarded me with a proud smile.

June looked down at the partially knitted sweater in her lap. "That's very kind of you, Sophie. I only wish I could spend some time with Mars. I had hoped to have some private time with him today while Natasha cooked."

"I know exactly how you feel." Mom placed a hand on June's shoulder. "It breaks my heart that my son and his family can't be here today."

My brother lived in Chantilly, a Washington, DC, suburb outside the Beltway. It wasn't too far as the crow flew, though it could be a good forty-five-minute haul in traffic. But this Thanksgiving, they'd driven to Connecticut to see his wife's family.

Hannah blurted out what I was thinking. "Give me a break, Mom; you just want to see Jen."

My brother's ten-year-old daughter was the only grandchild in our family and everyone doted on her.

Dad, always the voice of reason, chided gently, "Come now. You can't expect to see them every holiday. And don't forget, they'll be joining us for Christmas, which is more fun for a child anyway."

Mom seemed perilously close to pushing back tears. "It's just that I never get to see them. They're always so busy. Sophie, you see them more often than I do." Her face brightened. "Why don't we invite Mar—"

Oh, no! "Mom," I interrupted, "could you help me in the kitchen?"

She nodded at June and followed me.

Whispering, I said, "Don't you dare invite Mars and Natasha to dinner."

"Honey, you saw how sad June was. Is it really so much to ask?"

"Do you honestly expect me to entertain my ex-husband and his new girlfriend—who, incidentally, accused me of murder—at Thanksgiving dinner?"

"Honey, this is your chance to steal Mars back."

"Natasha did not steal Mars."

Mom patted me as though she didn't believe it. "There will be so many people you'll hardly notice." She sniffed. "And it will help me forget that Jen can't be here."

"No."

"Well, I must say that I'm very disappointed in you, Sophie. Where is your compassion? Their house burned and you can't even bring yourself to offer them one meal? I brought you up better than that. Besides, I have to see Natasha's mother every week at the hospital auxiliary. It's only good manners. If your kitchen burned down, I would expect Natasha to invite you." She paused. "And what's more, Natasha would do it because she has exquisite manners."

I would not let myself be manipulated. "No."

June poked her head into the kitchen. "I don't mean to interrupt, but Bernie lent me his cute little phone to call Mars. They've accepted your generous invitation. Now I'm going to call Andrew and Vicki."

June must have read the astonishment on my face because she added quickly, "They have nowhere else to go. Vicki's only living relative is a brother in Hong Kong. We've never met him. He didn't even come to their wedding."

Mars's brother and his wife, too? My eyes met Mom's in desperation. All of my former in-laws would be coming for dinner.

Mom shrugged like it was out of our hands. But she looked far too happy about it.

NINE

From *"A Natasha Thanksgiving"*:

For a dramatic centerpiece, hollow out eight small pumpkins. Randomly make holes in all of them with an electric drill. Be sure you drill matching holes on the sides so they can be joined in a circle. Use screws and bolts to fasten the pumpkins into a circle. Place a votive candle in each pumpkin and you'll have a sparkling showpiece for the center of your table or your buffet.

Hannah bounced into the kitchen, typically oblivious to the chaos in my life. "I'm taking a bath and doing my hair while Craig is out. Don't want him to see me in hot curlers."

I could have used some help, but if she was going to hog the only full bathroom for a while, she probably ought to do it now.

Dad grumbled a bit about Bernie having taken over the den. I gathered he'd planned to hide there with the newspaper. Instead, he and Daisy hit the brick sidewalks for a stroll.

Unlike Mars, who'd rather have died than spend the morning with three women in the kitchen, Bernie puttered about in his bathrobe, completely comfortable. He put on the kettle for tea, sampled cranberry sauce that had gelled, stirred roux for the gravy until it turned golden and smelled delicately nutty, and asked June about her sister.

I wondered if his unorthodox upbringing in so many different households had something to do with his ease and obvious desire to cozy up in the kitchen with us.

While she talked, June's knitting needles flew like they were on autopilot. "In the forties, an elegant socialite named Perle Mesta hosted intimate dinner parties for select guests in Washington. Legend has it that more than one international deal was sealed at her dinner table. She knew who to put together, you see, in a gracious setting, so that political deals could be worked out."

She paused to untangle Mochie's paw from her yarn. "Given that group of pompous political wannabes Natasha had at the house last night, I'd say she aspires to Perle Mesta fame." She tsked. "Explains why she had to sink her claws into Mars. Anyway, Faye never quite reached Perle's stature but she entertained Washington glitterati here. Things were different then. Women wanted jobs and entered the workforce, and being a domestic diva lost its glamour for a good many years. But that never deterred Faye. She put on her orange miniskirt and tie-dyed tops and hosted everything from séances to elegant midnight dinners. That's why the dining room is so large. She put the addition on the back of the house so she could accommodate big parties."

A mug of tea in his hand, Bernie walked over to examine Faye's picture. "We should hold a séance to see if we can contact her."

I bit my lip and waited to see if June would mention talking to Faye.

June simply smiled and said, "She never was the prettiest girl at the party but she sure was the most fun."

Time sped by with Mom and me arguing over whether basting a turkey actually makes a difference in moistness. I claimed it didn't and that opening the oven to baste only dropped the temperature. Mom insisted that drizzling the top with juices made for moister meat.

With the side dishes well under way, I faced the challenge of Thanksgiving hors d'oeuvres. Some guests don't want anything before the heavy meal but others choose to nibble. I mixed a batch of my light-as-air one-bite cheese puffs to bake in the oven as guests arrived. For those willing to eat a little bit more, I stuffed mushroom caps with a zesty crabmeat mixture.

All the dishes under control, I pulled on my sweater and popped out to the backyard with a basket and pruning shears. Though I hated to steal them from the birds, the orange pyracantha berries growing along the back fence would make a perfect centerpiece. Low enough for guests to see over, yet vibrant and cheery. I cut enough to fill several small vases. Natasha would have done something far more elaborate but I liked the simplicity of the berries. While I was out there, I righted the pots the Peeping Tom had knocked over.

Back inside, I pulled out one of Faye's ultra-long tablecloths of woven green, amber, and pumpkin plaid. When we inherited her sizable collections of china patterns and silver, I wondered what we would do with it all. Now I was thrilled to have a dozen matching place settings to use.

I felt certain Natasha had planned to use fancy-schmancy china and was almost sure that was the reason I chose sage-green earthenware plates and soup bowls. I added inexpensive wine and water glasses that I had bought because I loved the iridescent amber glass of the goblets. I bunched berries in three-inch vases and arranged them in clusters down the center of the table, mixing in colorful ceramic candlesticks.

Stepping back, I appraised the table. Festive and not at all stuffy. Perfect.

Mom peeked in the doorway. "It looks lovely, dear, but you need to add one more place setting."

I did the math again in my head. "No, it's an even dozen."

Mom gave me that look I knew from my childhood when she had a secret.

"Mom!" She didn't know anyone up here besides my brother, and he and his family were out of town. "Who did you invite?"

The doorbell rang. Perfect timing for Mom to avoid my question.

My stomach flip-flopped. I'd been dreading the moment Natasha and Mars would arrive.

Mom flicked a piece of fuzz off my shoulder. "Couldn't you have worn something that showed a little cleavage?"

What could she possibly be thinking? I didn't have time to contemplate it. I sucked in a deep breath of air, pasted a smile on my face, and answered the door.

Complete chaos ensued. Dad returned with Daisy, who shot into the house. Mars arrived with Natasha at the same time that the colonel and MacArthur strode up the walk followed by Craig.

They paired off quickly. MacArthur, the bulldog, romped with his old buddy, Daisy. Dad and the colonel commandeered the den.

Natasha, wearing her smiling TV hostess face, handed me a wreath of sugar pumpkins. A votive candle rested in each hollowed-out pumpkin.

"You didn't have to bring anything." I examined it closely. She'd made little holes for the light to shine through. "When could you possibly have had the time to make this?"

"It didn't take long. I borrowed a few things from the

hotel maintenance department. Thanksgiving's a slow time for them. They didn't mind." She held out her arms and cried, "Hannah!"

With barely restrained southern graciousness, she fussed over my sister. "I haven't seen you in years. Just as pretty as ever. You know I always said if I could have a little sister, I'd want her to be just like you."

Hannah introduced Natasha to Craig, which brought on a fresh torrent from Natasha. "Only seven months until the wedding? That's not much time. You have to tell me everything you're planning."

Little did Natasha know that a recitation of the details could last right up to the wedding day.

Hannah wore a buff-colored sweater set and tiny pearl earrings, a major change from her usual hot-pink clothes and bold jewelry. More of Craig's influence? Her blonde tresses bouncing from their hot curler treatment, Hannah ushered Natasha and Craig into the sunroom.

Mom suggested sending Mars and June into the living room for the private time June had wanted with her son but I stopped her and handed her the pumpkin wreath. "I'd like a word with Mars, if you don't mind. Would you find room for this on the buffet?"

She raised an eyebrow at me but acquiesced, grinning. "I'll help your dad serve cocktails."

Mars tilted his head. "Natasha said you'd try something like this, but I insisted we were past that. Sophie, hon, seeing you yesterday rekindled some feelings, but I'm not ready to leave Nat."

"You flatter yourself. I need to talk to you about June."

"Oh, no, not you, too. Nat thinks it's time for Mom to move to a home for the elderly."

"I don't want that, but I am worried."

He followed me to the kitchen entry. I held out my hand to stop him from going in.

We could hear June saying, "That couldn't be helped.

But don't you see, this is an opportunity to get Sophie and Mars back together again."

Mars muttered, "Aw, Mom." He walked into the kitchen and looked around. In a kind voice he asked, "Who are you talking to?"

She didn't drop a stitch of her knitting when she said, "Your aunt Faye."

Mars's eyes couldn't have opened wider if he had actually seen Faye's ghost. He kneeled beside her. "Mom," he said in the most gentle tone I'd ever heard him use, "Faye has been dead for several years."

June kept knitting. "You didn't think she'd leave this house, did you?"

"You think Aunt Faye's ghost is haunting this house?" Mars gripped the edge of the chair, looked up at me, and winced as he waited for her answer.

"Haunt doesn't seem right. That has spooky implications. I feel her spirit here."

Relief flooded Mars's face. "So you don't really hear Faye talking."

"Oh, no! I hear her very well. It's lovely having a visit with her again."

Mars bowed his head, no doubt to hide a worried expression. "Sophie and I don't hear Faye."

"Maybe you're not listening."

Mars rose and lifted his hands in a helpless gesture.

"Mom, you need to face reality. Faye is dead and Sophie and I are divorced. I'm with Natasha now."

"I know that. I'm not daft."

I tried, too. "June, it's lovely that you'd like to see us reunite but that's not going to happen."

June's knitting needles stopped and she turned her attention to Mars. "Not married to Natasha yet, are you?"

"No, ma'am."

"You see?" She grinned. "There's always hope."

Mars suggested they retire to the living room to talk

but on his way out of the kitchen, he pulled me aside. "Do you think Mom's losing it?"

"She seems okay otherwise."

"Let's not mention this to Natasha. She'll have Mom institutionalized by next week if she finds out Mom thinks she's talking to Faye. Especially now that Mom burned down half of her house."

"Are you sure your mom started the fire?"

"Nat's certain."

Their private time didn't last long. Mars's younger brother, Andrew, arrived with Vicki.

"Thank you so much for including us today," said Vicki. "We were at Natasha's last night when the fire broke out. It was awful. And we didn't have alternative plans. I had visions of us eating peanut butter and jelly sandwiches for Thanksgiving."

I was shutting the door when a timid knock came from the other side. A slight man with fine hair so blond it verged on white said, "Hello, Sophie."

TEN

Dear Sophie,

When my sister-in-law hosts family holidays, she gets up at four in the morning to bake bread. I work long days and with three kids, I need my sleep and don't have time to bake when it's my turn to host family gatherings. I hate it when my sister-in-law turns her nose up at my store-bought bread. What to do?

—Snoozing in Saltville

Dear Snoozing,

You need your sleep. Don't feel guilty about it. I make rolls or knots about a week ahead of time and I let my bread machine do the hard work. Even the busiest mom can find a few minutes to dump ingredients into a bread machine. Put it on "manual" and it will take the bread all the way through the first rise. Then take the dough out and shape it into rolls or cute knots. The kids can help with that. Place the rolls or knots on an ungreased cookie sheet. Cover with a clean kitchen towel and let rise (out of drafts) until they double in size. Remove the towel and cover the still raw dough with plastic wrap. Slide the entire wrapped tray into the freezer. If you need the tray or more space in the freezer, you can put them in a plastic freezer bag once they're frozen. When you need them, preheat the oven to 350 degrees, spritz the tops with water, and sprinkle a little salt on them before sliding the tray into the oven. They'll taste every bit as fresh as your sister-in-law's. But you won't be as tired as she is.

—Sophie

The man at the door seemed vaguely familiar. "May I help you?"

"You don't remember me? But I remember you." He bent toward me and spoke confidentially, "I cheered for you when you won the school hopscotch championship over Natasha."

Feeling stupid, I searched his face. He was talking about something that happened in fourth grade. Or was it fifth? Who was this guy?

Mom's voice sang over my shoulder, "Humphrey! I hope you didn't have any trouble finding the house."

Humphrey? That name went out of fashion before I was born. But I had known one Humphrey. I took a second look at him as he handed me a bottle of sherry.

"Humphrey Brown?"

"You do remember me."

I nodded. The truth was I hadn't thought about him in years. Evidently Mom invited Humphrey as her surprise guest.

The oven timer dinged and I left her to deal with him.

In the kitchen, Bernie peeked inside the oven. "Is this ready to come out?"

I put on oven mitts and was pulling Mom's sweet potato and marshmallow dish out of the oven when Vicki found me. "I don't mean to interfere, but Hannah and Mars are about to start a world war over medical insurance costs."

Swell. Mars loved to argue and he didn't always know when to let it go. "Bernie?"

"On my way, luv." Somehow in the bustle of guests arriving, he'd managed to dress and looked almost respectable except for the moppish hair.

"Oh! A kitten." Vicki stroked Mochie's head. "I always wanted a cat but my brother was allergic and so is Andrew. I seem destined to live life without a kitty."

She sighed and ambled toward me. Idly, she tore a corner off a bread knot and nibbled at it like a mouse. No wonder her trousers hung on her so beautifully. I'd have slathered the bread with butter.

I placed crispy golden cheese puffs on a glass serving platter and should have rushed them into the living room, but I was thrilled to have a minute alone with Vicki so I could pump her for information. "So what was the problem between Andrew and Simon?" I asked, pretending to be casual.

She swallowed a piece of the bread. "You remember— the television show."

"What show?"

Her face reflected surprise. "About, oh, my gosh, about the time you and Mars split up. You've heard of *Don't You Dare*?"

"That moronic TV show where people take ridiculous risks to win a million dollars?"

"That's the one. It was Andrew's idea. But he needed a TV producer with big bucks to back it. He went to Simon, who turned him down."

"But the show's still on."

"Simon stole the idea. It's been a huge success, well, except for that sad case where the girl lost her leg. If it hadn't been for that horrible accident, she would have won. My brother always says fate is a fickle mistress. She lost her leg, that cocky guy won a million dollars, and Andrew didn't get anything out of it. Not a cent."

Natasha barged into the kitchen and stopped abruptly. "I thought you redid this kitchen."

"We did."

"I wish you had called me, I'd have been happy to help. You should have seen the gorgeous kitchen in my country home." Her voice squeaked and broke. "Of course that's gone now." She fanned herself as if willing the tears away and then flicked her hand toward the stone wall. "You should have eliminated this, for instance. Kitchens should never contain rough stone or brick; they're impossible to clean."

Faye's picture swung to a slant but Natasha didn't notice.

Good thing she didn't know how old the stone was or that it had traveled here in the bottom of an ancient ship. I was about to point out that I didn't cook on the stone wall but choked back my words, determined not to start an argument.

"I feel terrible for imposing on you. The fire was a nightmare. We had guests when it started. You can't imagine the horror of watching your home burn." Her tone rose to a shrill pitch again. "And then we had to check into a hotel in the middle of the night."

Vicki walked past me and whispered, "I can't hear about this one more time."

I handed her the platter of cheese puffs. "Would you mind taking these in to the guests?" She took the platter and strode into the foyer.

"I'm glad no one was hurt." I offered a box of tissues to Natasha. She drove me batty sometimes but this wasn't a drama-queen act. Just thinking about the fire sent chills up my spine. I couldn't imagine how traumatized she must feel.

Natasha stared out the bay window and massaged her hands around a tissue in a nervous manner. "Sophie, I need to apologize."

She had my full attention. I couldn't recall Natasha ever having apologized for anything before.

"I may have been a bit hasty yesterday when I accused you of killing Simon. Not that you didn't have the motive or opportunity, but now I understand that things may not be the way they seem and I regret that I may have jumped to conclusions about your involvement regardless of how obvious it may have seemed at the time."

"Thank you, Natasha." I wondered what had happened to prompt the odd apology but I took the high road and didn't ask. It was enough that she'd thought about it and bothered to apologize.

I painted a second tray of homemade bread knots with a cold water wash, sprinkled chunks of kosher salt over them, and slid them into the oven.

Her shoulders relaxed like she'd been dreading her little speech. "I'm glad we got that out of the way. When you reach a certain level of celebrity as I have, it becomes so difficult to know who to trust. Who your friends are. It seems like everyone wants something from me. You're one of the few people I can reach out to, Soph."

Uh-oh. Wait until she found out about my anti-Natasha advice column. That would move me out of the trusted friend category and fast.

"I need a favor, Sophie."

Thanksgiving dinner was one thing, but they were *not* moving in with me, no matter what. I set the oven timer, picked up the gravy boat, and braced myself.

Her dark eyes full of fear, Natasha said, "The police are going to think that Mars killed Simon. I know you don't want that any more than I do. We have to help him, Sophie."

I nearly dropped the gravy boat. "Why would they suspect Mars?" Wild notions came to mind. Had they discovered blood on Mars's clothes? Had someone seen Mars come out of the conference room?

She cupped her hands along the sides of her face. "It's all my fault. I never should have agreed to be in the contest. But I didn't dream anything like this would happen."

I should have comforted her but the gravy base on the stove demanded my immediate attention by bubbling. "What did Mars do that would make them suspect him?"

"It's that terrible feud."

I couldn't help laughing. I'd forgotten all about it. "That was nothing but a publicity stunt." Simon's reporters routinely went through politicians' trash cans and invented scandalous stories. Mars had called him on it and Simon had fired back. In the end, they all won. Mars's clients got the kind of publicity they couldn't possibly buy, and Simon's cable network got better ratings when people tuned in to hear Mars and Simon rant at each other.

"It wasn't a stunt, Sophie. Congressman Bieler lost his bid for reelection because of the lies Simon's reporters invented. The worst thing is that the hatred between Mars and Simon was so public. Everyone knows about it."

I gave the gravy base another stir and checked the time. What I really wanted at the moment was Natasha out of my kitchen so I could concentrate.

"Please, Sophie? I thought you might have some ideas. Something we can do to convince the police that Mars isn't involved."

She had to be kidding. I couldn't even convince them that I wasn't involved.

"Would you take these bottles of wine into the dining room?" I asked.

Her eyebrows rose. "They're not decanted."

"Oh, no! What will we do?" I was sorry as soon as the sarcastic words left my lips. "Just take them into the dining room. Please?"

I breathed a sigh of relief when she complied. The

white wines didn't need decanting and the red was only a backup for guests who didn't like white wine.

Finally, a few minutes to concentrate on cooking. Without looking, I reached for a pot holder and encountered Humphrey's arm.

"Could I help you with anything?" he asked.

Did I have a task that would get rid of him, too? "No, thanks. Why don't you just visit with the others? We'll be eating soon." Provided I could get everyone out of my kitchen for a few minutes.

"I'll just keep you company, then."

He stood near the fire, his hands clasped in front of him. Each time I looked over at him, he smiled at me, his head jutting forward just a bit, like an eager vulture.

I couldn't stand it another second. I took the mushroom caps out of the oven and slid them onto a plate with a spatula. Tangy garlic wafted to me from the sizzling filling. Seizing Humphrey's hand, I towed him into the sunroom. "Honey, I wish I had the time to introduce you to everyone. But here's Mom." I released his hand and smiled at him. "She'll take good care of you and make sure you meet everyone. Won't you, Mom?"

Without waiting for a response, I handed her the mushroom caps and fled back to the kitchen. Mars and I had hosted plenty of parties when we were married and most of them came off quite smoothly. I could handle this, too. I just needed a few quiet minutes to finish everything.

Natasha returned and tapped me on the back. "You forgot to put out the place cards."

"There aren't any."

"You should always make place cards. How will we know where to sit?"

"Until this morning, I thought there would be six of us. Didn't seem like a major problem."

She explained, as if to a child. "Had you set out place cards you would have spared me the possible embarrassment of having to sit near June, whom I cannot abide at this moment since she burned down most of my house. I could have very discreetly switched them."

I couldn't help snickering and turned away from her so she wouldn't see. Was it June or me, the alleged murderer, whom she couldn't abide?

I collected myself enough to say, "Thank you, Natasha. I never realized place cards were for you to rearrange to suit yourself."

She ignored my sarcasm. "You should have prepared the leaves days ago. Don't you watch my show? You have to place them between heavy books so they'll dry flat." She sighed. "I'll just go out into your garden to see what I can use."

Just then Vicki sidled up to me and whispered, "I thought you should know that the cop from yesterday is hanging around outside."

"What?" I followed her to the dining-room window that fronted on the street.

Sure enough, Wolf stood on the sidewalk, watching the house.

"For pity's sake." I headed to the door.

"Sophie," she said, tugging at the collar of her silk blouse, "if he thinks you killed Simon, it's probably not wise to confront him."

Hers was the voice of reason but I ignored her. I hadn't killed anyone. I marched outside and straight up to Wolf. "If you're going to work on Thanksgiving Day, you might as well come inside and eat with us. That way you can keep a closer eye on me. I have a ton of guests. Believe me, I'm not going anywhere."

He appeared speechless and I felt pleased to have knocked him off his stride a bit. Maybe he'd have to rethink his convictions about my involvement in the murders.

He let out a warm laugh, as though releasing pent-up anxiety. "Are you sure you have enough food?"

"We'll make do." I didn't mention that I was beginning to think a twenty-five-pound turkey was mighty small.

The aroma of roasting turkey filled the air when we walked into the house. I hung Wolf's bulky leather jacket in the foyer closet and noticed that Vicki swiftly steered Andrew away from Wolf and into the living room with June. Craig scooted along behind them. But Bernie and Mars wasted no time asking Wolf questions about Simon's murder. They disappeared into the sunroom with him.

I didn't have the luxury of hanging around to listen. I needed to figure out how to stretch the soup to accommodate fourteen people and I had to fit another place setting on the table.

Natasha joined me in the kitchen, her hands full of moss and shriveled leaves. "Tell me you didn't invite that detective to join us."

"You'd prefer to have Wolf standing outside?"

She dumped the organic matter on a dish towel, wiped off her hands, and placed the tips of her fingers against her forehead in a dramatic gesture. "Simon's murdered, June burns my house down, no place cards, and now this. Why does everything happen to me? You have to ask him to leave, Sophie. I won't be able to eat a bite knowing that he's watching us."

I'd never seen Natasha so unnerved.

She grabbed a glass out of a cabinet, filled it with tap water, drank the whole thing, and held the glass against her forehead.

When she regained her usual poise, she said, "Do not seat me near the detective or June, please. Where is your golden pen?"

If I weren't an event planner, I probably wouldn't have owned a pen with gold ink. But I was and I kept one in my event emergency kit in my car and right about now, it was in a police impound lot somewhere. I didn't bother to explain. "I don't have one."

Natasha collected her towel of yard debris and headed for the sunroom. I could hear her ask if anyone had a golden pen.

I had bigger problems at the moment, like stretching the soup.

The pantry yielded just what I needed, though I had no idea how it would taste. I heated the contents of a box of organic roasted red pepper and tomato soup.

Giggling, Mom and June returned from the sunroom.

"What are you up to?" I asked.

"He's so handsome," said Mom. "He'd turn my head if I weren't married."

"Wolf?" He had a certain charm, though I thought he was a bit rugged in comparison to Mars's polish.

My question brought on more giggles. "We're talking about the colonel," Mom said. "He's attractive but too young for us."

"But that military bearing," June gushed.

Mom added, "And a full head of silver hair. You don't find that often at our age."

I shooed the swooners out of the kitchen with instructions to coax everyone to the dining room for dinner.

Donning thick oven mitts, I pulled the turkey from the oven and set it on the counter. Juices hissed inside the roaster. Working quickly, I placed the turkey on a grooved cutting board and finished the gravy with the hot pan juices. I dipped a spoon in the gravy to see if I should add salt. Who needed potatoes? It was delicious on its own.

Letting the turkey rest, I ladled creamy homemade pumpkin soup into bowls and poured a generous dollop of vivid red pepper soup in the middle of each. I inserted a knife into the top of each red dot and drew it through the silky pumpkin soup, creating a colorful heart. They looked gorgeous.

Bernie and Wolf helped me carry the soup bowls into the dining room.

I sank into a chair, thankful to finally have everyone

present and everything under control. Amid a chorus of "how prettys," Natasha muttered, "You're not serving my menu."

Humphrey sat halfway down the table. He stared at me with such intensity I wondered if he'd noticed that soup had been served. I averted my eyes and ignored him.

Natasha's face brightened. "You couldn't get squab. That's why you're not serving my soup." To the collected group she announced proudly, "Because of my recipe there's a shortage of squab."

Before I could try my daring mixture of soups, a series of crashes and thumps rumbled through the house and MacArthur barked nonstop.

"MacArthur and Mochie!" I jumped from my chair and rushed to the sunroom with Wolf on my heels. I'd forgotten about Mochie and had no idea how MacArthur would react to him.

Like little angels, Mochie sat between Daisy's front paws. A frustrated MacArthur barked at Mochie but the brave kitten didn't budge. With a one-word command, "Quiet!" the colonel silenced MacArthur.

But the odd thumping noises continued.

Hannah nudged me. "Do you know that woman?" She pointed to my neighbor, Francie, who was methodically tipping over my flowerpots and banging a stick against the side of my house.

"I'll take care of this." Wolf headed for the door.

"Let me see what's going on first." I ventured out into the cold, hoping she wouldn't use the stick on me.

"Francie, what are you doing?"

She straightened up and pushed straw-like hair off her weather-beaten face. "I saw a rat."

And I smelled one. "Are you the Peeping Tom?"

"There really was a Peeping Tom. I don't know why no one wants to believe that. They ought to. There've been two murders in town in the last two days."

I wondered if she had any idea that she was talking to the prime suspect in those murders.

I put my arm around her shoulders. "A big, strong police detective happens to be eating with us. How about you come in and join us?"

"I don't want to be a bother."

If she only knew the half of it. I wouldn't even notice one more person.

I steered her inside. "We're just sitting down to soup."

"I hope it's not that crummy broth Natasha's been spouting about on TV."

Everyone filtered back to the table and made room for Francie next to Wolf. I couldn't help noticing that Natasha had switched places with Mars so she wouldn't have to sit opposite June. Soup bowls, wineglasses, and spoons passed between guests as everyone chose new seats. So much for the place cards Natasha had crafted from leaves.

While they rearranged everything, I hurried to the kitchen and scraped the pots to make Francie a bowl of soup. I placed it in front of her and urged the others to eat before the soup was completely cold.

Within minutes I realized what was going on with Francie. She only had eyes for the colonel. And she wore a fussy blouse with a bow at the neck and a tapestry vest over top of it. She'd dressed for dinner. But she had to compete with my mom and June, who had engaged the colonel in an animated discussion about his charity work in Africa. I'd felt sorry for him, and then it turned out the man was a magnet for women over sixty-five.

My soup mixture went over big, which was a huge relief. When everyone was finished, Vicki and Hannah cleared the soup dishes and carried in creamy buttered mashed potatoes, green beans with crunchy almond slivers and jewel-like bits of roasted red pepper, crusty bacon-herb stuffing, cranberries spiked with a hint of Grand Marnier, and the gooey marshmallow-topped sweet potatoes Mom made specially for Craig. And last I brought in the turkey, which, in spite of Mom's surreptitious basting, was roasted to a crispy golden brown.

For the first time, I felt awkward and nostalgic about Mars's presence. In the past, Mars carved the turkey. I paused and glanced at him, wondering what to do.

He seemed thoroughly uncomfortable, which wasn't like him at all. Unflappable Mars took everything in stride. But he had unbuttoned the collar of his shirt and was using his napkin to dab his forehead. I stole a glance at Natasha, who seemed oblivious to Mars's discomfort, nattering on about a program she did on mushrooms.

Dad would have to carve the turkey this year. I hoped Mars wouldn't mind.

I flashed him a reassuring smile. But the color had drained from his face and he appeared dazed. He wasn't upset about being here for Thanksgiving. Something was seriously wrong.

"Mars?" I said.

Before I could set the turkey on the sideboard, Mars rose slightly from his chair. With sweat beading on his forehead, he coughed once and then collapsed.

ELEVEN

From "The Good Life":

Dear Sophie,

I love crispy turkey skin. It always looks wonderful when it comes out of the oven but somehow when my wife serves it, the skin is limp and unappealing.

—Crispless in Crimora

Dear Crispless,

I'd bet your wife covers the turkey with aluminum foil to keep it warm while you eat your soup. Covering the hot bird causes moisture to collect and the skin to lose its crispness. Just leave the bird uncovered and it will be as crisp as can be.

—Sophie

Natasha kneeled to tend to Mars. "Sophie, how could you?"

Mom shrieked, "Craig, Humphrey, do something!"

Wolf skirted the table to help Mars. "Call nine-one-one. Looks like a food allergy to me."

Mars didn't have any allergies. But even I could see he was suffering from something more serious than ordinary food poisoning. I set the turkey on the table, ran for the phone, and called an ambulance.

When I returned, Mars moaned and curled into the fetal position. He hacked and appeared to have trouble swallowing.

Natasha stroked Mars's head. "Please, Vicki, get Sophie to tell you what she gave him. Please?"

"You're being absurd. I didn't give him anything. If I had poisoned the soup, everyone would be sick." I was horrified to see more than one scared face. I threw my hands up in a hopeless gesture. "I didn't poison anything!"

The wail of the ambulance siren grew in strength. I gave up hope that I could be of assistance, flung open the front door, and ran into the street to flag them down.

The sight of another rescue squad raised goose bumps on my arms. Surely Mars wouldn't die, too. How could this be happening?

They brought a stretcher into the dining room and radioed the hospital. Wolf's presence made things easier. He knew the rescue crew and provided succinct answers to their questions.

When they asked Natasha if Mars had any allergies, she sheepishly turned to me. I shook my head. Within minutes they carried Mars out of the house and loaded him into the ambulance.

Natasha seized my arm and hissed into my ear, "I don't know why you would want to hurt Mars but make no mistake. I'll do anything to protect him." Throwing me an angry glance, she rushed out to follow the ambulance in her car. Bernie offered to drive June and bring her back later. Vicki apologized for having to leave and ran after a visibly shaken Andrew, who yelled for her to hurry.

I gazed around the yard at my remaining guests. The colonel, lonely heart Francie, pale Humphrey, creepy Craig, suspicious Wolf, my parents, and my sister. I wanted to go to the hospital with the others, but knew I shouldn't.

Dad slung an arm around my shoulders and squeezed. "He'll be all right. There's nothing you can do to help Mars now."

"We might as well get back inside and enjoy the turkey," I said with feigned enthusiasm. When we returned to the dining room, a police technician surveyed the scene. In the commotion, I hadn't noticed him arrive. Mom ushered everyone into the living room to wait.

Everyone except MacArthur and Daisy, who were whimpering at the table. Then I realized that Mochie had taken advantage of the chaos to jump up and help himself to turkey. Tiny as he was, he had chomped down on a wing and he pulled on it like a little tiger. I picked him up, along with the chewed-up wing, and called the dogs into the kitchen so they could share Mochie's ill-gotten treat. Wolf followed the dogs.

"Did you call your buddy to test for poison?" I asked.

He took a deep breath. "Be glad Mars had his reaction before we ate anything else." Wolf tugged loose a crusty piece of stuffing stuck to a pan and munched on it. "At least he only had to test the appetizers and the soup. Unless . . . did Mars come in here and taste anything while you were cooking?"

I tried to remember. "I don't think so." Various people had floated in and out of the kitchen. But the only one I could remember for sure was Natasha because she had been driving me crazy. So much for her theory about the cops suspecting Mars. Even they wouldn't think he'd poisoned himself.

Wolf picked at the stuffing pan again. "That's presuming he was poisoned at all. Could have had a reaction to something. Even something he ate hours ago for breakfast. The results will probably put you in the clear—for this one anyway."

I set Mochie on a chair and looked around. The cop, who had already investigated the kitchen, had been very neat. We'd stacked the empty soup bowls on the counter and they were now gone. Except for the smudge of a soup ring where bowls had been, I wouldn't have known he'd been in the kitchen at all.

After giving Mochie and the dogs their treats, I preheated the ovens to warm up the side dishes. They'd been sitting on the table cooling off for over an hour. The rest of my guests would probably get food poisoning.

Wolf threw a log on the fire and asked if he could help.

"Not unless you can speed up your cop friend."

He settled into a chair and Mochie jumped on his lap. "Do you invite your ex-husband and his family to all your holiday gatherings?"

I poured each of us a glass of iced tea, handed him one, and sat down opposite him. "That was just a confluence of bizarre events. Actually, the last couple of days have been that way. Are we in a full moon?"

In a very calm tone he said, "I don't expect many ex-wives would invite the women who stole their husbands."

I looked at him in shock. He didn't come right out and say it, but the implication hung in the air—only an ex-wife who was up to no good would invite the woman who broke up her marriage. I gritted my teeth and groaned. "Natasha did not steal Mars."

The police officer taking samples called Wolf from the doorway. They stepped outside to talk and I couldn't help spying on them from the kitchen window. Neither seemed worried or upset. If anything, they spoke calmly—business as usual.

I carried the reheated stuffing back to the dining room, where Mom collected discarded wrappers left by the rescue squad. Guilt nagged at me as we removed place settings. Mars could die, yet the rest of us were going to feast as though nothing had happened. I returned to the kitchen with Humphrey tagging along behind me.

"Thank you for inviting me."

I thought about telling him I didn't know he was invited, but that would have been unnecessarily rude. He seemed so frail and ghostlike with his pale skin and platinum hair. If I exhaled too hard, it might knock him over. "Glad to have you."

He reached out tentatively and placed cold fingers on top of mine.

It took all my willpower not to snatch my hand away.

He giggled. "I guess you'll think I'm silly, but I had such a crush on you when we were kids. I'm amazed you remember me. There were times I wasn't sure you knew I was alive."

I withdrew my hand fast and pretended to slap it to my chest in a completely stupid effort to appear surprised. "Kids! We were all so insecure back then." I struggled to recall details about him. "You were so good at . . . at . . ."

He stepped into my personal space, closer than I'd have liked, and bit at my bait. "Dissecting frogs."

I edged back, still trying to be friendly. "And look at you now. What is it you do for a living?"

"I'm a mortician."

It figured. Humphrey looked like he had stepped out of a blond *Addams Family* cartoon.

"You know, Sophie, I've always been so shy. I was never able to tell you how I felt, and now, to learn that you feel the same is like a miracle."

Where did he get that idea?

Wolf coughed, undoubtedly to let us know he stood in the doorway.

Humphrey's confidence melted and he shuffled out of the room, his head hanging down in embarrassment.

Wolf picked up the dish of sweet potatoes.

I wasn't sure how much he'd seen, but part of me wanted to be sure he knew that Humphrey got my feelings all wrong. "That probably wasn't what it looked like."

"Murder someone and it's my business. Your love life is your own business." He carried the casserole of sweet potatoes and marshmallows toward the dining room and I heard him mutter, "Though I can't see the attraction myself."

What did he mean by that? That he couldn't see Humphrey being attracted to me or me being attracted to Humphrey? I dashed after him but a dining room full of family and guests, including Humphrey, didn't seem the right place to question him.

For the third time, we sat down to eat. Dad carved the turkey and for a few minutes of passing and loading plates, we acted like a normal group of family and friends enjoying a holiday feast.

"Wolf, do you think Mars's poisoning has anything to do with Simon's murder?" Hannah brought us back to reality.

The soft clinking of silverware halted as we all froze.

Her question hung in the air, taunting me. If there were a connection, the killer had made a serious error. Wolf's field of hundreds of suspects at the stuffing contest would have been narrowed down dramatically.

Craig broke the awkward silence. "It's not a preposterous question. Mars's brother certainly doesn't make a secret of his feelings about Simon. And I understand Simon and Mars hated each other as well. Mars's whole family is suspect if you ask me."

"If the murders are related, then I guess Mars is off the hook for Simon's murder." Hannah speared a piece of turkey with her fork. "I mean, he wouldn't have poisoned himself. It must be one of the others. It can't be Natasha, so that leaves June, Andrew, and Vicki. Oh! And that Bernie fellow."

I watched Wolf. He was no dummy. He hadn't said a word but he observed the rest of us.

"My money's on Natasha." If she'd been younger, the brittleness of Francie's voice would have been chalked up to cheerleading. But at her age, it sounded grumpy and as though she'd had one Scotch too many. "Andrew isn't smart enough to do the dirty deed and deflect suspicion by being open about his disdain for the man. And June wouldn't poison her own son."

The colonel fed MacArthur a piece of turkey under the table. "Well, Detective? Do you have a suspect?"

Dad promptly knocked over his wineglass. I rushed to his aid and sopped up the wine with napkins. While I dabbed at the carpet, Wolf's cell phone rang.

He excused himself from the table but returned within seconds. His jaw had tightened. "I apologize for my abrupt departure but there's been a development in Simon's murder." His gaze shot to Francie. "They've found the suspected murder weapon."

TWELVE

From *"Ask Natasha"*:

Dear Natasha,

Last year I spent hours on Thanksgiving Day polishing the silver. By Christmas it was tarnished again. Isn't there a shortcut to cleaning silver?

—Tarnished in Tappahannock

Dear Tarnished,

I clean my sterling once a week. Use a soft cloth to rub it with a good-quality commercial silver cleaner. If you keep up with it by polishing it every week, it won't be such a chore and will always be ready for use.

—Natasha

Wolf watched my reaction when he said, "Fire investigators discovered the turkey trophy buried in Natasha's garden."

Francie slapped the table. "I knew it!"

"That can't be. There must be some mistake." Mom dabbed her mouth with a napkin. She had always liked Natasha.

"Mars!" I jumped out of my chair, nearly knocking it over. What if Natasha was the one who had tried to harm Mars? "She's with him in the hospital."

Wolf held up his hands. "I've got him covered. An officer is keeping an eye on him."

That was a relief. I hated that Wolf had to leave, though. He hadn't had much of a Thanksgiving. I loaded a plate with sliced turkey and a couple of rolls. "Give me a second, Wolf."

I hurried to the kitchen, found the mayo, and fixed turkey sandwiches, plopping a generous spoonful of cranberry sauce on each. In a rush, I folded waxed paper into small envelopes and slid the sandwiches inside so they wouldn't drip.

I wrapped the whole package in foil and handed it to him in the foyer, saying, "I guess I'm off the hook now?"

"Takes more than a couple of sandwiches to bribe me."

"You know what I mean. Now that the murder weapon was found at Natasha's, doesn't that mean I'm in the clear?"

He hefted the sandwiches in his hand. "I can't clear anybody yet, Sophie. Not a single one of you."

He opened the door and I watched him walk away. I'd hoped the matter would be resolved and that I might get to know Wolf a little better. But he'd just confirmed my worst fear. He thought the killer was one of us.

Could Natasha really have bashed Simon over the head with the turkey trophy? She'd certainly had the opportunity, but I couldn't think of a reason. Did she imagine she was protecting Mars? That didn't make sense. But if she didn't kill Simon, why would she bury the trophy in her yard?

"I'm glad he had to go. You should have seen the difference in everyone once he left."

I whipped around to find Humphrey holding the gravy boat. "Who? Wolf?"

"The second he was gone we all relaxed and started chatting. I volunteered to bring more gravy—just to get a moment alone with you." In the kitchen, I took the gravy boat from Humphrey and refilled it, wondering the whole time what kind of white lie I could concoct to diminish his interest. He stood so close to me that I could feel his breath on my neck.

"I could hardly believe my good fortune when I saw you yesterday. You look just the way you did in high school. Natasha was popular but she always looked straight through me, like I wasn't there. Nothing has changed, you know. She barely spoke to me today. You always smiled when we passed in the hall. And once you gave me your seat at lunch."

High school? We were in our mid-forties. Humphrey was stuck in a serious time warp. I handed him the gravy boat and lied. "You misunderstood Natasha. You know how it is, the prettiest girl never has a date. She's terribly shy."

"Really? I never would have guessed it. I'll have to make it up to her. Maybe at the stuffing contest. They will resume it, won't they?"

I had no idea, but if Humphrey was going to chase Natasha, I hoped they would hold the competition. I grinned at the thought of it.

Humphrey had just passed through the doorway. I grabbed the beige wool of his sweater. "Wait a minute. Where did you see me yesterday?"

"At the Stupendous Stuffing Shakedown."

I released his sleeve. He winked at me and walked to the dining room. I could hear my father asking Humphrey for gravy. In a fog, I crossed the foyer to the arched opening of the dining room and observed him. How long had he been watching me? Could Humphrey be the Peeping Tom? Would he have hired a private investigator to track me down?

"Sit and eat, Sophie." Mom waved me in. "Everything is delicious."

"And no one else has keeled over yet," added Hannah.

Craig snickered but he didn't hesitate to stuff his mouth with sweet potatoes.

I perched on my chair and sipped ice water. Halfway down the table, Humphrey ate daintily. Could someone so wan and meek be a killer?

"Humphrey," I said in as casual a tone as I could muster, "did you know Simon personally?"

"Good heavens, no. I don't meet celebrities until they're about to meet their Maker." Everyone else found his joke much funnier than I did. I felt tension leave my shoulders, though. He had no motive. I sat back, relaxed, and realized my remaining guests were enjoying themselves. Side dishes cluttered the table and conversation flowed. I helped myself to turkey and too many cranberries, one of my Thanksgiving favorites.

The colonel buttered a bread knot. "Don't worry about Mars, dear. That reaction he had is nothing compared to the trouble he's in over Simon's murder. Bad luck that Mars was so public about his disdain for Simon after that reporter went through the congressman's trash."

Craig stopped eating. "Mars Winston! No wonder that name sounded so familiar. I remember that. He accused Simon of promoting his personal political agenda through his media outlets. That was a huge scandal."

Dad helped himself to more stuffing. "Mars is too intelligent to kill someone after a public falling-out."

"Natasha isn't." The dry comment came from Francie.

The colonel sipped his wine. "I'm most fascinated by this murder of a private investigator. The police have reason to think there's a connection. Wouldn't surprise me. Simon was known for his ruthless business tactics."

"This is so exciting. It's just like one of those whodunit dinner games." Hannah gasped. "Could we do something like that at the wedding?"

I couldn't help myself, it was too obvious and I had to say it. "You want someone to be murdered at your wedding? What a lovely memory."

"Not for real. You know, a mock murder."

Had Hannah always been this crazed? Was there a disease called Wedding Euphoria that prevented brides from seeing anything else?

Fortunately, Mom changed the subject to MacArthur and we made it all the way through dessert without another mention of murder.

After dinner everyone pitched in to clear the table. If my mother hadn't been present, I'd have left the mess in the kitchen and joined my guests in the living room. But one of Mom's cardinal rules was that the cook didn't rest until the kitchen was spotless. She would bug me unmercifully if she thought there were still dirty dishes in the sink.

Mom must have worked some motherly guilt on Hannah, who flounced into the kitchen. "I'll load the dishwasher, but I'm not scrubbing anything. It would ruin my manicure."

Heaven forbid that should happen. While Hannah started cleaning up, I called Natasha's cell phone number. No answer. I tried Vicki's number next. Also no answer. I was dialing Andrew's number when Humphrey strolled into the kitchen.

He smiled as though all was right with his world. "I'm supposed to ask you to put on some decaf coffee. Francie and the colonel would like brandies, your father would prefer a port wine, and Craig wants whatever Hannah is having."

I nodded at him. "As soon as I get through to someone about Mars. None of them are answering their cell phones. I hope that's not a bad sign."

"They've probably been told to turn off their phones. They interfere with hospital equipment."

I hung up. "How do you know that?"

He flipped a milky white hand open, palm up, like he was surprised by my question. "I pick up bodies from hospitals every day."

I sank into a fireside chair. His words reminded me that Mars might be victim number three.

Humphrey fell to his knees like he was proposing. "You're still in love with Mars."

I wasn't, of course, but I was more than willing to let him think so. "Humphrey," I said . . .

Hannah chose that exact moment to burst out laughing. "Why does everyone think that? She's so over Mars. Do you think she'd have invited Natasha and Mars to dinner if she was still in love with him?"

Thank you, Hannah. I shot her an exasperated look.

Her eyes widened. "That's why you're so familiar. You're that kid who used to ride his bike back and forth in front of our house after school. Gosh, I didn't recognize you at first, but I felt like I knew you from somewhere."

Humphrey appeared flattered. "Let me give you a hand with those." He pulled on dishwashing gloves and began to scrub. "To be honest, I never thought anyone noticed me. I just confessed my childhood crush on your sister. Imagine my surprise to learn she feels the same way."

Why did he keep saying that? Surely I hadn't given him the wrong impression. I had to let him down nicely, but how?

Biting her upper lip to keep from laughing, Hannah turned slowly to look at me. "Imagine that!"

I rose. "I'm going to get the wine." Maybe if I left them alone, Humphrey would fall in love with Hannah instead.

The den, where Bernie had set up camp, had two entrances—one to the living room and one to the sunroom. I pushed open the door from the sunroom and the dogs forged ahead of me, trailed by little Mochie.

Bernie had left his clothes scattered about. His suitcase lay open on the floor next to an enormous duffle bag that had seen better days.

I pulled port and brandy from the liquor cabinet. My arms full, I turned in time to see MacArthur digging in Bernie's suitcase. I hissed at him but the bulldog kept after his quarry.

As I set down the bottles, MacArthur took off running with something sticking out of his mouth. Daisy and Mochie chased after him into the sunroom. Intending to cut them off by going the other way, I opened the door to the living room, where the rest of my guests chatted.

The clacking of dog toenails on the hardwood floors grew louder. MacArthur, still carrying something in his mouth, raced into the living room with Mochie riding on his back and Daisy in hot pursuit.

The colonel managed to catch the frantic MacArthur, and I hurried over to remove Mochie from the poor dog's back. Mochie jumped off before I got there. He leapt onto an empty chair and groomed his front paws as though they smelled offensively of dog.

MacArthur displayed no signs of injury but I noted that he remained close to the colonel. The delicious treat that had started the wild chase turned out to be a Toblerone chocolate bar.

I took it into the kitchen where Humphrey and Hannah worked side by side and threw it into a trash bin that none of the animals could reach.

Worried that Bernie might have more than one chocolate bar in his suitcase, I returned to the den. On my knees, I pushed back the items MacArthur had dislodged. When I flipped the suitcase shut, a newspaper article flapped halfway out. I opened the top enough to pull the paper loose and couldn't help noticing that it was about Simon. It was a short segment from the *Miami Herald* Food Section about the Stupendous Stuffing Shakedown and Simon's involvement.

I'd assumed that Bernie had come to Virginia straight from England, but there wasn't any real reason for my assumption. Still it disturbed me a little bit to think Bernie had known about the contest in advance and had bothered to keep the article. I stood up, irritated with myself for imagining that it meant anything. Bernie knew he was coming to town, saw the article, and ripped it out. Nothing sinister about that.

I collected the port and brandy and took them to the dining room where I kept the Waterford stemware Mars and I had received as wedding gifts. After serving everyone, I hustled to the kitchen to put on decaf organic Colombian coffee.

Hannah and Humphrey chuckled about something as though they were old buddies. But I had to give them credit, the kitchen counters sparkled and only a few items remained to be cleaned. Humphrey had even washed and dried the dreaded roaster and roasting rack.

At my request, he handed me a Rosenthal coffeepot that I kept in a high cabinet because I rarely had an opportunity to use it. I rinsed it out and poured in the hot coffee. In a matching bowl, I plopped a generous helping of whipped cream for those who felt they hadn't been sufficiently indulged. The coordinating creamer, ironically filled with nonfat milk, and the sugar bowl went on a tray with them. Humphrey carried it all into the living room.

Hannah snagged my arm. "He's very funny. Not much to look at, but you should think about going out with him. He's crazy about you."

If we'd been little, I'd have pulled her pigtail for saying such a thing. "You have to help me discourage him, Hannah. I'm not interested."

She picked up half the cups and saucers and headed for the door. "Don't be so hasty. I don't see anyone else lining up outside."

I followed her with the rest of the cups and saucers.

Dad poked at a crackling fire in the living room fireplace. MacArthur, Daisy, and Mochie stretched out in front of it, but MacArthur kept an uneasy eye on Mochie.

I poured coffee for everyone and had just taken a seat when we heard the kitchen door bang open. Bernie and June appeared in the living room doorway, bundled up in winter coats.

"Where's the turkey?" asked Bernie. "I'm starved."

He helped June with her coat and led her to a seat. She grasped the arm of the chair and lowered herself unsteadily.

Something was terribly wrong.

Mom stirred sugar into coffee and held it out to her. "You need some sugar, June. Haven't you eaten anything since you left?"

I couldn't believe no one had asked the obvious. I blurted, "How's Mars?"

June sipped at the coffee. Her shoulders sagged and she seemed to have aged twenty years.

I looked up at Bernie, who said simply, "Poison."

THIRTEEN

From "The Good Life":

Dear Sophie,

It's a tradition in my family to go shopping the day after Thanksgiving, then come home for yummy leftovers. But when I reheat the turkey, it's dry and tough. Any suggestions?

—Masticating in Martinsville

Dear Masticating,

Reheating turkey dries the meat. Take a tip from restaurants. Instead of heating the meat, heat the gravy. Slice the cold turkey and place it on warmed plates. Just before serving, pour hot gravy over the meat. It will be almost as good as it was right out of the oven.

—Sophie

"How could that be?" I felt like a noose tightened around my throat. No wonder June didn't feel well. Someone had poisoned her son.

"He'll be fine. They're keeping him overnight for observation, but the doctors said he would be okay." Bernie slid his coat off and tossed it over a chair with June's.

The colonel sat ramrod straight. "Rat poison?"

Bernie scratched the side of his face. "Actually, it turned out to be a nasty thing called muscarine. One of those odd coincidences. Because it's a holiday and there were staffing issues, one of the ER doctors happened to be a pediatric specialist. Recognized the symptoms because he'd seen it in a few children."

Francie smiled slyly. "Very clever. Poison mushrooms."

The colonel raised his eyebrows. "You're intimately acquainted with poisons?"

"You don't get to our age without learning a few things along the way. We picked our own mushrooms when I was a girl. My cousin died from eating a beautiful red-capped mushroom. Looked like it came right out of a picture-book fairy tale." Francie nodded her head. "Muscarine."

"But Bernie said Mars will be okay," I protested.

"Yes, by all means. He'll be right as rain by tomorrow." Bernie stood behind June's chair and motioned to me with his hand.

I followed him to the kitchen. "Is June all right?"

"She's as distressed as any good mum would be to learn someone tried to kill her son."

"And even worse, it had to be one of us who was here for Thanksgiving dinner."

Bernie frowned. "The doctor said it could have been in food he ate earlier in the day, at breakfast maybe."

"Unless he had breakfast with a whole lot of people, that sort of narrows it down to Natasha, doesn't it?" I felt guilty for even thinking it.

"She claims they ordered room service. Could have been poisoned in the kitchen or when it was being delivered."

"Is Natasha showing any symptoms?"

Bernie snorted. "Hardly. She's plenty nervous about something though."

I'd noticed that, too. Had she been on edge because she slipped poison into Mars's breakfast and was waiting for him to die? Natasha had her faults, but surely she wouldn't poison Mars. Still, the circumstances pointed to her. "Did the doctor say how long it takes before a person reacts to the poison?"

"There's the difficulty. Could be as little as half an hour or as much as six or eight hours. Depends on the dose and the variety."

Mom rushed in. "Sweetheart, I think it's time to unload the leftovers and serve a second go-round. Apparently the hospital dining service closed early because of the holiday."

The ovens hadn't fully cooled when I set them to preheat again. Then I stood in front of the refrigerator and handed Bernie one container after another.

"Any soup left?" he asked.

"Very funny."

"I'm not joking. It tasted delicious."

"We ate it all. The police officer had to take the bowls to get samples."

"Too bad. I'd have enjoyed a bowl."

I knew I hadn't tampered with the soup and even I wouldn't have dared take another bite now that we knew Mars had been poisoned.

Half an hour later, we gathered at the dining room table again. Those of us who hadn't gone to the hospital picked at our favorites, but Bernie and June ate proper meals.

The colonel placed his hand on top of June's. "Mars will be fine. He received prompt medical treatment and most likely won't have any lingering effects."

"You can't imagine what it's like to know someone wants to kill your son. And then to have the police suspect his own family—Andrew and Vicki and me. I never thought I would live to see anything like this."

After dinner, Mom helped June up to bed. The gallant colonel whistled for MacArthur, collected his walking stick, and insisted he walk Francie home in the dark. With a coquettish smile, Francie took his arm and strolled into the night.

Humphrey offered to help with the dishes, but it had been a long and strange day for all of us and, frankly, I didn't want to deal with his overtures. I assured him that he'd done more than his fair share of dishes and saw him to the door.

Hannah, Craig, and Dad retired to the family room.

Bernie and I made quick work of cleaning up the kitchen. I could barely keep my eyes open and headed for bed, but Bernie joined the others for a movie.

I slept restlessly, waking to think again about Mars and why anyone would poison him. At three in the morning, I padded down the stairs and found my mom and June in the kitchen. Daisy waited patiently for a crumb of crust from the pumpkin pie Mom sliced.

Mochie on her lap, June gabbed and as far as I could tell, Mom was ignoring her.

I nudged Mom. "June's talking."

"Sophie! I didn't hear you come in. Before you know it, everyone will be up. We're having hot milk. Want some?"

I poured more milk into the pot on the stove.

"Sweetheart, I've been trying to keep things light for Hannah's sake. This weekend with Craig getting to know us is so important to her. But tomorrow, you have to do whatever you can to figure out who's at the bottom of all this mayhem. I don't want to worry your dad, but, honey, even if Wolf does have eyes for you, you're a prime suspect. Is there anything I can do to help?"

"Mom, you do realize that June's talking?"

"Not to us. She's talking with Faye."

So much for Mars and me keeping that little secret. "Faye is dead. Don't you think that's unusual?"

"No, I talk to my father."

"Do you hear him talk back?" I whispered.

"Lots of people talk to loved ones who have passed on. Who's to say what's normal in that respect? I know my father is with me in spirit. For all we know he could be standing right next to us."

Between Faye and my deceased grandfather, the kitchen felt a little crowded.

Mochie leapt from June's lap and pounced on a tiny wad of aluminum foil. He batted it with his paw and played kitty hockey by racing after it and giving it another whack.

Mom handed me a plate with a piece of pie, topped by a droplet of whipped cream. "Wolf likes to eat, so he probably doesn't mind a few extra pounds on a woman, but, just the same, you ought to cut back a little bit before you get too chunky."

Where was Hannah when I needed her to distract Mom? "There's nothing going on between Wolf and me."

"If we'd known Wolf would be here for dinner, we never would have called Humphrey."

"We?"

"June and I." The corners of her mouth twitched down. "I confess. I'm horrified about the fire at Natasha's house, but the timing worked perfectly. June and I were conspiring to throw you and Mars together. We invited Humphrey because we needed someone to make Mars jealous."

June joined Mom at the kitchen table. "Didn't quite work out the way we planned."

A killer was on the loose and these two were playing matchmaker? "You thought Mars would be jealous of Humphrey? You couldn't pick someone with more sex appeal? Any appeal for that matter?" Heaven only knew what Mom had told Humphrey. That explained his mistaken impression that I had feelings for him.

"He's very pale, isn't he?" Mom addressed June. "His mother has that skin. Never spent a minute in the sun and looks ten years younger than the rest of us because of it."

Daisy whimpered at the kitchen door. I reached for the handle to let her out when a soft knock surprised us.

I opened the door and my neighbor Nina barged in, shivering from the cold. "I saw the lights on and had to join your midnight snack. Brr, it's cold out there. Got any of that Mozart liquor?"

"Chocolate liquor with pumpkin pie?" I said.

"Chocolate goes with everything," she assured me.

I pointed at the round bottle wrapped in gold foil and she poured her own drink while I cut more pie.

"Lots of whipped cream, please," she said. "I deserve it for putting up with my mother-in-law and her delusions that, since I'm a southerner, I ought to be another Natasha."

After handing Nina a piece of pie, I plopped more cream on my slice and joined the others at the table.

"Natasha tried to kill Mars," said June.

Nina's fork fell out of her hand and clattered onto her plate.

We filled her in on what had transpired.

"I knew it. She's too perky and perfect. Who's like that? Nobody can build a dining set from scratch and serve a ten-course dinner in the same day."

Mom spread a thin layer of cream across the top of her pie. "Natasha didn't do it." She gazed around at us. "You might not like Natasha and I'm sure you have your reasons, but that girl forged past all the terrible things that happened to her. She stayed focused on her career and deserves the success she's had. She's egocentric, I know, but I think a lot of successful people are."

June scowled. "It had to be Natasha. You know Andrew, Vicki, and I wouldn't poison Mars. And no one in your family would have reason to do so. That leaves Craig, the colonel, Francie, and Bernie. Not much of a lineup."

"If the police think it's related to the murders, then it all comes back to the dead PI that Sophie found," said Nina.

So much for keeping that from Mom. I explained in detail how I'd obtained Mochie. Mom took it better than I expected. "Then that's where you need to start. June and I will entertain everyone tomorrow. Nina, can you escape from your hostess duties?"

"I'd love nothing more."

"In the morning, you two pay a visit to the widow and see what you can find out."

～⁂～

After breakfast, I found Otis Pulchinski's address by searching for ocicat breeders on the internet. Dean Coswell, my editor, had forwarded e-mailed questions for "The Good Life." I answered enough to fill my column for the next few days.

We didn't want to disturb Mrs. Pulchinski too early, so Nina and I lingered over a second cup of coffee with my parents and June before driving to the northwest part of town.

Otis had lived in a town house that was part of a cluster of recently built houses. Spent leaves littered the tiny front yard and rust crept up a white van parked in the driveway. Nina pulled the Jag in behind it.

No one answered when I rang the doorbell. Nina tried it a second time and we heard it chime inside the house. I stepped back, off the raised stoop, and searched the exterior of the house. It didn't provide any clues about the owners. The red brick facade and Federal accents looked like all the other houses. But when I turned to go, I saw a curtain move in the window to the left of the door.

I motioned to Nina and knocked on the front door. "Mrs. Pulchinski? I . . . I have your cat."

A voice answered from inside the house. "What cat?"

"The one Otis had with him when—" I stopped abruptly. Why hadn't I prepared a way to say this?

The voice behind the door grew hysterical. "I'm not taking him back!"

Nina and I exchanged a look. She shrugged.

"I don't want to give him back."

With a creak, the door opened two inches. "Got him with you?"

"No."

"You wouldn't be lying, would you?" She swung the door open and eyed us with suspicion. A cloud of stale cigarette smoke enveloped us.

Ebony hair jutted from her head at odd angles and she'd applied a black eyebrow pencil with a heavy hand. A spandex-tight top and capri pants in a leopard print clung to her small frame. "That cat's nothing but trouble. Sold him twice, gave him away once, and everybody brought him back. Well, don't just stand there, doncha see I've got cats who'll run out the door?"

I wondered if she was confused and had another cat in mind. On the other hand, I wanted to keep my little Mochie and wasn't altogether unhappy that she didn't want him back.

We scooted in, taking care not to step on any of the inquisitive kitties. They were everywhere. Lounging in bookcases, sitting on top of the TV, milling around our legs. Chocolate, cinnamon, silver, and fawn and every one of them spotted, like an ocelot.

As was the furniture. Leopard print throws, pillows, chairs, even the slipcovers on the sofas sported spots.

"What are you going to do with him?" She took a long drag on a cigarette. "Take him to the pound?"

"I planned to keep him."

Mrs. Pulchinski couldn't hide her surprise but she recovered quickly. "Did Otis tell you he's a very valuable cat? Purebred ocicat."

I didn't think Nina was paying attention. She made no effort to hide her curiosity by taking in every detail of our surroundings. But she startled me by asking, "Then why doesn't he have spots like these cats?"

Mrs. Pulchinski motioned us to the sofas. She sat down and six cats immediately jumped on her, vying for her attention. "That's what makes him so expensive. He has the spots on his tummy but those stripes only appear once or twice in a dozen litters. The striped ones have"— she paused and considered her word choice—"outgoing personalities that make them very popular. I sell 'em for eight hundred dollars."

Mrs. Pulchinski watched our reaction with crafty eyes. Did she think we were complete dolts? I changed the subject before she could demand payment for Mochie.

"I'm very sorry for your loss. Were you and Otis married long?" I wanted to keep the conversation moving. The cops must have told her a woman found her husband's body. If she'd made the connection to me, she showed no sign of it.

"Spent fifteen years with the old coot." She dabbed at her nose with a tissue. "I don't know what I'm going to do for money. He had some big-shot clients and we were expecting the dough to roll in any day, but now all I have is my wonderful kittens. I hate to part with any of them but I have to live off something."

"I thought you were a breeder." I had expected to see photos of Otis, but all the framed pictures in the room featured spotted cats. Most of them professional photos of cats posed in front of becoming backdrops.

"I am. But it still breaks my heart to part with any of them. Especially that little sweetheart Otis gave you."

Did I have "idiot" written across my forehead? "I can't help wondering why he had the kitten with him the day he died," I said.

She searched the room as though she was looking for an answer. "Vet. Was taking him to the vet."

"Was he sick?" I asked. "Does he need medicine?"

This time she had a ready response. "Shots. Just needed his shots." She examined us carefully and her gaze locked on Nina's three-carat engagement ring. "You know, cats are much happier when they have a cat companion. You interested in buying a kitten?"

"No, thanks." I had a very bad feeling that I was about to write a check for Mochie.

"How about a PI? Either of you need to spy on your husbands? I'll give you a good price."

"You worked with your husband?" Nina asked.

Mrs. Pulchinski stabbed the butt of her cigarette into a glass ashtray. "You know how it is, all wives work with their husbands."

We must have looked skeptical because she rambled on. "Dumb old Otis got himself killed just when his business was drawing big customers. Politicians' wives take over when their husbands kick the bucket. I don't see why I can't carry on."

Nina scooted forward on the sofa and bent toward Mrs. Pulchinski. "Of course, you can. You have all his files, know who his clients are. It's a natural transition."

"Stupid cops came in here looking for files. They took the computer with them but it won't help them none. He wasn't dumb enough to keep anything about his clients in writing. Otis understood privacy. That's why they liked him."

I took out my checkbook. "Mrs. Pulchinski, I can't afford an eight-hundred-dollar cat, but maybe I can make a little donation to help you buy kitty kibble."

"That's right neighborly of you." She lit another cigarette. "Pen's on the desk."

Dust marked the spot on the desk where the computer had been. A coaster bearing the logo of the Stag's Head Inn, a dive I'd walked by, lay on the desk. She'd dumped her mail and, even though she wasn't exactly a straight shooter, I felt sorry for her. Bills spilled from the heap of letters, and I didn't see many hand-addressed envelopes in the way of condolences. She might be very alone in the world, except for her cats.

I found a pen in the top drawer and was making out a check when Nina leaned over my shoulder and gave the pile of mail a little push. Her unpolished fingernail tapped madly on a robin's-egg blue envelope.

Natasha's signature color.

FOURTEEN

Dear Natasha,

Due to my husband's job, we move every year. I hate to waste money on embossed stationery that I can't use up because it contains an old address. Is it totally horrible to make my own stationery on my computer?

—Computer Gal in Chilhowie

Dear Computer Gal,

Aren't computers wonderful? They offer us so many possibilities for scrapbooking and card-making. It's always most gracious to craft a card or note with your own personal message. I spend days working out my Christmas cards each year.

For those very few times when it isn't possible to craft an original card, keep some paper stock and matching envelopes on hand in your signature color. Handwrite a heartfelt message and it will carry just as much panache as embossed stationery.

—Natasha

Nina tried to slide the contents out of the envelope.

I smacked her hand away. I wanted to know what was inside, too, but it was just plain wrong to read someone's mail. My glare didn't stop her.

I glanced over my shoulder at Mrs. Pulchinski. Oblivious to Nina's shenanigans, she watched smoke rise from her cigarette.

Manipulating the envelope on the desk with one hand, Nina deftly flicked open a folded sheet of matching stationery. I recognized Natasha's perfect script immediately. A check for one thousand dollars lay inside. As far as I knew, Natasha hadn't bought any kittens lately. I had to give her credit, though. I never knew what to write on a card of condolence, but Natasha had written a gracious note praising Otis.

Nina's hand waved under my nose and pointed to the memo line of the check.

Natasha had written, "payment in full."

I left my meager check under the coaster so the cats wouldn't dislodge it right away and relied on Nina to slip Natasha's letter back in the envelope. I needn't have worried about Mrs. Pulchinski observing us. She slumped on the couch, the only sign of life the hand that held a cigarette inches from her mouth.

"Have the police found your husband's killer yet?" asked Nina.

I nearly choked. She might as well have introduced me as the number one suspect. Mrs. Pulchinski would catch on for sure and throw us out of her home.

"They think it's some woman he was checking out, but

I got my doubts. My Otis had smarts. Not many people ever fooled him. I think Otis come up against somebody as crafty as he was."

Certain she would make the connection between me and the police suspect, I hurried to wind up our visit by promising to take good care of Mochie.

Mrs. Pulchinski walked us to the door. "Thank you for coming by. I don't get many visitors. This meant a lot to me."

The door shut behind us and I felt terrible. The poor woman was distraught and we'd come to snoop.

Nina clutched my arm. "Can you believe it? Natasha's up to her neck in these murders. No wonder she was so quick to point her finger at you! We have to tell the police right away."

"If they have Otis's computer, don't you think they know already?"

We slid into the deep leather seats of her Jaguar and she started the engine. "You heard her. He didn't keep records on his clients."

Years of competing with Natasha left me with an instinct to malign her. I was hardly her best advocate. She was annoying; she thought she was always right and that she knew best. But I couldn't imagine her as a murderer. She was a perfectionist, harder on herself than those around her.

"I don't know. Natasha always does the right thing. Like sending a lovely note and payment in full to a widow who needs the money. That's typical Natasha. Everyone else will drag their feet paying the dead guy, but Natasha always does the right thing."

Nina glanced over at me. "What if she thought killing someone was the right thing? What if someone threatened Mars?"

Would she kill to protect Mars? She had implied as much. It just didn't add up for me. "Now you're grasping because you don't like Natasha."

Nina braked for a light. "Anybody other than Mars get sick at Thanksgiving?"

She had a point.

We turned right and familiar broad shoulders came into view. On the sidewalk in front of my favorite bakery, Wolf and Kenner were engaged in a heated discussion. I felt like ducking so Kenner wouldn't see me. No need, though, he wouldn't notice me seated in a car driving by.

Nina swung the Jaguar into a parking spot.

"What are you doing?"

She nodded toward Wolf and Kenner. "I know that detective. He might tell us what's going on in the investigation."

I shrank down in my seat. "Which one do you know?"

"The good-looking one. You should meet him. All the women who volunteer at the animal shelter are crazy about him." Nina opened the car door and called to Wolf.

Swell. "Nina," I said, "Wolf is the detective on my case."

It was too late. Wolf strode toward us. Reluctantly, I opened the car door and eased out.

"Nina Reid Norwood. I should have known it would only be a matter of time until you turned up involved in this mess." Wolf shoved his hands into his pockets.

Nina held her head in a coy tilt. "Sophie happens to be completely innocent and embarrassingly available."

I wanted to melt into the sidewalk.

"Thanks for clearing that up. I'll scratch her off the suspect list immediately," Wolf said with a grin.

Evidently they had known each other long enough to kid around. I hoped he'd think the part about me being available was a joke.

Nina straightened up. "Natasha's the guilty party."

Amusement faded from Wolf's face. "And you know that how?"

Nina ticked off reasons on her fingers. "She hired Pulchinski. She had the opportunity when Simon was killed and when Mars was poisoned. All we need is her motive."

"How do you know Natasha hired Pulchinski?"

Like a college girl flirting with her professor, Nina gave him a sly look and said, "We've been doing a little sleuthing on our own."

"You two stay out of this. Sophie's in deep enough trouble already and I don't need either of you mucking up my investigation. Is that clear?"

"What happened with the turkey trophy?" I asked.

"Wiped clean. No fingerprints. We're still running tests to see if there's blood on it anywhere."

"On the tail."

"Right now we only have your word on that. We don't even know for sure if it was the murder weapon."

"What about Mars? Was there poison in his soup?" My heart pounded. I didn't really want to hear the answer to that question.

"Don't have the results yet." He motioned over his shoulder. "I have to get back to Kenner. You two stay out of trouble."

We slid into the Jaguar. Despite the distance, I could tell Kenner's face had gone beet red again. Even if Wolf thought I might be innocent, the mere sight of me agitated Kenner.

Nina pulled her Jag into the traffic. "When this is over, you really should go out with Wolf. He's gorgeous and nice, too. A regular down at the animal shelter. Donates dog and cat kibble twice a month."

"If he's so great, how come no one has grabbed him?"

"Oh, that. It's just gossip, but the story goes that he was married and then he . . ."

Her voice drifted into a mumble.

"And then what?"

She took a deep breath. "And then he murdered his wife."

"Very funny."

"I told you it's just gossip. No one really knows what happened to her."

"You're serious? Something happened to his wife?"

"We know he was married. He doesn't wear his ring anymore and his wife isn't around."

"They call that 'divorce,' Nina."

"And he's not divorced. Either she ran off or she's buried in his basement."

"And you want me to go out with him? What a great friend."

"He can't really be a killer; he wouldn't still be on the police force."

"Who would know better how to get away with murder than a homicide detective?" I asked.

"He's such a nice guy. I'm sure there's a logical explanation."

So much for my love life. Simon had been murdered, Wolf might be a killer, and that left Humphrey, who had as much sex appeal as vanilla pudding.

Nina sped past the turn to our street.

"Where are you going?"

"Don't you think we should go to the hospital to warn Mars?"

"He's probably at the hotel by now." I couldn't believe I had to tell Mars about Natasha's connection to Otis Pulchinski. He would think I meant to put Natasha in a bad light to win him back. Still, he needed to know to protect himself.

Nina slowed and backtracked a few blocks to the hotel where the Stupendous Stuffing Shakedown had been scheduled to take place. She parked in front of the ballroom lobby. I stepped out of the car and leaned against it to steady my knees. I hadn't expected such a physical reaction.

"C'mon!" Nina already held the hotel door open.

I joined her, my pulse pounding from the memories.

She paused in the ballroom lobby. "Where's the door to the service corridor?"

"Nina, I don't think . . ."

"Is that it?" She forged ahead and peeked behind a door marked "Employees Only." She snapped her fingers. "Quick, before someone catches us."

Nina walked along the hallway ahead of me. "I want to see how Natasha did it. Is this the door to the conference room where she killed Simon?"

It swung open as she put out a hand to push against it. Nina squealed and jumped back.

Andrew greeted us in surprise. "Sophie! Nina! Sorry. Didn't mean to scare you."

I'd read a million times that the killer goes back to visit the scene of the crime. So, it seemed, did the suspects.

"Guess you're trying to figure out this stinking mess, too. You came through the main door the day Simon was killed, right, Sophie?" he asked.

I nodded and followed Andrew and Nina into the room where Simon died.

"I think Natasha bashed him over the head"—Nina acted it out—"and left by the back door where we came in. Then she ran around to the front and waited for Sophie to find Simon."

Andrew grimaced. "That back corridor leads into other conference rooms, too. She could have cut through one of those."

I wasn't sure I wanted to defend Natasha, but I felt obligated to point out the flaw in their reasoning. "Anyone else could have done the same thing. Natasha could have entered and left through the front door to the room, while the killer lurked in the service corridor, waiting for his chance to be alone with Simon."

Andrew squinted at me in disbelief. "It had to be Natasha. Who else would have poisoned Mars?"

I didn't have an answer to that. "Why would Natasha poison him? They're not married; she wouldn't gain anything."

"No? You don't think he's changed his will? You don't have to marry someone to inherit."

"Natasha has her column and her TV show. It's only local but she's making a decent living."

"When the police came to our house to question Vicki and me again, they wanted to know where we were when that PI was killed. That's obviously crucial. I hated Simon with a passion but when the killer offed the PI, I was in class to get my real estate license and Vicki was in her office with clients. Natasha's the only one without an alibi. She must be the one who murdered the dead PI."

A shudder ran through me. "Andrew, I found Otis dead. I found Simon's corpse and I cooked the soup. Do you think I'm the killer?"

A hush fell over us until Andrew blurted, "You? That would ruin my whole theory."

"No, it wouldn't," insisted Nina. "Natasha could still be the killer and Sophie just happened along every time."

Even I didn't buy that. It seemed too unlikely. "The important thing is to protect Mars. He has to be careful."

"I've tried to warn him about Natasha but he won't listen. Vicki and I are taking turns staying with him."

If I knew Mars, that wouldn't last very long. He wouldn't be keen on being babysat by his brother and sister-in-law. "What's the room number? While you two snoop down here, I'll have a word with him."

I took the elevator to the fourth floor and knocked gently on the door.

Vicki opened it. Relief swept away the worried look on her face. "Sophie. Oh, thank goodness. We're expecting that vile Detective Kenner."

The stress of the past few days showed in the bags under her eyes. I reached for her hand. Her fingers felt icy.

"I don't understand what's happening," she said. "I

think the police suspect Andrew of poisoning Mars. He would never do that."

"Of course not. The Winston brothers always stick together." I was about as enthusiastic as Vicki about seeing Kenner, though. I'd have to make this quick. "I came up to see how Mars is doing."

"Hi, Soph!" he called from another room. "C'mon in."

All things considered, Mars looked better than Vicki. Healthy color flushed his cheeks as he crossed to the sofa. He wore a cream-colored crewneck sweater and faded green trousers. If I hadn't known about the poisoning, I never would have guessed he'd been ill. He propped his feet on a coffee table and lounged comfortably on the sofa of what appeared to be a two-room suite.

"Nice digs."

"Natasha pulled some strings. Local celebrity and all that. How's Mom doing?"

"She's okay. We'll all be better once this nightmare is behind us." I perched on the sofa. "Mars, there's something you need to know."

His jaw tightened, an involuntary movement that he made when expecting bad news.

"Someone murdered a private investigator the day before Simon was killed. The police think there's a connection."

"I read about it in the paper."

I swallowed hard. "Natasha had business dealings with the dead PI. She hired him to do something for her."

Mars rubbed his hand across his mouth. "Are you absolutely sure? How do you know that?"

"I saw a check she wrote for his services."

"What would she need a PI for?" Mars asked.

"I was hoping you'd know the answer to that. Who did Natasha want Otis to check out?"

The color faded from his cheeks.

"Was it me?" I asked. "Did she hire Otis to follow me?"

Mars blinked at me. "Why would she do that?"

"The day he was murdered, Otis had my picture and name on the dash of his truck."

"Sophie, that's awful. I had no idea." He sat up and scooted toward me. "You should know that Natasha lawyered up the night Simon died."

FIFTEEN

From "THE GOOD LIFE":

Dear Sophie,

I'm supposed to bring a pie to my in-laws' home for a holiday meal. I think I can master the pumpkin filling, but the dough scares me to death. They turn their noses up at premade pie dough so that's out of the question. As the newest daughter-in-law, I want to please them, but I'm afraid this will be a disaster.

—Pie Novice in Pearisburg

Dear Pie Novice,

Your first holiday feast with new in-laws isn't the time to try your hand at pie dough. A graham cracker crust is just as tasty, much faster, and virtually goof-proof. To dress it up, pipe whipped cream around the edge. It will hide any uneven spots of crust and look gorgeous, too.

—Sophie

"She's been advised not to say anything, not one thing, to Wolf or Kenner," Mars said. "You need to do the same thing to protect yourself. They can twist the most innocent statement."

"I've called a lawyer but I haven't heard from him yet."

"Mike Doyle?"

"How did you know?"

"That's who's representing Nat. He was at our party the night of the fire. Good grief, it's been an awful week."

Vicki pulled a BlackBerry from her pocket. "I have a text message from Andrew. Kenner is on his way up to interview Mars again." She put the BlackBerry on the table and massaged her temples.

"Chill, Vicki." If Mars felt any fear of Kenner, he didn't show it.

"What about you?" I asked. "Are you talking to the police?"

"And take a chance on implicating Nat? No way."

I pecked Mars on the cheek, said, "Be careful," and hurried to the door.

Vicki threw her arms around me and held me close.

"Get some sleep," I said. "Everything will work out. It's only a matter of time until they find Simon's killer and then they'll leave us all alone."

She smiled weakly. "I hope so. I pray Andrew can keep his mouth shut for once instead of spouting off about how much he hated Simon."

Unwilling to risk a hostile run-in with Kenner, I took the stairs down to the ballroom level. Even though I knew Mars and Andrew well, Craig's observation about the Winston brothers haunted me. Could Mars and Andrew have joined forces to kill Simon?

Nina waited for me in the ballroom lobby, barely suppressing her eagerness. "Andrew and I talked to the housekeeping staff. After the cops took down the yellow police tape, one of the housekeepers found a key card on the floor that the police missed. She turned it over to the cops and says they were very excited."

"Who did it belong to?"

"She didn't know. She doesn't use the hotel computers for her job."

"A lot of people crowded in that room when Simon died. Still, it could be a lead. Think Wolf will tell us about it if we ask?"

Nina appraised me. "Maybe if you flirt with him."

I wasn't going that route. But maybe I should reconsider. Flirting worked pretty well for Nina.

The sound of approaching footsteps sent me for the door in an effort to avoid Kenner but Nina lingered.

"Sophie," she said, "look who it is. Hi!"

Dread welled in my stomach but I turned anyway.

Simon's driver, Clyde, strode toward Nina.

"Didn't you work for Simon?" she asked.

His eyes drifted toward me as I joined them.

"Hello, Sophie. Simon was more than a boss." Clyde mashed his eyes shut and rubbed his forehead. "I can't believe he's gone. I'd only worked for him a little over a year but he was great. I traveled the world with him, first class all the way. He treated me like family. There's nothing I wouldn't have done for him."

"The police must be keeping you apprised. What's the latest on his killer?" I asked.

He snorted. "You're a suspect. Don't worry, I'm inclined to think it was Natasha. She'd taken private meetings with Simon before the competition."

Aside from the implication that she might have been trying to sway his vote in the contest, it put her allegation that I had an unfair advantage in a whole new light.

Nina squinted at him. "What are you doing here?"

His eyebrows shot up and he smiled cynically. "I suppose I ought to ask you that question." He inspected her head to toe, stopping to take in the huge diamond on her finger, just like Mrs. Pulchinski had.

"We came to visit someone," said Nina in an irritated voice.

"If this is a contest, then I think I have you beat. I'm staying here."

His mild amusement only served to further aggravate Nina. I thought I'd better intercede.

"You're a lot like Simon, aren't you?"

"I consider that a compliment of the highest order. Simon was a great guy, a good friend." He looked down at the key card in his hand. "This has been very hard for me. I'm waiting for the police to release his belongings and the body so I can take him to England to be buried. We'd been living in London, you know. He loved it there."

In spite of his little game with Nina, I felt terrible for him. He'd lost a dear friend and his job and had the unenviable task of seeing to all the funeral details.

I choked out, "I'm very sorry, Clyde."

He nodded at us and walked away briskly.

Nina stuck out the tip of her tongue like she had a bad taste in her mouth. "What an obnoxious guy. I don't like him one bit."

She muttered about Clyde all the way home. When we parked in front of her house, I invited Nina in for a late lunch.

"Thanks, but I'd better get back to pretending I'm a perfect southern domestic goddess like Natasha."

Poor Nina. "What's for dinner?"

"Glad you asked—Veal Piccata with Angel Hair Pasta. Alfredo's is delivering it to your house. Call me when it gets there." She dug in her purse.

"My house? Why?"

"I don't want the monster-in-law to know I didn't make it. It's already paid for but here's money for the tip."

I was on the verge of pointing out that her mother-in-law would probably notice the absence of a garlic aroma in the air, but when I stepped out of the car, I saw a strange man open the side gate to my property and walk to the back of my house.

"Hey!" I ran across the street and into my backyard.

A team of people dressed in uniforms were searching the ground. Most of them crouched or kneeled. Raising my voice, I said, "Excuse me? What's going on here?"

Nina caught up to me at the same time Wolf appeared around the corner of the shed in the back.

He strode across to us waving a paper. "Sorry, Sophie. Search warrant for mushrooms."

"I used them all yesterday." I shouldn't have said it. I knew I shouldn't the moment it came out of my mouth. "That was a joke, Wolf."

"You need to work on your comedy routine."

A man bending under a pine near the fence shouted at us. Wolf jogged over, followed by Nina and me.

Two mushrooms grew in the shade. No more than three inches high, they bore bright red caps that drooped like elfin hats. Just as Francie had described them—worthy of a children's picture book.

Wolf gazed up at me. "Looks like you missed a couple."

"You can't think that means anything. I'm sure Nina has them in her yard, too. It's not like I planted them."

Nina frowned. "I've seen them in parks and near paths in woods. Anyone could have access to them." She raised her eyebrows at Wolf. "I bet there are tons in Natasha's garden."

"Don't worry about Natasha, her garden has been thoroughly searched."

"You closing in on her?" asked Nina.

Wolf stood up. "Hardly. You have no idea how many people hated Simon. That man cultivated enemies around the world."

Relief washed over me like a warm bath. "It's not just Mars's and my families then? You have other suspects as well?"

Wolf didn't answer my question. "We're almost done here." He promptly walked away, as though we'd been dismissed.

I closed my eyes. My teeth hurt from clenching them. I thought everything was going to get better—but a search warrant—that was bad news.

Nina threw a comforting arm around me and walked me to the kitchen door before she went home. I let myself in the house, grateful for the loving attention Mochie and Daisy demanded at the door. I petted both, praising them for getting along so very well.

June danced into the kitchen. "I thought I heard someone. How do I look?" She held out her arms and twirled around to show off a silk dress of vivid blue.

"Lovely." I tossed my jacket over a chair. "What's the big occasion?"

She placed her palms over her flushed cheeks. "The colonel invited me to dinner. He'll be here any minute to pick me up."

June had a date? I couldn't have been more delighted. She might talk with her deceased sister but I'd seen nothing else to indicate that June needed to live in a home for the infirm. The thought lifted my spirits and I gave her a hug.

"Did you see Wolf?" she asked. "He came with a search warrant for the backyard."

I didn't want to dampen her spirits with the news about the mushrooms he found so I just nodded. Through the bay window I saw Wolf and his crew get in their cars and depart.

"Where's my purse?" she said. "I thought I had it. Sophie, I'm a nervous wreck. I haven't been out with a man in a decade. Everyone goes dutch now, don't they? How do I know how much to pay? Do I ask him for the check or will he tell me the amount?"

I found her purse on the console in the foyer. "Think of it as dinner with a girlfriend."

"That's a good idea. Yes, I'm feeling calmer already." The doorbell rang and June cried, "I need a mirror. How's my hair?"

I grasped her upper arms gently. "You look great. Have a wonderful time."

I opened the door for the colonel. Dashing in a deep gray overcoat of fine wool, he handed June a peach rose. I was afraid the gesture might make her more nervous but she took it with gracious thanks and a flirtatious glance at the colonel.

When he helped her with her coat, I realized they made a striking couple, both with silvery hair, the colonel tall and authoritative in his bearing in contrast to June's gentle roundness.

I watched from the stoop as they left. A cold wind kicked up as the colonel's SUV drove away. Cloudy skies threatened to bring evening shadows early and I still hadn't eaten lunch.

Daisy wagged her tail and moved in for a dog hug when I closed the door.

"It's the first time we've had the house to ourselves in days, huh, girl?"

She followed me into the kitchen. I opened the refrigerator, so laden with leftovers that containers threatened to fall out. In looking for turkey to nibble on, I found two gorgeous pork tenderloins I'd meant to cook before Thanksgiving. I checked the dates on them. They were still good. Pork with cherry sauce, savory rice, and asparagus would be a wonderful break from Thanksgiving foods for my houseguests.

I took out the turkey, sliced off a few pieces, and shared my treat with Mochie and Daisy. The peace didn't last long. From the kitchen window I saw Nina dashing across the street, waving her arms like a madman. I opened the door and leaned out. "What is it? What's wrong?"

"The Peeping Tom," she panted. "He's in your backyard."

Daisy and I rushed outside. Daisy loped ahead into the increasingly dark backyard. Nina paused at the corner of the house. She peeked around the back. "He's there! He's looking in your sunroom."

I wanted to see a Peeping Tom about as much as I wanted to see a snake. Nina stood back and I peered around the corner of my house. The Peeping Tom wore a shabby jacket and an old hat.

Nina whispered, "I'll call the cops."

"Not yet." Something wasn't right. Daisy sniffed around the Peeping Tom without so much as a growl. "It's someone we know."

I heard Nina suck in air. "The killer! I knew it was Natasha."

I wasn't so sure it was Natasha but I thought we should find out. "I'm going to run straight back and cross to the other side of the yard. I'll stick to the shadows. It's getting so dark, I think I can do it without being seen. Give me about two minutes, then we'll sneak up on him from both sides."

Nina seized the back of my shirt. "And then what? What if it's not Natasha? We say, 'Oh, please, Mr. Peeping Tom, don't kill us'?"

She was right. We huddled by the side of the house. "You stay here," I said. "I'll get a fireplace poker."

But just as I took one last look around the corner, I came face-to-face with the Peeping Tom.

SIXTEEN

From "The Good Life":

Dear Sophie,

My husband says I make horrible tea because I heat the water in the microwave. I'm making a spiced holiday tea for a family brunch next week and he insists that I boil the water on the stove. We have a little bet riding on this. I say it doesn't make a difference. What do you think?

—Teetotaler in Troutdale

Dear Teetotaler,

While the microwave is great for hot chocolate, I have to side with your husband about tea. Microwaved tea usually tastes flat. For full body and flavor, bring your water to a boil on the stove and pour it over tea bags or leaves.

If you must microwave water, be very careful. It can easily overheat and explode extremely hot water on you and the microwave.

—Sophie

I screamed.

The Peeping Tom screamed.

Nina screamed.

Daisy finally barked, no doubt happy about all the excitement.

The Peeping Tom clutched at his chest. "Are you trying to give me a heart attack?"

Francie.

Not again. "Come on in, Francie." She'd better have a good explanation this time.

The three of us trudged back to the kitchen. Half frozen, Nina started a fire while I put on the kettle for tea. Francie took off her floppy hat and slumped in a chair to catch her breath. I should have been nicer but Francie's antics grated on me. I crossed my arms and counted to ten so I wouldn't be too rude when I demanded an explanation.

Nina rubbed her arms to warm up. "She started in the colonel's yard. I saw her creeping around in the back. By the time I ran downstairs, she'd snuck out the old service alley and crossed the street."

Francie raised her chin defiantly. "So what if I did?"

My anger subsided as I watched Francie, a pathetic figure, her hair mussed into spikes from the hat, her face weathered like an old sailor's. In spite of her brave front, she came across as small and withered.

"You've been the Peeping Tom all along, haven't you?"

She started to answer but Nina interrupted her. Pointing a finger at Francie, she said, "Don't give us any of the baloney you told the cops."

"There really was a Peeping Tom. Honest. I don't know who it was but it wasn't me."

Daisy placed her head in Francie's lap and Francie stroked her gently. Nina took the kettle off the burner and brewed three mugs of tea while I commenced with the interrogation. I pulled a kitchen chair in front of Francie's and sat down. "What were you doing?"

The corner of her mouth twitched. "Taking a short-cut."

"A shortcut that involved staring into my sunroom?"

Nina handed us steaming mugs of tea spiced with cin-namon and cloves and sat in the other fireside chair. "Okay, out with it or I'll call the cops the next time."

Francie flicked her hand at Nina, indicating she wasn't intimidated by Nina's threat.

I sipped the tea to warm up. The last time we caught Francie in my backyard she'd been dressed for Thanks-giving dinner. This time she wore loose, shabby clothing and a hat to hide her face. She wanted anyone who saw her to think she could be the original Peeping Tom. What did she want in my sunroom? Had she been checking to be sure no one was home?

Remembering how she'd barely taken her eyes off the colonel at Thanksgiving, I plotted a way to get her to talk.

I stood up and addressed Nina. "I guess I'll call the col-onel and tell him. He has a right to know that Francie has been prowling in his backyard and down his service alley."

The scowl on Francie's face turned to horror. "No! Don't involve him. I'll . . . I'll tell you the truth. But only if you promise me you won't tell the colonel."

Nina and I agreed to keep mum.

"I've been following him."

Nina burst out laughing. "You've been stalking the colonel?"

"I prefer to think of it as observing. Honestly, you girls are old enough to know you can't catch a man by just batting your eyelashes at him."

Nina covered her mouth with her fingers and I knew why. I didn't dare let our eyes meet. Suppressing a grin, I asked, "How does it help to observe him?"

"You'd be surprised what you can find out about a person. He sends out all of his laundry. Even his under-wear. A cleaning woman arrives every Monday morning.

He's very neat, though. I imagine that's from his military days."

"Francie," I said, "wouldn't it be easier to invite him over for dinner? You'd learn so much more about him that way."

"Not necessarily."

"That explains why you were in his yard poking around, but what were you doing looking in my windows?"

"I lost track of him. I thought I saw him walk over here. I went upstairs to change my clothes, but when I came down, I couldn't find him anymore. I didn't know where he went. I checked his house but he didn't appear to be home. The light in his mudroom was on; he always leaves it on when he goes out. Since I'd last seen him crossing to your house, I thought maybe you had invited him over for drinks."

My heart went out to Francie. I couldn't imagine being so lonely and desperate.

"The colonel has never caught you?" asked Nina.

Francie glowered at her. "Give me a little credit. Besides, the original Peeping Tom made it easier for me. If anyone saw me, they'd think it was the real guy back again." She looked around. "So where is he?"

I didn't dare tell her the colonel invited June to dinner. I couldn't break her heart that way. "He went out. He just stopped by for a minute."

"Where'd he go?"

At least I didn't have to lie. "I don't know exactly."

The knocker on the front door banged. Nina looked out the bay window. "That's my dinner." She rose to answer the door.

Francie's eyes roamed the kitchen. "Where's June?"

I chose my words carefully. "She went out."

Francie leapt from her chair. "Together! They went out together."

I didn't deny it. I couldn't.

Nina carried a pile of party-sized take-out containers into the kitchen. "Okay if I borrow some of your pots and pans so the monster-in-law will think it's homemade?"

"Of course."

Francie paced. "I've invested so much time. Then June arrives in town and boom, he's smitten with her immediately. How could this happen?" Francie's fingers curled into little balls. "Nobody trifles with Francine Vanderhoosen. Nobody. That . . . that . . . man!"

"Francie, calm down. It's just dinner," I said.

"Just dinner? When I think about the way I've been treated. Ooo. He'll rue the day he did this to me. I'm not keeping his secrets anymore."

Nina swung around. "Secrets? Do tell."

"I'll tell you something the police don't even know. The colonel went to see Simon the day he was murdered. And the colonel was there when Simon was killed."

SEVENTEEN

From "The Good Life":

Dear Sophie,

The holidays are upon us and what with decorating, writing cards, and going to school pageants, I have less time than normal. But family and friends expect more than a peanut butter and jelly sandwich for dinner. Any suggestions for something fast and festive?

—Frazzled in Fredericksburg

Dear Frazzled,

Pork tenderloins to the rescue. They're like the filet mignon of pork, delicious and easy to make. Better still, they go well with a variety of nuts and fruits if you feel like dressing them up. A whole tenderloin cooks in twenty to thirty minutes. Don't overcook them! They should be a little bit pink in the middle. You can pop them in the oven or cook them on the stove top. If you opt for a pan on the stove top, brown them first in olive oil and be sure to add some liquid like chicken broth or apple juice and cover tightly.

Need to speed up dinner? Cut the tenderloin into half-inch slices and cook on the grill or in a pan.

—Sophie

"How do you know the colonel was at the hotel the day Simon was murdered?" I asked.

"Haven't you been listening?" asked Francie, her expression incredulous. "I followed him."

"So you were there, too."

"Obviously."

"But why wouldn't the police know? They corralled us all in the ballroom."

"The colonel isn't an idiot. He left when word broke about the murder. Simply walked through the main lobby and out the front entrance. No one tried to stop either of us."

"Maybe he went to the hotel for another reason," suggested Nina.

"Not a chance. He knew exactly where he was going. Waited until that driver of Simon's left his side and then the colonel paid Simon a visit in the Washington Room."

I thought I caught an implausibility in her story. "If that were the case, Natasha would have seen the colonel coming or going."

"Not if she went in the back way. I would have seen her if she had come down the main hallway."

I frowned at her. "Then why didn't I see you?"

"I guess we had moved on by the time you found Simon. I was lurking behind a potted plant but I'd have noticed you or Natasha going into the Washington Room."

Nina appraised Francie with admiration. "Francie,

how'd you like to come over for dinner? My monster-in-law would love company."

Francie fingered the oversized sweater she'd worn under her jacket. "Dressed like this?"

"Go home and change first."

They headed for my front door.

"But one word about this being take-out and I'll spill everything to the colonel," warned Nina.

I followed them to the foyer and as they walked out into the early darkness I heard Francie say, "Deal."

I shut the door and returned to the kitchen to start dinner. After rinsing the meat and patting it dry, I seasoned it with salt, pepper, and thyme. The day I'd found Otis's body I'd bought fresh rosemary sprigs. I snipped the tiny leaves with scissors, enjoying the slightly piney scent. After sprinkling the meat with the rosemary bits, I rubbed the seasonings across the pork loins. Since the entire gang hadn't yet returned, I covered the two pork tenderloins with plastic wrap and placed them in the fridge. They wouldn't take long to cook. I'd wait until everyone had returned before starting them so they wouldn't dry out.

The heads of romaine in the refrigerator would provide a good base for a salad. I chopped crunchy pecans and tossed them with the washed and spun-dry lettuce. Using my favorite mini-whisk, I swirled together orange juice, rosemary, salt, freshly ground pepper, thyme, and olive oil for a vinaigrette but left it on the counter in its bowl. It would only take a second to dress the salad before we ate. If I dressed it now, the lettuce would wilt and become soggy. I chopped an onion and two cloves of garlic for the rice and set them aside. Next to them, I placed cottony dried sage, basmati rice, a knob of butter, and the pot. That would be ready to go in a flash.

Frozen cherries went into a small saucepan to which I added a little sugar, a splash of brandy, cinnamon, and ground cloves. The wintery scent of cinnamon mixing with cloves wafted into the air the minute the pot heated.

Bernie arrived home first. Daisy and Mochie clambered for his attention. He obliged them by kneeling on the kitchen floor. Daisy licked his face while little Mochie head-butted him.

When their excitement subsided, he stood and tossed his leather jacket on top of the jacket I hadn't bothered to hang up.

"I like your Old Town Alexandria. Has character. Walked over to check on Mars and then spent the afternoon roaming around a bit. Never had the time when I visited before."

I longed to ask him about the newspaper article I'd found. I stirred the thawing cherries and wondered how to steer the conversation to Miami. "Where's home these days?"

"Was living in London but I'm seriously considering a change. Mars thinks there are opportunities around here."

Rats, he didn't take my bait. "So what began as a vacation might become a permanent residence?"

Bernie poured himself a glass of orange juice. "Yeah, maybe."

I tried a different tack. "How's your mom?" She traveled a lot. Maybe he'd visited her in Miami.

"Met some bloke she likes and went to Hong Kong. Last I heard they were in Shanghai on business. She's likely to ring me any day now about another wedding. What's for dinner?"

If he wouldn't talk about Miami, I would have to be more obvious. "Miami Vice Rice and Pork Tenderloins."

"You Americans have odd names for food. I stopped over in Miami on my way here. Lovely to catch some sun this time of year but I don't recall seeing Miami Vice Rice on a menu."

The kitchen door opened and Dad walked in. "It's cold enough to snow!" He rubbed his hands briskly.

"Where are the others?" I asked.

He contorted his face in mock pain. "I begged them to drop me off. They had to see one more store."

Dad's coat landed on top of the jackets. The chair would topple soon. I swooped them up and hung them all in the foyer closet.

When I returned to the kitchen, Dad had settled into a chair. Mochie and Daisy demanded his attention but while he stroked them, he addressed Bernie.

"He's a nice enough guy." Dad didn't sound convinced when he said it. "Very polite. But I've never known another man to be so interested in his wedding."

"Craig?" I asked.

"Who else? I could understand if he planned the honeymoon, but over lunch today, the three of them discussed bows for the backs of chairs for forty-five minutes. I timed them." Dad stretched out his legs and leaned his head back against the chair. "The wedding is seven months away. I'm not sure I'll last that long if they keep this up."

"He's not macho enough for you?" asked Bernie.

Dad winced. "That wouldn't bother me. It's more like he's a chameleon. Like he says what he thinks we want to hear. I've spent a couple of days around him now and except for the fact that he's a doctor and he likes big droopy bows on the backs of chairs, I don't know anything about the man. I don't know if his parents are living or if he has siblings or what kind of car he drives or which sports he follows."

"Maybe he's trying hard to adapt, to please you," said Bernie. "It can be difficult to join a family."

I placed a lid on the pot with the cherries and let them simmer. "I know what Dad means. I think he's creepy. He's been spying on me since he arrived. I keep turning around and finding him there, listening, like he's gathering information."

"Spying?" Bernie chuckled. "That's the height of future in-law paranoia. Why would he do that?"

I was about to betray my sister, but I only had her welfare at heart. "Did you know they met through the internet?"

Dad's face went ashen. "Hannah told us they met at a party." He sprang from his chair. "Mind if I use your computer?" He didn't wait for an answer. Bernie and I trailed behind him into the den.

After a few swift keystrokes, Dad sighed with relief. "Here he is. Craig Monroe Beacham, MD. Internist . . . not much information . . . valid medical license in West Virginia. Hasn't been sued, went to medical school on the West Coast and did an internship in South Dakota. Nothing sinister."

I slumped back on the sofa. So much for that. I would do my best to be happy for Hannah. On her third try, she'd found a relationship the rest of us dreamed of. The kind of relationship some of us, like Francie, still chased.

"Dad, when you talked with the colonel yesterday, did he say anything about Simon?"

"The subject didn't come up. Mostly he told me about his efforts to bring medical care to underprivileged Africans."

Bernie sprawled on the other end of the couch. "What gives, Soph?"

"Apparently the colonel happened to be at the hotel when Simon was murdered."

The keyboard clicked as Dad's fingers flew across it. "This is impressive stuff. The colonel's received awards for his work. There are pages and pages about him." The clicking of keys commenced again. "Okay, now I've got something. Uh-oh. Remember the girl who lost her leg on that show *Don't You Dare*? Lots of allegations blaming the crew."

"That's reprehensible. Imagine being so sloppy that someone would lose a limb," said Bernie.

"It gets worse. The girl who lost her leg is the colonel's granddaughter."

EIGHTEEN

From *"Ask Natasha"*:

Dear Natasha,

In spite of my admonishments, my rowdy teenage son is always coming home with blood on his clothes. I've tried all kinds of commercial products, but the stains are usually dried and set by the time he comes home and nothing seems to work. What do you recommend?

—Bloody in Blue Ridge

Dear Bloody,

The conventional wisdom is to soak the stain with salt. However, I take a cue from the professionals. Not the professional launderers, the professionals who get blood on their clothes at work—firefighters and police officers. Hydrogen peroxide works best. However, with any stain treatment, always test an inconspicuous area first to be sure the color doesn't bleed.

—Natasha

"So the good colonel might not be such a splendid chap after all," mused Bernie.

"Could he have killed Simon to avenge his grand-daughter?" I asked.

Dad swung toward us in the desk chair. "If I thought someone rigged something to injure Jen, it might put me over the brink. That kind of thing can blur the lines of right and wrong and tamper with our natural inhibitions."

"Could he be the one who tried to poison Mars?" I asked, sitting up straight, alarmed at the thought.

"Andrew came up with the idea for the TV show." Bernie kicked off his shoes and removed his socks. "Perhaps the colonel meant to poison Andrew. That would have given him revenge against both of them."

Dad tented his hands and tapped his forefingers together. "He didn't say a word about being at the stuffing competition. Remember? At Thanksgiving when we all discussed the murder. Not a word."

"And being former military, one would suppose he has some training in how to kill. He'd have known where to lodge the blow that ended Simon's life. Did anyone else get the impression that the colonel was rather surprised by Francie's knowledge about poison?" asked Bernie.

"June!" I jumped up. "He took her out to dinner."

"Do you know where they went?" asked Dad.

"I haven't a clue." Why hadn't I asked? "What if he poisons June? Mars survived because he's young and strong, but June . . ."

Dad motioned for me to sit. "We're getting carried away. The colonel has no reason to harm June. Besides, it would be stupid of him to hurt her on the heels of poisoning Mars. We don't know that he killed Simon; we only know that he hid the fact that he was in the hotel when Simon was murdered."

"Your dad's right, Sophie. All three of us were there, but that doesn't mean one of us bashed old Simon over the head."

"Does June have a cell phone?" asked Dad.

"Don't think so. She borrowed mine the other day," said Bernie.

"Then there's nothing we can do. I think it's time we told your mom everything, Sophie." Dad put the computer to sleep.

I didn't want to start a fight between them but I thought I'd better be honest. "She already knows all about Otis and everything, Dad."

His face lit up. "That's my Inga. Plugging along like everything is fine."

Bernie nudged me. "Mind if I do some laundry, luv?"

"Help yourself. Washer and dryer are in the basement."

He hoisted the duffle bag and added the socks he'd taken off. "Daisy, Mochie? Coming to keep me company?"

As if they understood the exotic scents of a basement adventure awaited, they shot out the door ahead of him.

Dad and I rose and he wrapped his arms around me. "June will be fine, kiddo."

"I'll feel better when June is home, safe and healthy."

We walked slowly through the sunroom to the hallway.

"The cherries!" I'd forgotten all about them.

I rushed to the kitchen to check on them and heard the front door bang open. Thankfully, the cherries survived and their sauce had thickened nicely. I removed them from the burner and poked my head in the foyer.

The three wedding enthusiasts shed their coats.

Hannah handed hers to Craig and pulled off her gloves. "I'm so glad to be home. It's freezing out there."

I greeted everyone and returned to the kitchen to preheat the oven. Mom followed me, collapsed into one of the fireside chairs, and put her feet up on a stool. "I can't take another step. Honey, Mars called earlier while you were out. He asked June to come to the hotel tomorrow morning for a visit and then he's taking her shopping. Natasha has an important appointment and she'll be out. I think Mars is afraid for Natasha and June to be in the same room since things aren't so great between them what with the fire and Mars's poisoning. Neither trusts the other."

I couldn't blame him for trying to keep them apart.

Mom smoothed the pleats in her skirt. "Poor Natasha. When I think what that girl has been through in her life. She never seems to catch a break. It must be awful to be a murder suspect."

"It is," I said drily, whisking a spoon through the onions softening in the butter. Had she forgotten that her own daughter was a suspect? I spooned a generous tablespoon of sage on top of the cooking onions. The comforting scent of sage bloomed as soon as the herb hit the pan.

Mom leaned sideways to peer into the foyer. "Did Craig and Hannah go upstairs?"

"I think so." I checked the time and placed the tenderloins in the oven.

"What did you find out from the PI's widow?"

I added rice and broth to the translucent onions, popped the lid on top, and filled her in on Natasha's payment to Otis, the discovery of poisonous mushrooms in my backyard, the colonel's granddaughter, and June's date.

Mom clapped a hand over her mouth. "Lost her leg? That poor child. And now June is out with him. Too bad she didn't know about the granddaughter, she could have gotten the scoop. We'll make that her job tomorrow afternoon. She can invite the colonel for coffee and pump him for information."

"Assuming he doesn't kill her tonight."

"Nonsense. Any man clever enough to leave the hotel without being questioned by the police isn't going to blow it by poisoning his dinner date. That would be far too obvious."

The basement door, located in the tiny passage that connected the family room to the kitchen, swung open. Bernie emerged along with Daisy and Mochie. "Sophie, are you still doing Mars's laundry?"

An odd question. "Of course not."

"There were men's clothes in the dryer. I folded them and set them on the table down there."

"Did you do laundry?" I asked Mom.

"I've toured every bridal boutique in the greater Washington area. Who had time for laundry?"

I checked on the rice and the pork before venturing into the basement to see the mysterious clothes. I didn't have to look through them to know to whom they belonged. The day of the stuffing competition Craig had worn the black polo shirt on the top of the pile. What was he trying to wash away?

Daisy's heavy paws pounding behind me, I ran up the stairs to the kitchen. Craig couldn't be involved in the murders. He hadn't been in town when Otis was killed.

"Mom," I panted, "when you picked up Craig at the airport, did he come from the passengers-only area?"

"Dad and I waited in the car so we wouldn't have to park. Hannah prearranged to meet him in baggage claim."

Dad walked in and sat in the other fireside chair. "What's this?"

Mom frowned at me. "What are you saying, Sophie? That Craig didn't fly in from out of town?"

"Is it possible?" I asked. "Could he be involved in the murders? I dismissed him as a possibility because his connection was too remote. He barely knows us. How could he arrange it?"

"He was also with Hannah the entire time at the stuffing contest," said Mom.

"I saw him in the gent's washroom," said Dad. "He obviously escaped from her for a few minutes."

"And he managed to leave the hotel to bring back the French fries," I added.

"Sophie, you're talking nonsense. Hannah has been so upset with you. You're not very good at hiding your dislike of him. He's going to be family; you might as well accept him." Mom shot me a displeased look.

My eyes met Dad's but before I could say anything, Hannah and Craig joined us.

Mom deftly changed the subject to Daisy and Mochie and how well they'd adapted to each other.

While Dad opened a bottle of white wine, I set the table in the kitchen. Hannah would be happy to see the French country tablecloth and napkins she'd given me for my birthday. They coordinated perfectly with the amber and red jars of votive candles I placed in the middle of the table.

The others chatted amiably while I finished cooking and kept a wary eye on Craig. A doctor would know how to remove blood from his clothes and would certainly be smart enough to wash them right away.

I tossed crisp salad with the simple vinaigrette and divided it among salad plates. On top of the greens I arranged a few red onion rings in a circle. I sliced a juicy blood orange into thin wheels and centered one on each plate over the onions. Even Natasha would have admired the colorful combination.

I cut the hot tenderloins into rounds half an inch thick and placed them, overlapping one another, on the middle of an oval serving platter. A bouquet of onion and sage floated from the rice when I removed the lid. I fluffed the savory rice around the edge of the platter and spooned cherry sauce over the meat. The remaining sauce went into a bowl, to which I added a ladle.

The wind howled outside but the fire crackled, the kitchen smelled like rosemary, and the candles provided a soft glow for our cozy winter dinner. We devoured the remaining pecan pies and decadently fudgy brownies for dessert and used the last of the whipped cream to top steaming Kahlúa-laced coffee.

When we lingered at the table sipping our rich decaf coffee, Bernie vanished to the foyer and returned bundled in a loden green overcoat. "I'm going out for a bit. Have you got a spare key, Sophie? I don't want to wake anyone when I come back."

I handed him the key that used to belong to Mars. "Are you going to look for June?"

"I thought it might be a good idea."

He let himself out through the front door. From the kitchen window over the sink, I watched him saunter away and saw Nina walking a dog across the street. Pulling on a down jacket, I whistled for Daisy. Her leash securely attached, we trotted over to Nina.

I slowed as we approached since I didn't want to alarm the other dog. Not that I needed to worry. The golden retriever wagged his tail and pulled at his leash, eager to greet Daisy.

Nina laughed when he dragged her toward us. "Daisy, meet Duke."

Daisy held her head high, in reserved hound fashion, when Duke snuffled her jowls, but the golden's enthusiasm soon won Daisy over and her tail wagged, too.

"I'm fostering him because no one has adopted him yet. Must be because he's a mature dog and not a puppy. I can't bear to think what could happen to him if he doesn't find a home," said Nina. "He has lovely manners. Know anyone who would adore him and have the time to give him the attention he deserves?"

I promised to think about it.

We strolled under the streetlights, the night bitter enough to discourage most casual walkers. Anyone out tonight had a good reason for it.

"Duke and I just walked Francie home. She's a gas. I think my monster-in-law was horrified by her," said Nina with glee.

"Did she calm down about the colonel?"

"Not at all. That man is going to pay for not being interested in her."

I told Nina about the colonel's granddaughter. "You don't think . . . Francie couldn't be the killer."

Nina's laugh echoed down the empty street. "Are we talking about the same wiry little woman who lives next door to you? She couldn't throw a man in a Dumpster."

"She could if she had help."

"You mean that story about following the colonel might be a bunch of baloney that she made up for our benefit?"

"What if they operated as a team and that's why she went ballistic over his dinner date with June?"

"She loves him so much that she agreed to help him kill Simon to avenge his granddaughter? Why would he poison Mars? Or kill Otis?" Nina sounded doubtful.

No matter whom I considered, it always came back to the same thing. Lots of people held grudges against Simon, but when Otis and Mars were factored in, nothing made sense.

Nina gripped my sleeve. "Quick!" She opened the gate to the colonel's service alley.

The dogs ran in, eager to sniff MacArthur's territory. Nina and I followed.

She closed the gate behind us and we peered over the top.

A figure in a dark coat ambled up our street.

"Not Francie again," I groaned.

"I don't think so. Not this time."

Apparently my unbridled suspiciousness was infectious. Even Nina had begun to overreact.

"It's not illegal to stroll. I think you're losing . . ." I stopped mid-sentence. The person on the other side of the street had slowed to study the houses. Not uncommon in Old Town, except in frigid weather. An icy finger ran down my spine when he observed my house. The light in the kitchen glowed, backlighting my parents and Hannah as they sat at the table in front of the bay window.

"I have to warn them." I reached for the gate latch.

Nina held her arm out to stop me. "There's a second person."

The one observing my family made no effort to hide. But another figure darted along the sidewalk among shadows where the streetlights didn't reach. I suspected Francie immediately. But a quick look at her house revealed someone passing behind closed curtains. This time Francie was in the clear.

The person watching my house turned toward us, ostensibly to observe Nina's house. Nina and I gasped at the same time.

NINETEEN

Dear Sophie,

My boyfriend says there's nothing that compares with sleeping on a feather bed. Is that a mattress filled with feathers? Or is he confused and sleeping on a comforter?

—Featherless in Ferrum

Dear Featherless,

A feather bed is similar to a down comforter, but you sleep on top of a feather bed. It goes over the top of your mattress. Some people put them under their fitted sheets but I use mine on top because I like the way it fluffs up around me. Either way, be sure to place it inside a duvet cover that can be removed to be washed. I have to agree with your boyfriend—there's nothing quite like snuggling into a lofty feather bed on a cold night.

When you shop for one, be sure you don't feel any
nasty quills that could jut out. It should be lightweight
but never thin. Ideally, it should loft up like a cloud.

—Sophie

The brisk wind blew her hair back, leaving no doubt
about her identity. The streetlight illuminated Natasha's
face.

"Where's the other guy?" whispered Nina.

I'd lost track of him, too. "We should tell her she's being followed."

"What if it's Mars?"

I hesitated. What if Mars thought she was the killer?
What if he suspected her of having an affair? "What if
it's not Mars?"

Natasha ambled to the end of the block and stopped
again.

"This is creepy," said Nina. "It's like she's casing the
neighborhood for burglary."

I still couldn't locate the second person. Where had he
gone? Natasha abruptly changed direction and headed
back—toward us. I opened the gate and let Daisy out first.
If the mysterious stalker prowled nearby, Daisy would
surely pick up his scent and growl. Nina followed me
through the gate and the two of us met Natasha on the
sidewalk in the middle of our block.

She might believe I poisoned Mars, but I had to tell her
the truth in case she was in danger. "Natasha," I whispered, "someone's following you."

"Probably a fan. They're so cute. It happens to me all
the time."

"Do your fans stick to the shadows so they won't be
seen?" I asked.

"Sophie, haven't you had enough drama? Do you mean

to scare me? I can't imagine why you'd make up such a thing."

"She's telling you the truth," protested Nina.

Natasha pulled her coat tight around her. "Then where is he now? I don't see anyone out here but you two."

"Exactly what are you doing here?" Nina didn't ask, she demanded. "It's a little cold for an evening walk."

Natasha released a sigh. "If you must know, I've been having trouble sleeping. I guess the murders and the attempt on Mars's life have taken a toll on me. I thought a brisk walk might help me calm down and sleep."

The news that she was being followed probably didn't do much to calm her nerves. "Maybe we should walk you back to the hotel," I said.

Natasha turned on her sweet TV persona. "Don't you worry your little head about me. I'll be fine." With a quick wave of a gloved hand, she strode away in a big hurry.

"Did you buy it?" asked Nina.

"Not a word."

"Me, either. I'm going to call the police about that other guy. The least they can do is drive through the neighborhood a few times."

"June is going to visit Mars tomorrow morning. Natasha will be out at an important appointment."

"We should follow her."

Exactly what I was thinking. "Eight thirty in the morning early enough?"

"Have coffee ready."

The bright lights of an oncoming vehicle lit the street. I swiveled around but still didn't see the person who'd been following Natasha. I could only hope our presence discouraged him and that he wasn't tailing Natasha now.

We watched as the oncoming car pulled over to the curb and parked and the colonel stepped out and walked around the car to open the passenger door like a gentleman. I felt a weight fall off me when June hopped out, safe and sound.

She waved at us. "Hi, girls."

The colonel escorted her to the front door of my house. They kept their voices too low for me to make out what they were saying, but there was no mistaking the goodnight kiss they shared.

Nina elbowed me like we were little kids spying on a big sister. "Isn't that sweet?" she whispered. She turned and punched me in the shoulder. "Why didn't we introduce him to my monster-in-law? She'd have forgotten all about me."

"Did she figure out that you didn't cook dinner?"

"Francie distracted her. I don't think she gave it any thought. Hmm. Do we know any other single men their age?"

Grinning at the thought of matchmaking for her demanding mother-in-law, I said good night and headed home, passing the colonel as he crossed the street to his house. Despite the cold, he was humming.

By the time I reached the kitchen, June was entertaining everyone with tales from her date. "He's so refined. We ate in an exotic Moroccan restaurant—with our fingers! You should have seen the belly dancer." She lifted her arms and waved them around as she glided across the floor.

While June changed out of her pretty dress, Hannah helped me put out spiced nuts, nachos, zesty homemade salsa, crackers, and a heavenly soft goat cheese with Italian herbs. I licked a dab that clung to my finger and was tempted to scoop up more of the tangy mixture to lick. Dad mixed a batch of his famous whiskey sours and poured a Scotch for Craig.

We passed the rest of the evening playing cards. Craig lost more often than anyone else and after a while, I suspected that he was losing on purpose. It didn't matter, but it piqued my curiosity. Did he think he would win us over by losing?

Normally, I'd have stayed up with Hannah, but tonight I went up to bed when June and my parents retired, hoping it didn't mean age was creeping up on me too fast. Chalking my fatigue up to the murders and the hectic pace of Thanksgiving Day, I gratefully snuggled between my down comforter and my feather bed. Daisy nestled at the foot of the bed and Mochie pawed at me until I lifted the comforter and he could crawl underneath it.

I woke briefly around one o'clock and thought I heard Bernie walking around downstairs but drifted off again quickly.

In the morning, I thought I was the first one up, but I could hear soft murmuring when I reached the bottom of the stairs. June sat by a small fire in the kitchen fireplace, talking again. To Faye, I presumed. I said, "Good morning," and started breakfast. My presence didn't seem to bother June. Mochie jumped into her lap and except for the fact that she was talking to a dead person, it made for a sweet scene.

Nina showed for surveillance duty at a quarter past eight. Clad in black jeans, a zip-front black velour top that clung to her curves and black running shoes dotted with rhinestones, she stood at my kitchen counter pouring organic breakfast blend coffee into a stainless-steel travel mug.

As I entered the kitchen she glanced over her shoulder at me and nearly spilled the coffee. "You have to be kidding! Who knew there was a uniform for sleuths?"

I had dressed the same way, except my black sweatshirt hung loosely, disguising any shape beneath, and little gold stars decorated my shoes. "Pour me one of those, too, will you?"

I wrapped leftover croissants in aluminum foil and stuffed them into a canvas tote along with a bag of organic white cheddar cheese puffs.

"Where's the wedding party?"

"Upstairs, getting dressed. Even Bernie was up early this morning."

Nina carried the coffee, I carried the snack tote, and we left quickly, before we had to explain our plans to anyone. At the hotel where Mars and Natasha were staying, Nina took a parking ticket and circled slowly through the dim garage in search of Natasha's robin's-egg blue Lexus.

"Do you have a signature color?" I asked.

Nina sputtered. "A what?"

"Like Natasha. Everything is robin's-egg blue. Her Christmas card last year was in shades of green with touches of red but she still managed to get one tiny bit of robin's-egg blue in the picture. It's her signature color."

Nina sniffled as though she were crying. "I wanted robin's-egg blue but it was taken. I can't believe it has a name," she muttered. "I just thought Natasha was obsessed with blue. Hey! We didn't miss her. There's her car."

Sure enough, on the fourth floor of the garage sat the blue Lexus with license plates that read NATASHA. At least she made it easy for us to know we found the correct car.

Nina parked in a nearby spot where we could watch the elevator doors as well as the Lexus. An hour later we'd eaten all the croissants, made a substantial dent in the cheese puffs, and had only sips of coffee left. Surveillance, even with your best buddy, was boring.

"Maybe she walked." Nina smacked the dashboard. "We should have parked outside."

Another fifteen minutes went by before the elevator

doors opened and Natasha strode out. She wore three-inch heels, a camel turtleneck, and a matching skirt with a persimmon-colored cape draped loosely over her shoulders. She intended to impress someone.

Nina started the engine. "She stills struts like a beauty queen. Just watching her be so perfect makes me itch all over."

I was afraid Natasha might notice us, but she didn't pay us any attention at all as she stepped into her car and pulled out of her parking spot.

In the garage Nina hung back a good distance, making me wonder if she'd done this before. But as soon as Natasha passed through the gate at the entrance, Nina hit the gas pedal. She paid for parking in one swift motion as the Lexus turned left. In hot pursuit, Nina swung onto the street, but a khaki-colored, soft-top Jeep pulled out in front of us.

Nina hit the brakes hard. "What's your hurry, buster? At least his stupid car will block Natasha's view of us."

Parade-style, the robin's-egg blue Lexus, the beige Jeep, and the dark green Jaguar drove slowly through King Street, the heart of Old Town. Tourists strolled along the sidewalks, stopping to gaze in store windows. Brunching diners inside restaurants looked out over passersby.

Including Bernie.

I craned my neck to see better. It was Bernie, for sure.

"Nina." I grabbed her arm. "Is that who I think it is with Bernie?"

Heedless of the traffic, Nina slammed the brakes and stopped in the middle of the street. "Mrs. Pulchinski. Oh, that can't be good. How could Bernie know Mrs. Pulchinski?"

Good question. One that produced goose bumps on my arms. How long had they known each other? Did he know Otis, too?

Nina pressed the gas and hurried to catch up to the Jeep. In a few blocks, we would be close to home. "You don't suppose they're having an affair?" she asked.

In all the times Bernie visited, he'd never brought a girlfriend. Somehow I imagined him with a more sophisticated type than Mrs. Pulchinski. She wasn't much older than us, but she wasn't the type I'd have picked for Bernie. On the other hand, Bernie, in spite of all his international travels, drifted from one job to another and was definitely a beer-and-pretzels kind of guy. Maybe Mrs. Pulchinski was his type.

I didn't like what I was thinking. But I couldn't find any other explanation for Bernie and the dead PI's wife to be having brunch together. Were they romantically involved? Or was their meeting a business transaction related to murder? Could he have killed her husband? But he didn't have any reason to kill Simon. Maybe the two murders weren't related. *Not Bernie!*

Nina winced. "It's not easy when the suspects are people you know. How could Bernie have possibly met her?" She drew in a sharp breath of air. "Do you think Mrs. Pulchinski was at the stuffing contest? Maybe she killed her husband and Simon."

Nina was right about one thing: I wanted to think that a stranger like Mrs. Pulchinski committed the murders. It was too upsetting to imagine Natasha or Bernie could have been involved in anything so heinous.

"Will you look at this?" Nina said. "We could have stayed in your kitchen and waited for Natasha to cruise by."

We drove by our homes but Natasha didn't stop. At the corner of our block, she took a left. The Jeep zoomed straight ahead.

Nina slowed down the Jag and hung back. "Now that we could use the cover of the Jeep, it's abandoned us." We turned and drove at crawling speed to keep Natasha at a distance.

Natasha parked around the corner from our block, prompting Nina to mutter, "What's she doing?"

Her head down, Natasha concentrated on something inside her car when we drove past and slid into a parking space farther down the block.

Nina drummed the dashboard. "I don't think she saw us."

"Wouldn't matter if she did. We live here. We have every right to happen to be in the neighborhood."

Nina adjusted the rearview mirror so she could watch Natasha. "She's getting out."

I opened the car door and crept out, ready to follow her. I peeked over the roof of the car.

Natasha's heels clacked along the uneven brick sidewalk. Not the best place for three-inch heels. I'd have twisted my ankle in ten seconds. She walked past the alley that ran along the rear of Nina's and the colonel's properties and turned the corner onto our street.

"Do you think she came to spy on us?" asked Nina. "Maybe she's the Peeping Tom."

"Not a chance. She's not wearing burglar chic."

Nina peeled out of the car and we scuttled up the sidewalk. When we peered around the corner of the Wesleys' house at the end of our block, Natasha startled us by standing only a few feet away.

"Oh, no!" Nina flung her back against the side wall of the Wesleys' house. "It can't be. This is the worst!"

I looked again. Natasha was speaking with a man dressed in Old Town chic for men, khakis and a navy blazer with prominent golden buttons. I was close enough to see a monogram etched on them.

"That's Blue Henderson," she hissed.

"Blue? What kind of name is Blue?"

"He's one of the biggest real estate agents in Old Town. He sold us our house. Don't you get it? She's shopping for a house on our block."

"Don't screw up your face that way," I whispered. "Besides, there's nothing for sale."

"If Blue Henderson is here, something's for sale. This can't be happening. Not on our block. There must be dozens of houses for sale in Alexandria. Why does she have to look here?"

Nina had to be wrong. Maybe Natasha and Blue bumped into one another and were just being friendly. I peeked around the corner again. Blue led Natasha up the front stairs of the Wesleys' house and opened the front door for her.

"Have you been inside?" I asked Nina.

She looked miserable when she said, "Double lot, gorgeous old gardens, stunning moldings everywhere."

In other words, Natasha would love it. And ruin the historic charm by renovating with modern Italian appliances.

Natasha and Mars living under my nose—not exactly what I had hoped for. I turned around and scanned the next block. Weren't any houses for sale over there?

A flicker caught my eye and, with a jolt, I realized someone clad in burglar black lurked in the deep shadow of a basement entrance on the next block over.

I tried not to stare as I murmured to Nina, "Check the basement apartment next door. Could that be the guy who followed her yesterday?"

"It's sure not Francie." Nina fumbled in her pocket for her cell phone. "I'm calling Wolf. I think the cops blew me off last night when I reported her stalker."

We strolled casually in the direction of Nina's house and ducked through her service gate. While she left a message for Wolf, I searched the street for the man we'd seen. He hadn't followed us. Except for the rustling of dried leaves in the breeze, nothing stirred.

"Why aren't the cops available when we need them?" Nina snapped her phone shut. "Follow me, we'll cut through the alley." We jogged through Nina's backyard and burst out her rear gate onto the alley.

His back to us, the stalker was leaning against the Wesleys' rear fence. It was the perfect place to attack an unsuspecting Natasha when she walked to her car. She wouldn't have noticed him until it was too late.

TWENTY

Dear Sophie,

Other people who get married receive too many toasters or blenders. For some strange reason, I now have seven crystal vinegar decanters. Believe me, I don't use that much vinegar. What else can they be used for?

—Vinegary in Vinton

Dear Vinegary,

I adore those little decanters or cruets because they're so useful and elegant. You can use them to serve cream with coffee as well as for various liquors to add to warm drinks. Barbecue sauce in crystal adds a classy punch to your table. And if a family member has dietary restrictions, serving his special sauce in a crystal decanter makes it much more tasty.

—Sophie

The stalker turned, his hood shielding all but the smallest slice of his nose from view. He saw us and bolted.

We tore after him, raced through the alley, and came to a full stop where it met the sidewalk.

I didn't see him anywhere. Not even a flash of black disappearing around a bend or into a garden.

Nina rasped, "There!" She pointed at him lurking behind a tree and he took off again.

We chased after him. He rounded the corner to the next street and we kept going.

Our running had become a fast stagger by the time we reached the corner and saw him step into a Jeep and speed away, his tires squealing. The Jeep looked suspiciously like the vehicle we'd followed through Old Town earlier.

"Did you see his face?" asked Nina between gasping breaths.

"No. Did you get the license plate?" I huffed.

"Me? I was busy watching Natasha so we wouldn't lose her. You were the passenger, did you get it?"

"I was thinking about Bernie."

My breath came hard and heavy as we trudged back. I hadn't run like that since I was a kid. No wonder my pants were too tight.

As we neared Natasha's car, she strode around the corner, her cape billowing in the breeze. She extracted a purse from the cape, and continued walking, head down with one hand in the purse, no doubt hunting for her car keys.

She looked up when she reached us, surprise evident on her face. "Have you been running? Girls, you have to work up to that kind of exertion. The two of you can hardly breathe. And really . . . dressing alike? How odd."

I didn't mince words. "Natasha, you're definitely being stalked."

"Not that again." She surveyed the empty street. "You have got to get a hobby." Her eyes widened. "This is about me and Mars. How stupid of me not to recognize that sooner. You're trying to gaslight me. That's not very nice, you know."

"Natasha, pay attention. There've been two murders and I don't want to see you get hurt." I really didn't.

Nina blurted, "What are you doing touring the Wesleys' house with Blue?"

Her question caught Natasha off guard, but only briefly. "Surely you didn't think Mars and I would live in a hotel forever."

I'd been too busy concentrating on murder to give their housing issues much thought. I'd assumed they would return to Natasha's country estate in a week or two. At least we now understood her interest in our street last night. She must have walked over from the hotel to check out the Wesleys' house.

"Mars never should have sold you his interest in Faye's house." Natasha unlocked her car. "I've needed a town home. Now that the country house is uninhabitable, it seems the right time to make that purchase."

She shot Nina and me a look of haughty disapproval. "You really ought to get involved in a charity. People do kooky things when they have too much time on their hands."

I felt like lunging at her. We'd chased away her stalker, saved her from goodness knew what kind of harm, and she dismissed us like we were nuts.

I could almost breathe normally when I stared down into the backseat of her Lexus.

The contents on the seat took my breath away again.

A huge packet bearing the name of a local nursing home rested in the back. Poor June. The cheerful couple on the glossy cover didn't make me feel any better. I wondered if Mars knew about it.

Nina made one last effort. "You may not have noticed

him, but we've seen him following you twice now. You're definitely being stalked and you're a fool to ignore us."

Natasha didn't flinch. "Apparently I am being stalked—by you two."

She slid into her car with an elegance I could never have mastered, especially in those heels. The engine purred and she drove away without a glance back.

Nina sputtered, "Can you believe that woman? We probably saved her life and she still doesn't believe us."

Natasha had spent her youth hiding feelings of inadequacy. She'd had plenty of practice covering up her emotions. But I couldn't help thinking of her reaction to Wolf at Thanksgiving. She hadn't been able to conceal her nervousness then. Whatever was going on, Natasha was up to her Audrey Hepburn–esque neck in it and I suspected she knew perfectly well that she was being stalked.

We walked back to our homes and I could see why Natasha longed for a house in Old Town. Front doors bore harvest wreaths, and pumpkins and gourds decorated front stoops. The graciousness of another era infused the old red brick of the houses and the sidewalk. Smoke from a fireplace perfumed the crisp air. I could hardly believe that we were caught up in some kind of murderous web.

Daisy met me when I opened my front door, her tail wagging in a happy circle. I bent for a giant dog hug and heard voices in the kitchen. I peeked in. June, Mars, and my parents chatted amiably.

"Sophie, sweetheart, you're just in time for lunch. We thought we'd make turkey sandwiches and warm up your delicious stuffing." Mom slid out of her chair next to Mars at the kitchen table and patted it. "Come join us."

I wasn't sure if I should bring up Natasha's stalker in front of everyone. "Is anyone else here?"

Mom put the kettle on. "Bernie left quite early and Hannah and Craig went to see an exhibit on the evolution of the computer at the Smithsonian. The colonel will be coming for coffee with June around three."

I perched on the chair next to Mars. "We have to talk."

"Do you want us to leave?" asked June.

"We're all in this together." I looked into Mars's eyes and said, "Natasha and I have had our issues, but please know that I'm not saying any of this out of malice or revenge or jealousy."

Mars sat back, his eyes apprehensive.

I ticked items off on my fingers as I spoke. "Natasha hired Otis to do something for her. The turkey trophy, which I'm sure was the murder weapon, turned up in Natasha's garden. And now someone is stalking Natasha."

"What? How would you know that?" asked Mars.

"Nina and I have seen him following her twice. At least we think it's the same guy. We've never gotten a good look at his face. We warned her about him, but she acts like we're making it up."

Mars rested his elbows on the table and rubbed his face. "That explains a lot. She can't sleep and she has no appetite. No wonder. Poor kid probably thinks she'll be the next victim."

"She denies that she's being followed. I'm very afraid for her," I said.

June gently stroked Mochie on her lap. "Mars, son, I have thought and thought about the people who attended Thanksgiving dinner and no matter how I envision things, I always come back to Natasha—she's the one who poisoned you."

Mars groaned. "Mom, that makes no sense. Why would she do that?"

"Maybe she figured out that it's you who leaves wet towels on the bathroom floor," I said.

Mom tried to hide her smirk and Mars attempted to glare at me but couldn't help laughing.

Something else had been bothering me and I decided

this was a good time to bring it up. "About the fire . . . could Natasha have set her house on fire to cover up some kind of evidence?"

"I don't think Natasha could ever bring herself to burn the home she worked on so hard." Mars shook his head. "Someone else might have set the fire, though I don't know why."

"It wasn't me!" June protested with such vehemence that Mochie sprang from her lap in alarm.

"Honey, I think it's time you told Wolf all this." Mom poured boiling water over a tea strainer on top of a Royal Worcester teapot.

"Not without your lawyer present," insisted Dad.

"You're lawyering up?" Mom asked, fear in her tone.

"Face it, Mom. I found both of the corpses. Had their blood on my clothes. And Mars was poisoned in my house. I'm right up there in contention for killer of the year with Natasha."

"I guess the fire and moving to the hotel and then being poisoned distracted me," said Mars. "We have to get to the bottom of this. We can't take chances on one of us being the next victim. And the police won't leave any of us alone until they have the killer."

I recognized Mars's expression. He wore the same determined look when his candidates' popularity numbers tanked.

"Natasha and I are moving in with Andrew and Vicki today. Just until we find a place to live. Our hotel bill is growing astronomically. The move won't be a big deal since almost everything we own has to be laundered and cleaned." Mars's eyes met mine. "As soon as we move, I promise I will make the murder priority number one."

Mom set the remaining turkey in front of me. "Slice while you talk."

Over an early lunch of Thanksgiving leftovers, we discussed various suspects and theories, none of which satisfied any of us.

When we finished, Mars and June left in a hurry to do some shopping before June's sleuthing date with the colonel.

Mom loaded the dishwasher and I whipped up a cranberry spice Bundt cake to serve when the colonel arrived.

While it baked, I forced myself into the living room to be sure it wasn't a wreck. If there was one domestic chore I hated, it was cleaning. I'd hired a service to clean before my parents arrived, but dust had begun to settle on tabletops again, and my most hated job, washing the kitchen floor, awaited.

I plumped up pillows and dusted the tabletops in the living room. Fortunately, I didn't use the living room often and it stayed relatively serviceable.

The fireplace mantel and window moldings shone a glossy white when I turned on a couple of table lamps. A designer had suggested to Mars that yellow wasn't just a power color in neck ties, so Mars insisted on buttery yellow walls. We argued for days over upholstery for the sofa and chairs. Mars won with a fabric the color of summer squash for the sofa. Blood orange pillows that coordinated with the yellow plaid I'd insisted on for the chairs interrupted the shades of yellow.

I should have vacuumed or run a dry mop around the hardwood floor but time didn't permit. The dining room needed tidying, too. It connected to the living room through a twelve-foot-wide opening. Faye knew what she was doing when she built the addition. The living room and the dining room felt larger as a result of the opening between them and provided terrific flow for parties.

I returned to the kitchen, removed the cake from the oven, and placed it on a rack to cool while I walked Daisy. On our return, Mom flitted around the kitchen, as nervous as if the colonel were her suitor. She'd even turned the cake out of the pan for me while I was out.

I ground Viennese coffee beans that smelled heavenly. While the coffee brewed, I shook powered sugar into a small bowl and squeezed in a tiny amount of lemon juice. Using a miniature whisk, I mixed the two, adding a little more lemon juice until it reached a drizzling consistency. I scooped up a dollop with the whisk and let it ooze onto the top of the cake. It formed a white glaze on the top and dribbled down the sides. I cut a portion of the cake into slices and convinced myself that I really should taste one. Moist, not too sweet, with just the right burst of tartness from the cranberries. I arranged the slices on a plate and took them into the living room.

I was returning to the kitchen when June arrived, breathless. "I had no idea it was so late." She hurried to her bedroom to freshen up for her gentleman caller.

In the kitchen, Mom poured the coffee into the china pot that I so rarely used. She added it to a tray with sugar, cream, Battenberg lace napkins, and china.

The brass knocker sounded and Mom's hands flew to her hair. She fluffed it and then flicked a quick hand over her outfit in case any crumbs or fuzzies clung to her.

I watched from the kitchen doorway when Mom received the colonel. She took his overcoat as June descended the stairs, her cheeks flushed.

"Sophie," said Mom, "would you be a dear and fetch some Irish whiskey from the den?"

I snuck into the den through the sunroom and discovered Dad comfortably seated on the sofa, his sock-clad feet on the coffee table.

He held his forefinger up to his lips. The door to the living room remained slightly ajar and we could hear every word said between June and the colonel. My father had become a spy.

I shouldn't have done it, but I listened, too. Their conversation about their dinner the night before would have bored anyone.

I found the liquor and returned to the kitchen. Mom

poured a small amount into a petite crystal decanter and added it to the tray. I carried it all into the living room and set the tray on the table. June and the colonel sat on the sofa side by side. June poured coffee and Mom looked on from the dining room. I gently took Mom's arm and escorted her into the foyer.

"They're so sweet together," she said.

"You can't just stand there and watch them." Apparently spying was in my genes. "I never knew you and Dad were so snoopy."

"Where is your dad?"

"Spying in the den."

"That sneak! What a great idea." Mom hustled down the hallway toward the sunroom.

I was certain she didn't want to miss another word.

I tidied the kitchen, glad that I didn't have to cook dinner. When Mom announced I would be hosting Thanksgiving, I ordered tickets to the Ford's Theatre production of *A Christmas Carol.* I hadn't planned on June and Bernie, of course. Bernie would have to entertain himself and I'd gladly give my ticket to June. The theatergoers would be eating out and, to be honest, I looked forward to a quiet evening to catch up on my column.

Even though I wanted to take the high road and wait until June reported to us, the den pulled me like an impossibly strong magnet. I wandered to the sunroom and poked my head into the den.

Mom nestled against Dad on the sofa, her feet on the coffee table beside his, his arm around her shoulders. If I hadn't known better, I'd have thought they were watching a movie on TV.

I could hear June saying, "That Simon must have been a horrible man. He cheated my Andrew out of millions of dollars."

"Ruthless. The man had no scruples whatsoever," the colonel responded. "There's one fellow who paved his own path to hell."

"Did you know him?" I marveled at the innocence in June's voice.

At that moment, Daisy galloped along the hallway. I rushed through the sunroom to the foyer to see what was going on.

Bernie was hanging his coat in the hall closet. "Where is everyone? This place is as quiet as a tomb."

"June is entertaining the colonel in the living room." I was too embarrassed to admit that my parents were spying in the den. Besides, I had some careful questions of my own to craft. I needed to find out what Bernie was doing with Mrs. Pulchinski. "Come in the kitchen and I'll make you an Irish coffee."

Bernie followed me. "Splendid. What have you been up to all day?"

It was the opening I needed. "Funny you should ask."

A soft banging distracted me.

"What is that?" asked Bernie.

I traced the sound to a kitchen cabinet. The door bounced open ever so slightly and shut again. "There's something in there."

"Must be a rat. Have you got an iron skillet?" asked Bernie.

"It's in there with the rat."

Bernie scanned the kitchen for a weapon. "How about a broom?"

I fetched one that hung on the wall of the basement stairwell.

"You open it and I'll be ready." Bernie gripped the broom tightly and held it up over his shoulder.

I flipped the door open and jumped back.

With a complaining mew, as though he were asking what took us so long, Mochie stalked out.

Bernie and I broke into laughter. This was definitely the cat everyone brought back to Mrs. Pulchinski. I scooped Mochie up and danced through the kitchen holding him in the air. The banging of the door knocker interrupted our gay relief. Still holding Mochie, I pranced into the foyer and opened the front door.

Wolf stood on the stoop and regarded me with a serious look. Not even the sight of Mochie broke his stern demeanor. "I need to speak to a Bernard Frei, who I believe is currently residing here."

TWENTY-ONE

From *"Ask Natasha"*:

Dear Natasha,

I'm having a party Thanksgiving weekend and want to decorate the staircase in my small foyer. What can I do besides cheesy swags and bows?

–Harried in Herndon

Dear Harried,

One of my favorite decorations is simple and quick. Collect twenty or so colorful leaves from your yard and place them between the pages of an old book for a few days so they'll dry flat. Buy enough clear glass votives to place one on each step of your staircase. Using rough twine, tie one of the pressed leaves around each glass. Some will be too large and stand taller than the glass but that's okay. If you don't have time to press the leaves, you can vary this by substituting berries or interesting twigs. Don't worry about hiding the rough knot or bow, that's part of the charm. Place a

candle in each glass and light. When your guests arrive,
they'll enter to a seasonal cascade of festive lights.

—Natasha

"Bernie?" Fear clutched at me. I wanted to imagine there
was a logical explanation for his brunch with Mrs. Pulchinski, but Wolf's demand dampened that hope.

Bernie emerged from the kitchen.

I invited Wolf in and the two men shook hands.

"We'll speak in your sunroom, if you don't mind."
Wolf headed in that direction with Bernie behind him.
Mochie ran ahead of them. My poor parents were stuck
and would hear the conversations on both sides of
them.

I should bring Wolf and Bernie something to drink. It
was the hospitable thing to do and it wouldn't hurt if I
happened to overhear something while I carried it in to
them.

Irish coffees were out of the question. Bernie needed
to be sober when he answered Wolf's questions and Wolf
was clearly on duty. Working fast, I put on more of the
Viennese coffee. While it brewed, I sidled along the hallway to eavesdrop.

I could hear Bernie saying, "I don't see what's so unusual about it. I was invited for Thanksgiving, not the
days before. One doesn't want to be the guest that smells
like stinking fish. Besides, I had some banking to do in
the city and I didn't know quite how far away Natasha's
grand country estate might be."

"What kind of banking?"

"Changing pounds to dollars. And I had a rather com-
plicated transaction for my mum. She needed funds from
an account in England wired to her in Shanghai."

I hurried back to the kitchen, poured two mugs of coffee, quickly added sugar, cream, napkins, and spoons to a tray and carried it into the sunroom.

When I walked in, Wolf said, "Exactly when did you arrive in Washington?"

Bernie took a mug of coffee from me. "Thanks, Soph. I flew in the day before the contest. That would have been . . . Tuesday morning."

"How did you choose the hotel?" When I held out a mug to Wolf, he waved me away. I set his mug on the glass-topped wrought-iron side table next to him and left the tray on the oversized ottoman I used as a coffee table.

"When I talked to Mars on the phone, he mentioned the stuffing contest. I saw an article about it in the *Miami Herald* and thought it would be most expedient to stay in that hotel Tuesday night. Mars and Natasha would be there on Wednesday and I could follow them back to Natasha's place in my rental car. Frankly, Detective, I don't see why any of this matters."

I assumed I wasn't supposed to be present and feared Wolf would throw me out any minute, so I backed slowly to the door.

"Did you know Simon Greer?"

Bernie leaned back on the sofa and casually crossed a leg over his knee. "I never met the man."

I lingered in the doorway, guilt banging at my conscience.

"Did you see him when he was dead?"

"That's rather ghoulish, isn't it?"

"Let me make this easy for you. Were you ever in the Washington Room?"

"I presume that's the place Simon set up camp? No, I had no reason to hunt him down."

"Even after he was dead?"

"What are you suggesting? That I mutilated his corpse? Tampered with evidence?"

Wolf's back was to me. I wished I could see his expression.

He said, "The key card to your hotel room was found in the Washington Room."

Bernie scratched the back of his neck. "Is this some absurd American method of prompting a confession? Because it's not working."

Good move, Bernie. Aggravate the man with the handcuffs. I waved my hands at Bernie and shook my head in dismay.

Wolf didn't miss the twisted grin on Bernie's face or the fact that his eyes focused on me.

Without turning, Wolf said, "I'd appreciate some privacy, Sophie."

Appropriately chastened, I slunk into the hallway.

My conscience worked overtime. Wolf clearly did not want me to listen. But if I remained completely quiet, I could hear from the hallway and he wouldn't know about it. I should do the right thing and return to the kitchen. Or I could dust the pictures hanging in the hallway . . .

"Where is everybody?"

Mars! I scurried to the kitchen before he gave away my location.

Wearing black gloves and a leather bomber jacket that resembled Craig's, he roughhoused with Daisy.

"Very snazzy. New duds?"

He peeled off the gloves. "Everything we own reeks of smoke. I had no idea that smoke alone could do so much damage."

Mochie zoomed into the kitchen and flew onto the table, where he watched Mars. Mars tossed the new jacket over a chair, stroked Mochie, and turned his attention to the kitchen counter. "Is this the cranberry cake I like so much?"

I could take a hint. I cut a piece for him and poured coffee into two mugs. He didn't bother to sit down. He retrieved a fork and ate while standing. "Is Bernie here? I want to borrow his rental."

"Wolf is questioning him in the sunroom."

"About what?"

"Where he was, what he did, and why the key card to his hotel room was found in the conference room where Simon was killed."

Mars set his coffee down. "They're desperate. When they question someone from England who didn't even know the victims, they're reaching."

I hoped Mars was right. I hated to think that Bernie could be involved somehow. Between England, Hong Kong, Shanghai, and Miami, his world, like Simon's, was much larger than mine. Unfortunately, it wasn't out of the realm of possibilities that he'd hired Otis and come here for a specific reason.

Mars checked his watch. "I can't hang around here long. Have you seen his car keys?"

"You can't just steal his car."

"It's not stealing between Bernie and me." Mars spied the jacket Bernie left in the kitchen. He took a long swig of coffee, picked up the jacket, and felt the pockets. "Aha!"

"What's wrong with your car?"

"Nothing." He fumbled in his pants pocket and tossed his keys onto the counter. "In case Bernie needs to go anywhere." He reached for the last bite of cake.

I snatched it away and held it as a bribe. "What's going on?"

"I don't need that last bite, you know."

"Of course you don't." I cut another tiny slice and added it to the plate. I waved it under his nose but pulled it back when he reached for it.

"Okay, but no sharing this with Wolf. I didn't know that Nat hired Otis until you told me. She shares almost everything with me, but she skipped that, which worries me. There's only one other thing that she won't tell me.

I tease her about it all the time, but it didn't matter until now. Once a week she turns off her cell phone and disappears for a few hours."

I handed him the plate with cake on it.

He ate a piece before continuing. "It never bothered me before. Everybody needs some private time, right? But now that she's being stalked, I'm afraid she's gotten herself into a mess and doesn't know how to handle it. That has to be the reason she hired a private investigator. It all fits together with the not sleeping and the lack of appetite."

I was glad he told me but didn't quite understand. "What's that got to do with Bernie's car?"

"I'm going to follow her. Maybe I can identify her stalker. If nothing else, I'll know where she goes every week. I need Bernie's rental so no one will realize it's me—at least not right away."

Wolf's voice filtered to us from the hallway.

"Gotta go." Mars snarfed the rest of his cake. "Not a word to Wolf." He grabbed his jacket and gloves. "Oh, and if Andrew comes in here looking for me, you don't know where I am." He rushed out into the cold without bothering to bundle up.

The door clicked shut seconds before Wolf walked into the kitchen.

"Are you seeing anyone?" he asked.

I wanted to interpret his question as flirtatious but his demeanor was definitely angry cop. "Nina told you . . ."

"Never mind what Nina said. I want to know if you're dating anyone."

"No." Did he mean Humphrey? I thought he'd misconstrued Humphrey's words on Thanksgiving when he walked in on us in the kitchen. "Humphrey appears to be suffering from delusions stemming from a childhood crush, but it's nothing."

Wolf raised his chin. "Don't be so quick to dismiss him. Anyone else? What about Bernie?"

What did he mean about dismissing Humphrey? "Bernie is an old friend. He was Mars's best man at our wedding."

Wolf stared into the fireplace, deep in thought. "That's right. Can't forget about Mars. What did you do after the stuffing contest?"

Clearly, romantic thoughts had not been the source of his questions about my love life. "You should know. I was driven down to the police station to relinquish my clothes."

"And after that?"

"You were here Thanksgiving Day. Maybe you didn't notice all the food? I was home all night cooking and baking."

"You didn't go out for dinner, to get take-out, make a quick grocery run?"

His line of questioning annoyed me, mostly because I didn't understand what he was getting at. "You have my car, remember?"

He loosened his tie. "Is there anything you'd like to tell me?"

"I'd like to know why you're asking these odd questions."

"Thanks for your time." He headed for the front door and let himself out.

So much for Mom's theory that he was sweet on me. And then it hit me. He was trying to figure out who might have buried the turkey in Natasha's yard. It could have been me or someone who liked me enough to do an important favor for me. After all, as far as I knew, I was the only one who remembered seeing the bloody turkey trophy. He thought I'd planted it.

The kitchen door opened behind me and Andrew stuck his head in. "Where's Mars?"

I didn't have to lie. "I don't know."

"His car's outside, he must be here somewhere."

"He left the car here, but I don't know where he went."

"Shoot!" Andrew came in and shut the door. "How about Mom? Is she here?"

"She's entertaining the colonel in the living room."

"I think I'll join them."

I placed my hand against his chest to stop him. "There might be a little romance brewing. You wouldn't want to spoil that."

"At her age? You're kidding me, right?"

"How about a piece of cake?" Maybe that would distract him.

"Sure." He plopped into a fireside chair. "Did Vicki tell you I'm going to become a private investigator? Yeah. I've been watching Wolf, it's not that hard. Andrew Winston, detective. Sounds pretty cool. I've been following Mars. He doesn't know, so don't tell him. You know, to protect him in case the killer goes after him again."

I handed him a plate of cake and said, "Definitely cool." Mars obviously knew that Andrew was tailing him. I couldn't help wondering what Vicki really thought about Andrew's latest career plan.

"I'm way ahead of the game. I've got this murder all figured out, well almost, and Wolf is still working on it. And he has people helping him."

Pouring his coffee could wait. I perched on the other chair, anxious to hear Andrew's theory. "Spill it."

"It's elementary, my dear Watson. The killer talked Francie into making that scene outside so everyone would leave the table and he could poison Mars's soup. But, you ask, why would he want to kill Mars? He didn't. He meant to kill me because I knew too much."

I had a feeling Andrew intended to drag out his story for his own amusement so I rose and fetched his coffee after all.

"You know how they say the killer always revisits the scene of the crime? On Thanksgiving morning I went over to the hotel looking for Mom. She'd left Natasha's house in a snit the night before and all. But in my new profession as a private detective, I stopped to check out the Washington Room where Simon was killed. There was yellow tape up but that never applies to those of us in the profession. And who did I see there? Craig, surreptitiously looking for something."

I hadn't expected to hear Craig named as a suspect. I thought for sure Andrew would point a finger at Natasha. "Have you told Wolf?"

He beamed with pride. "Give away my secrets? No way. I'll reveal the killer when I'm ready. I'm so good at this. I can't believe it's taken me this many years to figure out that detective work is what I was meant to do."

"Are you absolutely sure it was Craig?"

"Not a doubt in my mind. He wore running shoes and a big sweatshirt from Georgetown U."

That cinched it for me. Craig left here to run and clearly ran over to the hotel for some reason. But there were major holes in Andrew's theory. "Why did Craig kill Simon?"

"Because . . ." Andrew raised his index finger. ". . . I haven't figured out that part yet."

A major omission. "If Craig meant to kill you, and Mars was never a target, then why are you following Mars?"

"In case I'm wrong."

Sounded like he had as much confidence in his theory as I did. Still, Craig's behavior disturbed me. He washed the clothes he wore when Simon was killed and he went back to the scene of the crime the next morning.

Andrew sipped coffee so deep in thought that he paid no attention to the tinny ringing in his pocket.

"Andrew." I tapped his knee. "Isn't that your cell phone?"

"Oh!" He flipped it open. "Hi, dear." He jumped up

and placed his plate and mug on the counter. "Stay there but outside." Panic registered in his voice. "I'll be home in a jiffy."

He snapped the phone shut. "Vicki went out for groceries and when she came home, the house had been ransacked!"

TWENTY-TWO

From *"Ask Natasha"*:

Dear Natasha,

My mother insists that a host should always provide a toothbrush for each overnight guest. Do I leave them in the bathroom in the package unopened? On their pillows? It all sounds sort of dime-store tacky. Should I provide toothpaste, too?

—Hopeless Hostess in Harrisonburg

Dear Hopeless Hostess,

A luxurious bathroom basket should await each of your guests. I roll fingertip towels and washcloths of long-staple Egyptian cotton and place them in the basket along with one new and unopened battery-operated toothbrush and a tube of toothpaste. Gentlemen receive a tiny bottle of aftershave and ladies get perfume. Don't forget a loofah and a personal bottle of scented shower gel. In the summer, it's extremely thoughtful to add powder. I always include a

magnolia-scented soy candle and a carved soap, both in
my signature color of robin's-egg blue, for guests to take
home.

—Natasha

"Wait," I said. "I'll come with you." Vicki could probably use someone to lean on.

I dashed to the den, poked my head in, and whispered to my parents, "Give my Ford's Theatre ticket to June. I'll fill you in later." Without waiting for a response, I rushed to the front door to catch a ride with Andrew.

When we arrived at their house, Vicki sat on the stoop, the collar of her fleece jacket turned up against the wind. Andrew parked in haste and ran up the walk to the town house before I'd managed to remove my seat belt. By the time I reached them, Andrew held Vicki in a bear hug.

"Are you all right?" I asked.

Andrew released her and Vicki placed a hand on her chest. "My heart's still pounding, otherwise I'm fine. How lucky that they'd left by the time I came home. At least I think they had. The cops are in there now and I imagine we'd have heard if they discovered anyone in the house."

I followed them inside. The lovely dining and living rooms were a mess. Sofa cushions lay on the floor. Drawers hung open and shards of a lamp spread across the hardwood floor.

"Mrs. Winston?"

I turned out of habit, but Wolf meant Vicki.

"Can you tell if anything is missing?"

"I'm not sure. I haven't been upstairs yet."

"When we're through fingerprinting, I'd like you to do a thorough inventory."

"I assume your presence means you think this is related to the murders in some way," I said.

Wolf pulled a pen from his breast pocket. "These days I respond to anything involving a Winston."

He'd been so curt today that I wondered what was up. Had I done something to offend him? When we'd first met, he'd been sweet with Mochie. What happened to change his demeanor? I wished he would open up and tell me what he'd learned.

"Do you realize that Natasha and Mars are also staying here?" I asked.

The news startled Wolf. "Anyone else living here?"

While Vicki answered Wolf, Andrew pulled me aside and whispered, "Do you think it could have been Craig?"

"Sorry, but he's touring museums with Hannah. I think she'd notice if he left her."

Andrew snapped his fingers. "I may have to rethink my theory."

No one had closed the front door, and when I turned around, Natasha stood in the doorway, her large eyes taking in the situation. Vicki spotted her and rushed to Natasha's side to explain. Panic registered on Natasha's face and she bolted for the stairs, but Wolf blocked her.

"Not yet. When the officers are finished, I'd appreciate knowing if anything is missing."

Natasha backed away from him as though he'd threatened her.

Wordlessly, she tugged me outside. "Every time I think nothing could possibly get worse in my life, some horrible thing like this happens."

Her shoulders slumped and I felt sorry for her. I was going through similar troubles, but at least I hadn't lost my home and no one was stalking me.

"They're going to use this opportunity to search our stuff, you know. No warrant needed." She groaned.

I patted her shoulder and wondered what kind of stuff she had that worried her.

"Sophie, you have to help me. This situation with June

is becoming serious and Mars closes his eyes to it. He refuses to see that she's confused and needs help."

Her statement caught me off guard. Considering the magnitude of Natasha's other problems, I expected her to forget about June. In any event, I wasn't going to let Natasha talk Mars into moving June to a nursing home.

"She's behaved normally at my house." Most people didn't talk with the ghosts of their siblings, but I hoped Mom was right about that. Maybe a lot of people did it in private.

Natasha squared her shoulders and placed her fists on her hips. "I stopped by Nordstrom to buy new clothes, since the smoke from June's fire rendered everything unwearable, and I found her in the teen section buying clothes completely inappropriate for a woman her age."

"Like what?"

"Like lacy tops and frilly skirts."

"You'd rather see her dressed in somber prints and black orthopedic shoes?"

"She bought a silk slip!" Natasha's nostrils flared.

I didn't understand why a silk slip indicated a disconnect with reality. "What's wrong with that? The expense?"

"It's sexy!"

At the risk of further annoying Natasha, I couldn't help laughing. Thanks to the colonel's attention, June felt good about herself. Instead of thinking about holing up in a nursing facility, June had romance on the mind.

"What if she were your mother? Would you feel the same way then?" I regretted my words immediately. Natasha had always been sensitive about her mother. They couldn't be more different.

"Why do I bother thinking you're my friend? You're impossible." Natasha stomped to her car and drove away.

Guilt kicked in. We all nursed stress as a result of the murders and the investigation. At the moment, poor Natasha probably felt everything in her life had gone haywire and there wasn't a thing she could control and put back on track. She needed help.

I strolled up the steps and into the foyer, where Wolf spoke with Andrew and Vicki. Mars would hate me, but Natasha's life might be at stake. I would never forgive myself if she was killed and I hadn't said anything. "Wolf, someone is stalking Natasha."

Simultaneously, Vicki, Andrew, and Wolf said, "What?"

Mars probably hadn't had a chance to tell Andrew and Vicki about the stalker. They, more than anyone else, deserved to know now that Natasha would be staying with them.

"Nina and I have seen him twice."

"This is terrible!" Vicki's hand flew over her mouth in terror.

Wolf squinted at me. "Why didn't you tell me?"

"Nina called you. She reported him to the police the first time and said she thought they blew her off. The second time I heard her leave you a message."

I could tell Wolf was angry with himself. He'd probably been working long hours on the murders and hadn't paid enough attention to his voice mail. His ears burned red and he strode away.

Andrew took a deep breath. "This changes everything." He looked at Vicki. "Was the guest room ransacked, too? The burglar might have been looking for something in Natasha's possession." Without Wolf there to stop him, the self-appointed detective pounded up the stairs.

"Are you sure you're okay?" I asked Vicki.

"Just a little shaken. I'll be fine. Thanks for coming over with Andrew. I'm worried about Natasha, though. A stalker! She never said a thing to me about it."

"Now that she's staying with you, maybe you can talk with her privately and find out what's going on."

Vicki promised to tell me if she gleaned anything from Natasha. When Wolf called Vicki from another room, I decided I was only in the way and said good-bye.

I walked the ten blocks home, glad for a few minutes alone. Porch lights flicked on as darkness settled over Old Town. Each block seemed worthy of a Christmas card picture as warm lights began to glow inside the ancient homes. As I ambled up my block, Mars arrived in Bernie's rental. I waited for him to park and we walked to the house together.

"Did you know someone broke into Andrew's house?"

Horror crossed Mars's face. "Was anyone hurt?"

"I just came from there. Everyone's fine."

In spite of my assurances, he called Andrew on his cell phone. When he snapped it closed, he said, "What's happening to us?"

Daisy and Mochie demanded our attention the moment we opened the kitchen door. Dressed for an evening at the theater, my parents and June waited for Hannah and Craig in the kitchen. Bernie leaned against the counter, a half-eaten sandwich in his hand.

"Hear you have an admirer." Mars hugged his mother.

June's cheeks flushed. "Maybe a little bit."

"Is he going to the play with you tonight?" he asked.

"They're sold out. We tried to get a last-minute ticket but couldn't." June turned to me. "Are you sure you don't want to go, dear?"

"I can go anytime. I'd rather you had fun. What did the colonel say about Simon?"

"He never came right out and admitted he went to the hotel. However, he confirmed that the lovely young woman who lost her leg is his granddaughter. A terrible tragedy. She taught mountain climbing in the summer and skiing in the winter. Very athletic. It looked like she would win the contest on Simon's show."

Dad fidgeted in his chair. "They'd rigged some sort of contraption over a dramatic gully that the contestants had to cross. A rope snapped when she was on it; somehow her leg tangled in the rope and it cut off the blood supply. They couldn't save it."

"The colonel blames this on Simon?" asked Mars.

"He thinks the show was rigged," said June. "The problem is that the rope disappeared so there's no evidence. Simon claimed the remaining contestants burned the ropes in a cleansing ritual that night. The colonel has been doing research to try to prove that Simon's crew staged his granddaughter's accident."

"That's horrible." I cringed at the thought. "She could have died. Losing her leg was bad enough."

"Simon was always ruthless. He left chaos and death behind him everywhere. No honor or decency or regard for human life. Money drove everything he did." Bernie couldn't hide the bitterness in his voice.

I finally posed a question that had been nagging me. "Do you think he asked me out to irritate Mars?"

"Could be." Mars laughed. "But I wouldn't have killed him over you, honey."

"So what happened with Natasha today?" I asked Mars.

"You won't believe this. She went to a soup kitchen."

"To contact someone." I'd tried so hard to believe Natasha couldn't have killed Simon. Had she hired someone to kill him? Had she hired Otis to find a paid assassin for her?

"It looked like they knew her. She put on an apron and dished out dinner. I don't know what to make of it."

"Maybe she spotted you and drove there on purpose to throw you off," suggested Dad.

"Or maybe she works at the soup kitchen every week when she disappears. But why keep it a secret?" Mars gazed at us like we had answers.

"She's looking for her father," Mom said quietly. "You were so young, Sophie, I don't think you understood the impact on Natasha. She was only seven when he left. Her mother couldn't afford the mortgage on their pretty house over on Elm Street and she couldn't sell it without his

signature. The bank foreclosed and her mother filed for
bankruptcy. I'm certain Natasha felt it was her fault he
abandoned them; children so often do."

"But that happened over thirty years ago," I protested.

"Don't you understand? His leaving was the driving
force in her life. That's why she strives, to this day, to be so
perfect. It's also the reason she always competed with you."

"Oh, please." My mom, the shrink.

"You weren't competitive by nature, but you had everything she didn't. A dad and siblings and a nice house.
And you gave her a run for her money. You were both
good at the same things. You didn't mean to but you made
her reach a little higher, work a little harder, and when she
kept one-upping you, it turned out you had a competitive
streak in you after all."

"That explains a lot," Mars teased, "but I'm with Sophie. Hard to believe she's still searching for him after all
these years. And why would she think she'd find him at a
soup kitchen? He could be a multimillionaire."

"I imagine her mother painted a fairly dim picture of
him," said Mom. "She was probably brought up to believe that he was a ne'er-do-well."

"Why do you think he left?" asked Mars.

"Berrysville is a small town, You can imagine the
rampant gossip. Some people thought he had another life
somewhere else. Others think he died and no one knew
who he was. I think he felt too much pressure."

"I'd have run away from that pushy woman, too." Dad
made a face like he'd sucked on a lemon. "Natasha's
mother wouldn't be easy to live with."

The phone rang, interrupting our conversation. I scurried to answer it.

The coordinator of the Stupendous Stuffing Shakedown
asked if I could participate in the contest on Monday.
Simon's TV network decided to go forward with it after
all. I checked my work schedule to be sure I could fit it in.

I assured her I would be there and hoped the others would be able to compete as well. Before hanging up, she said, "And as a precaution, we're providing all the ingredients this time. All you have to do is show up and make stuffing."

Mars was leaving when I returned. Mom closed the door behind him and said, "Why can't we ever manage to get him over here at the same time as Wolf?"

"Surely you don't think Mars is the killer?" I asked.

"Goodness, no. But I want to shake up Mars a little bit. He would have to be pheromonally challenged not to feel the attraction Wolf has for you."

Not anymore. "Mom, Wolf is watching me because I'm a murder suspect."

"Think what you like. Wolf looks at you like you're an ice cream sundae with extra chocolate on top."

I shot my dad a pleading look. "Didn't you hear the way Mars talked about Natasha? We're not getting back together, Mom."

"She's right, Inga. Mars is very concerned about Natasha."

The corners of Mom's mouth pulled back in disapproval. "In that case, you'd better start dressing sexier for that Wolf of yours. And it wouldn't hurt you to use eyeliner and brighter lipstick."

~~~

I adored having my family around, but when the door shut behind them and quiet reigned in my home, I felt tension ebb away. The play and dinner would keep my parents, Hannah, Craig, and June out until eleven or so. Bernie left when they did but was somewhat hazy about his plans. I couldn't help wondering if he had a date with the widow Pulchinski.

Before indulging myself in a long bath, I hit the den to catch up on my column. Questions poured in from readers.

Coswell wrote me suggesting I set up a website to handle some of the overflow. The response to my column delighted me. Excited as I was about the prospect of a web page, it would have to wait a couple of days until my family went home.

I put the column out of my mind as I left the den. I needed to think about the murders. The killer had to be stopped before another one of us fell victim to him. Wolf was probably a great detective, but I knew everyone so much better than he did. I had to be overlooking something, some tiny clue to the identity of the killer. As though she knew what I had in mind, Daisy trotted upstairs. Mochie followed us.

I ran water in the tub and poured in vanilla-scented bubble bath. Mochie perched on the edge, fascinated by the growing foam that disappeared when he touched it. While the tub filled, I undressed and tossed a bathrobe on the vanity in case someone returned unexpectedly. I sank into the warm water and focused on the murders.

I figured I could eliminate my parents, sister, and June from my list of suspects. Wolf and Humphrey also seemed unlikely candidates. Wolf might have killed his wife but so far I hadn't heard about a connection between him and the victims. Humphrey seemed too wan to undertake a murder spree. He could have hired Otis to trail me and he could have killed Simon after he asked me out, but I was neither vain enough nor stupid enough to believe anyone, even smitten Humphrey, would take such drastic action on my account. I was no femme fatale.

Bernie didn't appear to have a motive, unless he was involved with Mrs. Pulchinski somehow. Since he'd been living abroad, he came in low on my list of suspects. But the timing of Bernie's visit seemed a bit more than coincidental and I still couldn't shake the image of him in the restaurant with Mrs. Pulchinski. Nor could I dismiss the fact that he'd been at Natasha's house the night of the fire and present when Simon died.

The colonel, on the other hand, had both the motivation and the opportunity to kill Simon. I hadn't connected him to Otis yet, but he'd been very interested in Otis's death at Thanksgiving dinner. And Francie had been the one who reported a Peeping Tom. Could the two of them be in cahoots?

Mars and Andrew both hated Simon. Both had been present in the hotel when Simon was murdered. Either of them might have known or worked with Otis. Mars had warned me about Simon on the day he was murdered. Had Mars hired Otis to follow me? That didn't make sense. The Mars I knew could become furious, but he ranted and paced. He would never kill anyone. Would he clean up after his brother if Andrew committed murder? He might. And while I couldn't see Vicki being irrational enough to kill Simon because of the way he'd treated Andrew, I supposed that was a possibility.

And that brought me to Natasha. She hired Otis for something and met privately with Simon. She was prone to drama but she'd displayed uncharacteristic nervousness on Thanksgiving, especially when she discovered Wolf would be joining us. Had she lost her tight self-control and let Simon have it? Either she killed Simon or she knew something.

Had I omitted anyone? Craig. The outsider. The one least likely to have a connection to any of us. Yet he spied and eavesdropped, and even more suspicious, he returned to the scene of the crime. Hannah would be furious if she knew what I thought of Craig.

My relaxing bath had been anything but. The killer and the person who tried to poison Mars was clearly one of us. I closed my eyes and tried to unwind, but Daisy alarmed me by barking and running down the stairs. For a moment I thought Bernie might have come home, but Daisy stopped barking and I decided she'd probably heard Francie knocking around the backyard again.

When the phone rang, I lay in the bath and debated

whether or not to answer. My indecision lasted longer than the caller's patience and the ringing ceased.

And began again. I still didn't bother to get up. But when it rang a third time, I feared the worst, stepped out of the tub, and wrapped a towel around me. The phone stopped ringing before I could answer. I was on the verge of checking the caller ID when it jangled again and I finally picked it up.

Nina's voice said, "There's someone in your house. Get out now."

TWENTY-THREE

From "THE GOOD LIFE":

Dear Sophie,

I've inherited a collection of copper pots and pans from my aunt-in-law who is downsizing. They're gorgeous, but I never use them because I hate cleaning the copper. She'll be offended if I give them away. Any suggestions?

—Copper-phobic in Coeburn

Dear Copper-phobic,

If you decide to use them, make it easy on yourself by keeping a salt shaker and a vinegar cruet by your sink. Shake on a hefty dose of salt, add a splash of vinegar and the tarnish will clean up as if by magic.

   If you still don't want to cook in them, hang them over your cooktop or display them on a baker's rack as a beautiful decoration.

—Sophie

Terror gripped me unlike any I'd ever known. I was on the second floor. I couldn't leave the house without walking down the stairs. Where was he? Had Nina called the police? Had the intruder hurt Daisy?

Clutching my towel, I padded softly to the stairs and listened. I heard a chair scrape across the floor. I tiptoed down the stairs, trying to remember where they squeaked. At the landing in the foyer, relief flooded over me. Daisy wagged her tail, panting and perfectly fine. I picked up Mochie and peered around the entrance to the dining room.

Panic hit me full force. The intruder, dressed in baggy gray sweatpants and a sweatshirt, was pawing through the silverware drawer. Seeing the intruder scared me silly. He could have all the silverware he wanted as long as he didn't hurt any of us.

Moving stealthily, I crossed behind the opening to the dining room, toward the front door, and safety. A floorboard creaked under my bare foot and the intruder turned around. He wore a Paula Deen mask and Paula's friendly smile took on the sinister appearance of a fake clown smile. I screamed and lunged for the door. My fingers trembled and I fumbled with the lock. Seconds passed like an eternity but I swung the door open, called Daisy, and ran onto the front lawn.

Police sirens pierced the quiet night. My wet skin prickled in the freezing winter air. Two squad cars pulled up and blocked the street as Nina ran to me with a fuzzy bathrobe and a huge blanket. She held Mochie while I gratefully donned the bathrobe and dropped the wet towel to stand on. At least it was an improvement over the freezing brick of the sidewalk.

Two police officers rushed into the house. Wolf arrived minutes later. His face grim, he stopped to ask me what happened. "I don't like this," he grumbled. "Not one bit."

"Do you think it could be the same person who broke into Vicki and Andrew's house earlier?" I asked.

"I don't think it's a coincidence."

When the house had been searched, Wolf and Nina ushered me into the kitchen to warm up. My teeth chattered, partly from the cold but mostly from sheer terror. One of the uniformed officers called us into the sunroom where the door to the backyard stood ajar.

"I presume you didn't leave the door open," said Wolf. "Any sign of forced entry?" He stepped around the door to examine the exterior and the lock.

The uniformed cop said, "Either it was unlocked or her intruder picked it."

Wolf scrutinized me from head to toe. Even though I wore the robe Nina brought me, I felt exposed and vulnerable. I'd pinned up my hair haphazardly for my bath and my feet were bare.

He shut the door and studied the sunroom, still not saying a word. I followed his gaze. Nothing had changed since he sat here earlier with Bernie. I hadn't even taken the tray into the kitchen yet or removed their coffee mugs to be washed.

"How big was the intruder?" he asked.

I felt foolish. All I could see in my mind were the baggy sweats and the mask. "I don't know. I was a little panicked."

Wolf walked out of the sunroom, down the hall, and up the stairs to the second floor. Nina and I followed.

"Where's the bathroom?" he asked.

I pointed to the open door.

Wolf paused in the doorway, taking in the unfortunate green-and-black tile I longed to rip out. He crouched to examine my wet footprints on the tiny squares of green tile Faye had installed decades ago. When he rose, he dipped his hand in my bathwater. Only then did it dawn on me that he didn't believe my story.

"Do you really think that I'd have made this up and run out into the freezing night wet and wrapped in nothing but a towel?"

"I don't know what to think about you anymore."

"I can't believe I told Sophie she should go out with you," Nina said. "She's not fabricating anything, I saw him. She has a witness." Nina jabbed her forefinger toward her throat. "So there."

Wolf folded his arms across his chest and I wondered if he realized how intimidating he looked when he did that.

"Where exactly was he when you saw him?"

Nina threw her shoulders back and lifted her chin. "He was crossing through the kitchen. I was walking the dog, outside on the sidewalk, and I saw him through the bay window of Sophie's kitchen. That precise enough for you?"

"That wasn't even a good stab at lying," said Wolf. "You don't have a dog."

Nina's cheeks flamed. "I'm fostering one. You can ask Karen down at the shelter."

I thought I saw a flicker of a grin on Wolf's face, but he suppressed it quickly.

"Don't worry, I will."

I patted Nina's arm. "He thinks I'm the killer. He thinks Bernie's the killer. He probably even thinks Mars is the killer. It's a good thing you didn't join us for Thanksgiving dinner or he'd think you were the killer."

Wolf showed no emotion in spite of my deliberate barb. "You're so right. Mars hasn't been excluded."

"But why not?" This was ridiculous. "Surely you don't think he poisoned himself?"

"Desperate people have been known to take desperate measures. What better way to throw suspicion off himself? Everyone would feel sorry for him and assume that he couldn't be the culprit."

"Sophie! Sophie!"

A man's despairing call echoed up the stairs.

"Who's that?" asked Nina.

I shrugged and the three of us hurried to the landing to peer down.

In the foyer, at the bottom of the stairs, Humphrey tangled ineptly with one of the uniformed officers. "Unhand me, you heathen!"

"Wolf, tell him to let Humphrey go." I charged down the steps with Wolf and Nina behind me.

"What are you doing here?" I asked.

"I happened to be driving by and saw the police cars. Naturally, I was concerned. Thank goodness you're not hurt." Humphrey tucked his shirt in and straightened his overcoat. "What happened?"

Nina held out her hand to Humphrey. "I don't believe we've met. I'm Sophie's best friend, Nina."

Humphrey took her hand. "And I'm Sophie's beau. Oh, how I love saying that."

Wolf groaned. "You two can knock off the we've-never-met-before routine. I'm not that stupid."

"But," Humphrey stammered, "we haven't met before."

Wolf cast a disparaging look in my direction and stalked away.

I left Humphrey and Nina in the foyer and followed Wolf into the sunroom.

A third police officer must have arrived while we were upstairs. He dusted fine black powder over the door handle and the lock.

"You get the dining room yet?" asked Wolf.

"Loads of prints. A few good ones."

I tugged at Wolf's sleeve and towed him into the den. I switched on the desk lamp and shut the doors. My hands on my hips, I drew myself up as tall as a short person can and demanded, "What is your problem? You won't believe anything I say. You won't even believe Nina, who clearly isn't a suspect, or poor Humphrey, who barely has the moxie to look you in the eye. We can't all be the killer. What is wrong with you?"

Wolf studied me silently. He gripped my upper arms, pulled me to him, and kissed me. A long and surprisingly sensual kiss. And then he left the room. Just left me there, wanting more.

It took me a few seconds to recover. I floated out to the foyer and asked Nina and Humphrey, "Where's Wolf?"

Nina motioned toward the front door. "He took off."

I rushed out to the front stoop but the taillights on his car were already pinpoints in the night.

The uniformed officers came up behind me. One of them said, "We'll apprise you of the results. In the meantime, keep your doors and windows locked and call us if you see anything unusual."

I closed the door behind them.

Humphrey wiped his brow. "Can you imagine, that detective barged into the funeral home and frightened the staff half to death by asking questions about me. They think I'm some sort of crazed wild man now."

"I'm sorry you wound up involved in this mess, Humphrey." If Mom hadn't called him to make Mars jealous, he wouldn't have the police lurking around his place of business asking questions.

A shy smile lit up his face. "That's all right. I think most of them thought I invented you. When he showed up and started asking questions, at least they knew I wasn't making up stories about my love life."

Nina's eyebrows shot up and she looked at me with curiosity.

"What did you tell them?" I asked, afraid to hear his answer.

"How we've known each other since grade school and we had secret crushes and now, fate has intervened and thrown us together again and we're dating."

Fate, thy name is "mother." No wonder Wolf didn't believe me. A bunch of people I'd never met told him Humphrey and I were in a romantic relationship.

Humphrey slipped his car keys into his pocket and removed his coat. With dismay, I realized that he intended to stay awhile. Nina would go home and I would have to deal with Humphrey on my own. Why couldn't I be stuck with Wolf? On the other hand, Humphrey was better than nothing. I didn't relish the thought of being home alone at the moment. I'd interpret every squeak and thump as an intruder.

"Sophie," said Humphrey, "how well do you know this Bernie fellow?"

"He's an old friend."

"I've been doing a little checking up on him. Frankly, I'm not sure he's the sort of person you should invite to sleep over."

Sleep over? Did Humphrey think I was intimately involved with Bernie? I opened my mouth to deny any such thing, "It's not li . . ." and realized that Bernie might be just the ticket to discourage Humphrey. "He's stayed over many times."

"He's a bit unsavory, don't you think?"

Nina listened with an amused expression.

"Are you jealous?" I asked.

"Good heavens, no. I'm simply concerned about your welfare. Did you know that he spends his evenings at the Stag's Inn?"

Nina's forehead crinkled. "Where have I heard that recently?"

"Mrs. Pulchinski's desk. She had a coaster from the Stag's Inn."

A spark lit her eyes. "Quick, go change," said Nina, picking up the phone. "I'll do anything to get out of the house."

"What . . . you mean go down there?" asked Humphrey. "I hardly think that's advisable. It looks like a frightful establishment." I dashed upstairs to change clothes while listening to Humphrey trying to dissuade Nina.

Remembering Mom's advice, I pulled on a fluffy cucumber-green sweater with a deep V-neck in case we ran into Wolf. Humphrey wouldn't make a fly jealous but, all the same, it wouldn't hurt to look kissable. After Christmas, I would have to shed those extra pounds, but for now, trousers with an elastic waist would have to do. I ran a brush through my hair, added a smidge of lipstick, and I was ready.

Bundled against the chilly air, we walked along the ancient sidewalks past enticing restaurants and upscale bars. I sensed Humphrey's hesitation when we left King Street. The side street, though less busy and somewhat dimmer, was evocative of colonial times and quite charming. Four blocks down, we turned into an old alleyway.

Humphrey balked at the dark alley. Without bright street lights, it seemed dingy. I'd been by in the daylight, though, and it wasn't as shabby as it appeared when lit only by the few lamps on the back doors of the buildings. It added to the allure of the the Stag's Inn that the only entrance was through an alley.

"Couldn't we go to one of the nicer, clean places we passed earlier?" asked Humphrey.

"We could." I took his elbow and propelled him along the cobbled passageway. "But we wouldn't get the kind of information I want. You're the one who's worried about Bernie. Don't you want to find out what he does down here?"

He stopped again in front of the pub.

A weathered door of wormy chestnut, braced by substantial forged-iron hinges, reminded me of medieval England. Black forged iron that matched the hinges formed the hook holding a lamp to the left of the door. Due to the thick bubbled glass, it provided little illumination. Growing impatient with Humphrey, I dropped his arm and followed Nina inside. I suspected he'd hate waiting in the alley more than entering the inn with us.

I hadn't expected the interior of the Stag's Inn to be

murkier than the alleyway. While many of the chic bars
and pubs of Old Town were in historic buildings, the in-
teriors used the patina of age in an elegant manner or had
been modernized. The owners of the Stag's Inn hadn't
attempted either.

A low ceiling, ostensibly supported by heavy beams,
gave it a slightly medieval flavor. The place might have a
certain charm in a better light. It reminded me of the days
when cigarette smoke created a haze in bars and I wondered if they sought that old atmosphere or if their electric
wiring wasn't up to code and they didn't dare plug in more
lights.

Small tables lined the right wall and an enormous bar
spanned the left wall for a considerable distance. The bartender and a good number of patrons turned to check us
out when we entered. I felt as though we'd walked through
some kind of time-warp portal that had transported us to
a different land.

Even brave Nina whispered, "This better be worth it."

We found a table in the back, under shelves decorated
with empty ale bottles bearing British labels. As we shed
our coats, Humphrey pleaded with us to leave. In truth,
the clientele of the Stag's Inn didn't seem all that different from the people patronizing the classier bars on King
Street. They probably didn't receive invitations to White
House dinners, but then neither did I.

A stout waiter who could easily lift any one, or possibly two, of us and toss us out the front door, took our
order. Nina and I opted for Whitbread India Pale Ale.
Humphrey asked for chamomile tea until I gave him a
little kick.

The stout man didn't return. Instead, a man with a
week's beard growth plopped three glasses of Whitbread
on our table. He pulled up a chair, turned it around, and
straddled it. Ignoring Humphrey, he asked, "You ladies
new in town?"

I figured Nina could handle him, and I rose to do my

own sleuthing, but Humphrey seized the sleeve of my sweater.

"Where are you going?"

There was probably only one place he wouldn't go. "The ladies' room."

He released his grip. "I'm going to time you. If you're not back soon, I'll break down the door."

I didn't think that would be necessary. Out of Humphrey's view I ambled to the bar, trying to look casual. The bartender plunked a coaster in front of me.

"I'm looking for an Englishman named Bernie."

He didn't seem perturbed by my quest. In a British accent he said, "Haven't seen him tonight. Harold, 'ave you seen Bernie?"

I heard someone say no, but the bartender had the courtesy to tell me, "He hasn't come in yet."

Two bar stools down, a woman swiveled in my direction. "What do you want with Bernie? He's already got a girl if that's what you have in mind."

She didn't sound British. Deep South, I thought, Louisiana maybe. In comparison to the low cut of her dress, my sexy sweater seemed tame enough for Sunday school.

"Shut up, Brandee."

I wasn't sure who said that until she playfully smacked the arm of the man next to her.

He spoke with his back to me, hunched forward, his elbows on the bar. "Don't mind her; she's been chasing Bernie since he arrived in town."

No question that he was a Brit.

"Do you know when that was?"

The bartender squinted. "Otis was killed Tuesday. I think Bernie showed up on Friday. Hasn't been in Alexandria long."

"You knew Otis?" I asked.

"Sure. All the regulars knew Otis." The bartender wiped a glass.

"Who . . . who do you think killed him?"

The Brit with his back to me rotated to eye me. "You a cop?"

A cop would be inept to ask such a blatant question. "No, a friend of Bernie's."

"A friend of Bernie's who knew Otis." He scratched a sideburn that would have been at home on Elvis Presley. "You know Otis well?"

The woman with the dipping neckline giggled. "She's not his type."

"Only in passing," I said.

The Brit spewed beer from his nose. He wiped his face with his sleeve. "You must be a friend of Bernie's, that's what Bernie said about Simon Greer."

I felt like a cold wave hit me. "What exactly did he say about Simon?"

"That he hadn't really met him, which is bullocks."

TWENTY-FOUR

From *"Ask Natasha"*:

Dear Natasha,

When my husband's friends visit for an afternoon of football viewing, our home theater looks like a junkyard in minutes. It makes me want to pull out my hair. How can I get these guys to clean up their act?

—Tech Fan in Toms Brook

Dear Tech Fan,

Banish beer cans. Buy a set of pilsner glasses and pour the first round yourself. Don't allow bags and plastic containers to migrate out of the kitchen. Serve the chips in silver bowls and dips in hollowed-out artichokes or boules. If you surprise them with elegant hors d'oeuvres served on proper platters, they'll have fun and you'll be the hostess they remember.

—Natasha

I wasn't sure what bullocks meant but I gathered the British guy didn't buy Bernie's denial of knowing Simon. "Why is that bullocks?"

"It's a well-known fact that Bernie's stepfather killed himself."

I was stunned. Bernie had never mentioned anything of the sort. "You must know Bernie very well."

"Naw. Bernie's stepfather was a highly respected gentleman. The circumstances of his death were quite well known in certain circles." He took another swig of beer.

"What circumstances?"

"He was brought to the brink by a competitor. A man of questionable ethics who used devious business practices to spin Bernie's stepfather into the ground. He lost everything. His country manor, the land that had been in his family for generations. He lost it all and took his own life because of a young entrepreneur named Simon bloody Greer."

I finally understood the full impact of his sad tale. Bernie blamed Simon for the death of his stepfather. "Are you suggesting Bernie killed Simon to punish him?"

"That's a bit of a leap. But I don't believe him when he says he didn't know Simon."

At that moment Humphrey grabbed my upper arm so hard his thin fingers felt like talons. "What are you doing?"

"Huh?" I was still trying to process the new information about Bernie. Part of me felt terrible about the tragedy of his stepfather's death, but at the same time, I now knew that Bernie had a motive. I had been so sure he wasn't involved.

I thanked the Brit and stumbled toward the table where Nina was speaking animatedly with a young man sporting a mohawk. He strode away before I sat down.

Humphrey didn't bother to take a seat. "I think we should go. That last guy was, well, I wouldn't want to see him again until he needs my services."

"No way," said Nina. "Otis's death started the sequence of events. If anyone here knows anything about his clients or his business, we need to hear it. That guy you're afraid of is sending over someone who knows all about Otis."

Humphrey reluctantly sat next to me. "After this one, we're going home."

I braced myself for an unsavory character. But no amount of bracing could have prepared me for the man who sauntered toward us. Other patrons called out greetings and jesting barbs to him. The man with the moppish hair and lopsided grin turned the empty chair around and said, "Sophie, Sophie, Sophie, what do you think you're doing?"

My pulse pounded in my head. How could Bernie be the local expert on Otis? How could he know all these people? No wonder Wolf questioned him. My spirits plummeted.

Surely Mars's best friend hadn't tried to poison him. Did Mars suspect Bernie of killing Simon? He must have known about the stepfather. Would Mars have told me about his suspicions? Maybe that was the real reason Mars had taken Bernie's car. Could the story about Natasha and the soup kitchen have been a diversion? Had Mars borrowed the car hoping it would contain clues?

"Bernie," I hissed, "what are you doing here?"

"The same thing you are, I imagine. Gathering information about Otis."

I wanted to believe him. I wanted so very much to think his motives were pure and that he meant to help us find the killer. But I couldn't overlook the fact that we'd seen him brunching with the widow Pulchinski. I searched his face, desperately wishing I could read his intentions and know if they were benevolent or evil.

Nina cut to the chase. "What have you found out?"

Bernie turned and raised his hand to signal a man at the bar. Medium height, bald with bushy eyebrows, and brawny enough that I would want him on my side in a fight. He sauntered over, a giant mug of beer in his hand.

"Ambrose," said Bernie, "tell my friends what Otis told you."

Ambrose sat down. He took a long swig of beer and rested the mug on the table, never letting go of the handle. "Wish one?"

I couldn't tell how drunk he was. He hadn't staggered to the table from the bar, but if he was slurring his words that badly, I wondered if we'd hear an accurate representation.

"All of them."

That simple sentence went a long way in redeeming Bernie. He might rely on a drunk for information, but he didn't intend to hide anything from us.

Or had he paid the drunk to lie?

"I told that idiot Kenner that Otis was sleeping with Wolf's wife."

"The one who's missing?" I asked.

Clearly pleased with himself, Ambrose said, "Yeah, boy! And I told Wolf that some political type wanted his ex-wife tailed."

"Are either of those true?" asked Humphrey.

"Not the one about Wolf's wife."

Bernie prodded Ambrose. "Now tell them what Otis really said to you."

"He said he knew that being a PI would pay off someday and that his ship would come in soon. Bought all the boys a round of drinks that night."

I sat back in disgust. That meant nothing.

"And?" Bernie reached over and helped himself to a slug of my beer.

"And that the bigger and richer the client, the more they'll pay to keep things quiet."

I folded my arms across my chest and thanked my lucky stars I hadn't paid for these brilliant insights. So far, the only thing I'd learned was another reason for

Wolf to doubt my innocence. He probably thought Mars was the political type having his ex-wife followed and that I had killed Otis to prevent him from revealing a dark secret he'd uncovered.

I'm not much of a poker player. Either my face showed how unimpressed I was or Bernie could read my thoughts.

"Tell them about the cat," he said.

Ambrose snickered. "Oh, yeah. His wife had this kitten she couldn't get rid of and it was driving her nuts. She'd been bugging him to take it to the pound, but ol' Otis had a soft spot for the little guy. Said he'd found a lady who could give it a good home but she didn't know it yet."

"He targeted me? He wanted me to have Mochie? Why? He didn't know me."

Bernie threw me a smug look.

Ambrose stared into his empty beer mug like he was searching for one last drop. "Ole Otis knew a lot about people who didn't know him. He was good at his game. He was only sorry it had taken him so long to figure out how to make big money at it."

"Oh, no." Humphrey kicked me under the table and motioned with his head.

I looked up.

Wolf was heading straight for us. His demeanor grim, he said, "Sophie, I need a word with you, please."

Like a twelve-year-old at my first dance, I scooted around the table and imagined that he might lead me to a cozy nook for another kiss. I couldn't suppress a smile and I was glad I'd listened to my mom and worn a sexy sweater.

Wolf escorted me out of the pub. "I want to apologize for my behavior."

I melted. He realized he'd been abrupt and gruff. I admired men who could see their flaws and knew when to apologize. I stepped toward him and was about to place my hand on his coat when he said, "I never should have kissed you. That was inexcusable and unprofessional."

So much for that. Even my sexy sweater hadn't made a difference. I consoled myself with the thought that maybe he did murder his wife. "There are a few things I should tell you. I should have done it earlier but well, I took off too soon," he continued. A chilly breeze penetrated my sweater. In spite of his obvious inattraction to me, my heart raced. I was afraid of what he was going to say.

"You were probably right about the turkey trophy being the murder weapon. We found traces of blood on the tail, as you said, and according to the medical examiner it's consistent with Simon's injury." I stood up a little straighter. I'd been vindicated on one tiny item but it felt good. At least he knew I didn't make it up.

"What about the soup?" I asked.

"We found the poison in only one soup bowl. That doesn't clear you or implicate you."

"Wolf, I've been wondering about blood spatter. You interviewed all of us right away. If one of us had been the killer, wouldn't he have had blood spatter on his clothes?"

Wolf's head jerked back. Apparently my question surprised him.

"I'm always underestimating you, Sophie. But it's not unusual for blood spatter to be absent in cases where the victim is killed by a single blow to the head. That's what we think happened to Simon."

But I hadn't known that and the killer might not have, either. He might have worn a dark shirt and rushed to wash it—just in case.

"We've been a little slow processing everything because of the holiday. I'm sure they'll get to your clothes next week."

I'd forgotten all about them. "How about my car? My folks will be going home soon and I'll need transportation for work."

"Better rent one. I doubt they'll turn it over to you until the perpetrator is in custody." He focused on the door of the inn and said softly, "And that could be a while. What are you doing here?"

"Asking questions."

"Suspect everyone, trust no one," said Wolf.

"That's a terrible attitude. Your suspects are my family and friends. I'm not turning on them."

Wolf flexed his fingers while he thought. "Sophie, this would be so much easier for everyone if you would tell me what you're hiding."

The same old tune again. "I don't have any secrets. Believe me, Mars did not hire Otis to have me tailed and I'm not in a relationship with Humphrey."

"Look, Sophie, I've seen the tapes from the grocery store—"

"Then you know I didn't do anything."

He studied me in silence before saying, "I know that Otis approached you in the parking lot and that you waved your hands at him and ran away, into the store."

"Because he was trying to pawn Mochie off on me."

"And I know that when you came out, you scanned the parking lot like you were looking for him."

"Because of Mochie. I changed my mind while I was shopping. I wanted to take him to Nina to be sure he'd get a decent home."

"That's not how it looks on the tapes."

This was ridiculous. "I can't help that. What about the film in the rear of the store? Doesn't it show the killer?"

"There aren't any cameras on the rear of the store. All we know is that you ran from Otis and then looked for him nervously when you left. Did he threaten you?"

"Only with a kitten." I flung open the door and stalked back into the pub. There was no point in subjecting myself to more of that nonsense. Wolf obviously didn't want to believe me.

I wondered if I'd said too much. I couldn't incriminate

myself because I hadn't done anything, but Mars and my dad were probably right about getting a lawyer. I should have done that from the beginning. I'd wanted to cooperate with Wolf because I found him attractive. How stupid of me.

"Let's go." I said to Nina and Humphrey, as I picked up my coat and put it on.

Humphrey jumped to his feet. "Did he work you over? Are you all right? I should have come with you."

I didn't have the patience to deal with him. My temper flared, partly out of disappointment over Wolf and partly because I'd hoped the tapes would vindicate me. I ignored Humphrey and charged through the crowded pub.

Standing by the doorway, Wolf watched me, but I didn't care. I shoved by him and burst out the door. Outside, I gulped cold air and waited for Nina and Humphrey. It didn't take them long.

"We stopped to tell Bernie we were leaving," said Nina.

I calmed down while we walked home. As we approached my house, I realized I should have asked Humphrey where he parked so we could have walked him to his car and I wouldn't have to pretend to be polite and invite him in. Maybe it wasn't too late to try. I stopped on the sidewalk in front of my house and was about to address Humphrey when Nina hissed, "Stalker. In the bushes in front of your house."

TWENTY-FIVE

From *Live with Natasha*:

In the summer, I love to harvest fresh raspberries and other fruits, like peaches and black currants, from my garden to make liquors. It's surprisingly easy to do using fruit, sugar, and vodka. The liquor needs to sit for a few months so the flavor can develop, which means it's ready just in time for those blustery winter nights. Delicious over homemade ice cream or straight in a cordial glass. Add a festive bow to the bottle and it makes a very thoughtful one-of-a-kind gift.

I was in no mood to deal with any more of this nonsense. But at that moment the last thing I wanted was to call the police and face Wolf again. The lantern by my front door lit enough of the bushes to reveal movement in the branches. If I yelled, the lurker would probably take off running.

"What do we do?" I whispered to Humphrey and Nina. Nina whipped out her cell phone.

I reached for it and snapped it shut. "We have to find out who it is. Nina, you block him on the right, Humphrey . . ." I doubted Humphrey could stop a flea but he was all I had. "You take the left. I'll act like I'm saying good night to you and walk straight to the door."

"Are you insane?" Humphrey whispered in a higher pitch than I'd have thought possible.

I didn't give him a chance to argue. Projecting my voice, I called out "Good night! See you tomorrow," and headed for my front door. Keeping my eyes on the bushes, I tried to hold my head straight so the man in hiding wouldn't know we were on to him. When I was almost at the stoop, Mars stepped out of the shadows.

"Are you trying to scare us to death?" My heart raced. "Why are you lurking outside the house?"

"I wasn't sure who was with you or who might be home. Hi, Nina. We need to talk, Soph—"

Humphrey charged from the left, a pale blur that intersected Mars at his knees.

Mars crumpled to the ground.

"Stop, Humphrey! It's Mars. It's okay," I shouted.

I couldn't tell which one moaned louder. Nina and I helped them stand. Humphrey rubbed his shoulder but forced a smile. "I always wanted to be a football hero."

Mars grumbled, "I need a drink."

"I should go." Humphrey dusted himself off. "It's been a most adventurous evening." He leaned in for a kiss.

I evaded him by pulling away. I jammed the key into the lock and turned it. "Thanks for going with us, Humphrey."

Mars staggered into the house. This was the third time he'd been by today. Did he really need to talk or was he making up excuses to come over and see me?

"I think everyone's still out." I motioned feverishly for Nina to come in. She hurried in after Mars, and I could tell she was pleased to be included. When I closed the door, Humphrey was limping toward the street.

Mars waited for Nina and me in the kitchen. "Sit."

We draped our coats over a chair before taking seats at the kitchen table. Mars unzipped his new leather jacket, placed a package wrapped in plain brown paper on the table, then slammed down a photograph. The glossy enlargement showed Clyde, Simon's driver and bodyguard. He stood casually, with one hand on his hip, and wore an embarrassed smile like he found it silly to pose for a photo.

"Too bad he's so obnoxious; he's not bad-looking," said Nina.

Mars glared at her. "I found it in Natasha's briefcase."

"You were snooping?" said Nina.

"Yes, I was snooping. Somebody's stalking her, somebody poisoned me, and she hired Otis for heaven knows what reason." He paused and said in a hushed voice, "I was afraid Nat might be having an affair."

"And you think this picture confirms that?" I asked.

Mars paced. "What else can I think? Fairly incriminating evidence, wouldn't you say?"

"So she has this picture. It's not like he's nude or anything." Nina craned her neck. "Where was this taken? It looks like the Jefferson Memorial."

I examined it again. The round structure behind him didn't leave much doubt about the location. "Pretty recent, too. He's dressed for fall weather."

Mars punched his fist into an open hand. "What do I do? Do I confront her? Do I leave her?" He paused and held the back of a chair. "Do I pretend nothing ever happened and just go on?"

I flipped the picture over, but the back side was plain white photographic stock. "Could Natasha have taken this picture?"

Nina and I bent over it.

"I don't see any reflections." Nina's mouth twisted doubtfully. "There's nothing incriminating about it. Mars, this picture alone isn't evidence of an affair."

"You two are a gas," Nina continued. "How many other men would go to their ex-wives when they suspect their girlfriends of cheating?"

Mars sighed. "We're divorced, Nina, not archenemies."

"What's in the package?" asked Nina.

"Don't protest, Sophie, you need this," said Mars as he slid the package toward me. "I got one for Nat, too."

I unwrapped the brown paper to find a Taser.

"They're not easy to buy, but a client of mine came through for me. It's like a stun gun. It won't kill an adult, but it'll incapacitate one long enough for you to get away."

Nina chirped up. "I want one, too. I'll pay for it. Can you get me one?"

I didn't like guns, but I'd decided long ago that I should carry mace in my car since I regularly came home late at night after events. This was another step in the direction of a gun.

"Sure. I think my source can procure one more. I want you to carry it with you, Sophie. Your folks will be going home soon and you'll be here all by yourself. I don't know what we're up against, but strange things are happening around you and Nat. I knew neither of you would carry a gun. This is the best alternative I could come up with."

As if on cue, the front door opened and a cold draft floated through the kitchen. Judging from the lively chatter, the theatergoers were returning and had enjoyed their evening.

Mars snatched the picture from the table and hid it in his jacket. "Don't tell Mom. She already hates Nat."

I glanced toward the foyer to be sure June wasn't in earshot. "Natasha's pushing to put her in a home."

Mars couldn't have looked more miserable. "She keeps telling me Mom can't live alone anymore. That she'll burn her own house down if I don't have her put away."

"I don't suppose she could move in with you and Nat?" I asked, only half teasing.

He blanched. "I couldn't take the two of them in the same house. Don't you think there've been enough murders? C'mon, Nina. I'll walk you out to be sure Humphrey doesn't jump you."

Mars paused to peck June on the cheek before leaving with Nina.

While the theatergoers changed clothes, I poured red wine and spices into a pot for a grog to warm them. On a baking sheet, I placed slices of Italian peasant bread and slid them into the oven to broil for a quick black bean bruschetta. Suspecting that June would like chocolate chip cookies, I prepared a tray of them from my freezer stash.

Bernie came home in time to share our midnight snack by the blazing fire in the kitchen. While the others discussed the play, I thought about Bernie and his stepfather and Mrs. Pulchinski, and eyed him surreptitiously. He was listening to the conversation, his expression as animated as if he'd been there. At one point he turned his blue eyes on me, and caught me watching him, but instead of shying away, he flashed me a dazzling smile.

I wanted to believe that someone with such easygoing charm couldn't possibly kill anyone. That wasn't true, of course. But by the time we turned in, I'd decided I didn't need to worry. If Bernie intended to murder one of us, he'd had plenty of opportunities already.

❧

I woke to the thundering of the door knocker. Daisy whined and pawed at me and Mochie stood on the edge of my bed, alert. Whoever was banging the thing must have been trying to wake us for some time. I glanced at the clock—two thirty in the morning. I didn't bother with a robe and ran down the stairs in my single-girl flannel pajamas. The person outside tried again.

Bernie emerged from the den, yawning, and wearing

only sweatpants. I could hear murmuring behind me and glanced back to see that the caller had awakened everyone. My parents, Craig, Hannah, and June watched from the second-floor landing. I unlocked the door and flung it open, afraid the killer had struck again and someone needed help.

Instead, a bleached blonde wearing too much makeup stepped inside and dropped a shiny purple raincoat on the foyer floor. Posing seductively in black stockings, garters, and underwear that left nothing to the imagination, she arranged her long hair so it draped over her shoulders. She looked at Bernie and said, "So which one of you is the colonel?"

"The colonel!" June cried, dismay in her voice.

"I'm afraid you have the wrong house." I picked up her coat and held it out to her.

"No, I don't." She reached for the coat and withdrew a piece of paper from the pocket. "Right here. See?"

What I saw was my address and the colonel's name.

I opened the door and pointed. "The colonel lives on the other side of the street."

Pulling on her coat, she giggled and said, "My bad."

After she left, June walked down the stairs and slammed the door behind the blonde. June hurried to the kitchen to look out the window and we all followed her. The blonde strutted across the street in heels that had to be five inches high. The raincoat couldn't provide much warmth against the winter air. She must have been freezing.

"He can't be serious. The colonel is such a proper man." June clenched her fists.

I signaled my mom. "Since we're all up, why don't we go in the sunroom for a nightcap?" Mom took June's arm and steered her away from the window. I shooed everyone else along behind them.

I could hear June saying, "She was nothing but a tart.

A common tramp. The kind you pay for services." She had that right. I was sorry the tart had awakened everyone. If it had just been Bernie and me, we could have kept the colonel's little secret.

Bernie followed me into his sleeping quarters and pulled on his bathrobe. I handed him a bottle of sherry and another of Grand Marnier, one of Hannah's favorite indulgences. Bernie picked out a bottle of Scotch and hauled them into the sunroom while I retrieved cut-crystal sherry glasses and colorful cordial glasses from the dining room.

I carried them on a silver tray and almost stumbled over my own feet in the hallway. Someone had turned off all the lights. I understood why when I reached the sunroom. Mom had lit candles and Dad had plugged in the lights he'd helped Mars and me install years ago. The tiny Christmas lights twinkled on the arched glass ceiling like stars.

The romantic mood didn't comfort June, though. "I thought the colonel was a respectable man, like my dear husband. I'm overwhelmed with disgust when I contemplate what's going on at his house this very minute."

"We're all surprised." Mom handed June a glass of sherry. "It's just as well that you found out now. You could have gone on for years not knowing the truth about him."

"It's so repulsive to think of him ordering that girl like a . . . a side of beef." June tugged her lavender bathrobe closed around her neck and held it there with one hand.

"No woman wants a man like that. He's definitely not the gentleman we all thought." Mom settled into a love seat next to Dad. "I don't blame you one bit for being upset."

"What did Mars want so late?" asked Hannah.

I shot her a grateful smile for changing the subject. The sooner we distracted June, the better. And then I remembered that Natasha might be having an affair. That would distract June but not in a good way.

"He brought me a Taser." That wasn't a complete lie. I didn't like misleading anyone, but this time I thought it more important to cheer up June. "For the nights when I come home late from work."

I scored. My simple lie generated a lively discussion between Mom and June on how they could throw Mars and me together more often. Before long Craig and Hannah drifted up to bed, followed shortly by my parents and June. Daisy had stretched out in the sunroom with us, but I hadn't seen Mochie in a while. I found him in the kitchen, sitting on the bench in the bay window looking out as a hearse drove by.

TWENTY-SIX

From "The Good Life":

Dear Sophie,

My mother-in-law complains that my Thanksgiving decor looks too much like Halloween. Must be those rotting pumpkins by the front door. What can I do that will please her?

—Desperate in Dumfries

Dear Desperate,

Instead of hiding your favorite photos in scrapbooks, make duplicates of pictures with an autumn theme. A memorable hike to see the leaves changing, the kids playing in piles of raked leaves, a beautiful garden of colorful squashes and pumpkins ready to be harvested, even a photo of dear mother-in-law visiting. Put them in frames that carry out the seasonal theme and bring them out each year after Halloween. Cluster them on a sideboard or entry hall table for an instant decoration and a lovely reminder of fun times that you can add to each year.

—Sophie

I watched the hearse drive away, hoping it wasn't some sort of horrible omen. Carrying Mochie, I returned to the sunroom. Bernie had decided to watch the tiny TV in the den. Since he didn't intend to sleep yet, I joined him and began downloading photographs of the stuffing competition from Dad's camera. I knew it was a long shot, but he might have caught something of interest. Like Natasha kissing Clyde.

Thumbprint-sized images showed immediately. I scanned through them. Mom and Hannah at a bridal salon. Picture after picture of bridal gowns. I assumed Hannah wanted to remember the dresses and asked Dad to snap photos. Finally, a picture of the Stupendous Stuffing Shakedown banner that hung across the entrance to the hotel.

I viewed picture upon picture of Mom and Hannah. Craig showed up in a couple of them, but both times he'd turned his head and was barely recognizable. Dad had also taken some shots of Natasha, her creative baskets of ingredients behind her, and a few of Wendy and Emma and their work spaces as well.

If only Dad had been photographing the Washington Room or one of its entrances. Even though I hadn't expected to find anything earthshaking, I couldn't help being disappointed. I printed out two sheets of tiny thumbnails to examine in the morning when I'd be more alert.

The printer hummed and I looked over at Bernie. Snuggled in a down comforter, he snoozed peacefully with a snoring Daisy next to him. I put the computer to sleep, turned off the TV and the sole light on the desk. I left the thumbnails on the kitchen table and tiptoed up to bed with Mochie racing ahead.

━━━━❧❧❧━━━━

In spite of a sleepless night, I rose early on Sunday. The rich aroma of coffee wafted to me as I walked downstairs to the kitchen. June sat by the fireplace, pouches under her eyes. I suspected she hadn't slept well after the colonel's middle-of-the-night date stopped by.

She muttered, "I never expected this of him."

Wearing a silky robe, Mom studied the thumbnails I'd left on the table. I tapped her shoulder and whispered, "Is June talking to Faye?"

Mom nodded. "And check out Mochie."

The kitten sat in front of the stone wall, staring at it as though listening to something. I shivered. "You don't think he can hear Faye?"

Mom shrugged. "Who knows?"

I poured a mug of coffee for June. She needed a jolt of caffeine. She took it with a smile but continued to mutter.

"I'm glad you're up early," said Mom. "There's something I need to tell you."

I poured coffee into a mug, added milk, and when her back was turned, plopped in sugar. I didn't need any more lectures about my weight. "What's up?" I asked, sitting down next to her.

She glanced at June and whispered to me, "I saw Vicki embracing a man at the stuffing contest."

I hadn't expected that. "What did he look like?"

"Nice enough. Brown hair. At the time I thought it might be that driver of Simon's, but I'm not sure. Oh, honey, do you think that has anything to do with the murders? I should have mentioned it sooner, but with all that's happened, it went right out of my mind."

Clyde? Did Vicki know about Natasha's affair? "What kind of hug was it?"

"Friendly, but there was something odd about it, like they didn't want anyone to see them."

"Maybe it was an old client. Someone she met through her marriage counseling service?" Loads of people hugged at the contest. Vicki knew a lot of people, had counseled hundreds.

A knock at the kitchen door caught us off guard.

To my utter surprise, Francie walked inside and presented me with a white bakery box tied with a glittery gold ribbon.

"I brought muffins for brunch. Cranberry nutmeg, walnut mincemeat, and pumpkin spice." She plunked the Sunday edition of the local paper on the kitchen table and removed her jacket. "Are you the only ones up?" She moseyed toward the coffee and poured herself a cup. Looking out the window over the sink, she said, "Sure is dead out there this morning."

Brunch? I didn't remember planning a brunch. The mere mention of it reminded me that I had ignored my company. Normally, I'd have planned all the meals in advance and even prepared a few dishes that I could pop in the oven so I wouldn't have to abandon my guests to prepare them.

We could pull together eggs and bacon and whip up apple-cinnamon French toast. Thank heaven the freezer and pantry were well stocked. Could Mom have mentioned brunch to Francie?

Wearing sweats, Dad ambled in and stopped short. "Didn't realize that we're having company. Pardon me while I change."

Mom and June followed suit, but Francie didn't mind. She tossed kindling in the fire, lit it, and made herself at home in a fireside chair, her nose buried in the paper. At least I didn't have to worry about entertaining her.

I found a basket big enough for the muffins, lined it with a white lace-edged napkin, and placed the muffins inside. While Francie read, I peeled and sliced firm

Granny Smith apples and melted butter in a large pan. The apples plopped into the melting butter with a sizzle. I added a liberal dose of brown sugar, sprinkled cinnamon over the top, and gave the entire mixture a few good turns to blend it all. With the burner on low, I put the lid on and left the apples to simmer while I set the dining-room table.

Mochie zoomed past me into the living room. Daisy followed cautiously, as if she expected Mochie to change direction any second. Instead he jumped onto the sofa, gazed around, and then flew back toward Daisy and me in the dining room. I spread my arms and blocked the table, hoping to discourage Mochie from leaping on top of it. But at the last moment he veered to the right and halted abruptly in front of the buffet.

His bottom raised, Mochie flattened his chest to the floor and struggled to reach something under the buffet. I decided a mouse would run from him so I let him entertain himself by trying to bat out what was probably a major dust bunny while I set square white plates on an apricot tablecloth.

Natasha's pumpkin wreath had started to cave in on itself. I carried it into the kitchen and tossed it in the trash. I retrieved a large rustic basket made of twigs, filled it with hard ruby pomegranates and rosy pears, and carried it, along with a bag of assorted nuts in the shells, to the dining table. I placed the basket in the center, ripped the bag open, and scattered nuts around the basket, throwing a generous handful on top of the fruit.

Something rattled as it spun across the floor. Daisy pranced after it. Mochie squeezed out from under the buffet, his belly flat, his whiskers white with dust-bunny fuzz. He ran to his new toy, which Daisy sniffed cautiously. Mochie batted it across the room, where it spun before rolling to the outer wall, raising the excitement level of his game. I spoiled his fun by retrieving it for a closer look.

Made of some sort of brassy metal, the cylindrical object measured about two and a half inches long and less
than an inch in diameter. Both ends were rounded. Whatever it was, it had not been made to stand on end. Highly
polished stones decorated it in between swirls of tiny
golden beads.

I detected a thin line near one end and gave it a twist.
It opened easily to reveal a hollow compartment. A
creepy feeling came over me. My dread grew when I realized that Mochie was staring at something behind me.
I whipped around in time to see Craig watching me again.
I closed my hand over the object so he wouldn't see it and
suppressed my initial instinct to ask him, not very nicely,
why he liked to spy on me.

Choking back my annoyance, I asked, "Hungry?"

"Sure smells good. Can I help you with anything?"

I would have sworn his eyes focused on my clenched
hand when he asked. Mostly I wanted to get rid of him so
I could close the little vial and cram it in my pocket away
from His Nosiness.

"Would you bring the basket of muffins from the
kitchen?"

He didn't comply immediately. I suspected he knew I'd
found something and that I was hiding it. My blood pressure rose in the few seconds that passed with us in a
standoff. I had the upper hand, though. No matter what
he'd seen, he couldn't exactly tackle me and wrestle it
from my hand with everyone else in the house.

As I stared him down, it occurred to me that he rarely
showed emotion. He acted sweet and endearing around
Hannah, but he must be a great poker player because he
never displayed anger or frustration or any negative feelings. No matter how much he wanted to fit in and be accepted by our family, it didn't account for his amazing
self-control. I didn't trust him and I didn't like him.

At long last he left, presumably to fetch the muffins. I
turned my back in case he was trying to fool me, twisted

the top onto the peculiar vial, wrapped it in a napkin, and stuck it in my pocket.

Although I still found an occasional item from the days when Faye had owned the house, it seemed unlikely that the vial could have lain on the floor all these years without being noticed. But what a perfect little poison container. It fit easily in my pocket. No one would have noticed it in the palm of a killer's hand. Or was I leaping to conclusions?

When Craig returned, I had finished setting the table. I smiled nicely, thanked him for his help, and rushed back to the kitchen so I wouldn't have to be alone with him. Mom had the French toast under control, so I opened two packages of preservative-free bacon and laid the slices on the griddle. The mouthwatering aroma of crispy bacon would surely rouse Bernie.

I struggled to act normal but I couldn't help watching Craig. Had he intended to look for something in the dining room? Did the vial belong to him? Did he have a reason to poison Mars?

Ten minutes later, the entire household gathered for brunch in the dining room. But the phone rang before I could take my first bite. I chose not to answer. The machine could pick up and we would all enjoy a peaceful brunch.

The knock on the door a few minutes later was more difficult to ignore. When I opened it, Nina burst in. She hadn't bothered to wear a coat over her dressing gown.

"You won't believe this—my monster-in-law saw the colonel being loaded into a hearse last night."

"Did we hear that right?" Dad asked from the dining room.

It was too late to hide it from June. Nina bustled into the dining room and I followed.

"I'm still in shock," she said.

I watched June. Would she be able to deal with another blow?

"Good Lord! The man must have had a heart attack last night when his tart visited," said Mom.

"Or someone killed him."

"Sophie, why would you even think that?" Mom asked.

"Don't you think it's a bit much to be coincidental? We know he was at the stuffing challenge. He spent Thanksgiving Day with us. Whoever killed Otis and Simon must have killed him, too."

Dad murmured, "I'd rather believe the tart did him in."

June looked down at her fingers, folding and unfolding her napkin.

Francie lowered her forehead to a quivering hand. "This can't be happening."

"The hearse!" I said. "Before I went to bed last night I saw a hearse driving down the street. The tart must have found his body."

Nina picked up a piece of bacon and chewed on it, "What tart?"

I set a place for Nina while Hannah explained about the tart's arrival during the night.

"That old codger. Who'da thought it?" Nina helped herself to French toast and apples.

Francie slumped against the back of her chair. "No! It can't be. It's not possible."

"What about MacArthur?" I asked Nina. What had the tart done with him last night when the colonel was taken to the morgue? Had he been left alone in the house? "Francie, do you know how to get into the colonel's house?"

Francie pursed her lips as she gazed around the table, evidently debating how she should answer. "I'll go with you."

We pulled on coats and walked somberly across the street.

The sun shone, the cold air felt clean and crisp, and it was impossible to imagine that the colonel wasn't with us anymore. We opened the gate to the service alley and rounded the back of the house. Francie lifted a terra-cotta flowerpot and slid a key out from underneath it.

I unlocked the door and found MacArthur waiting eagerly inside. A leash hung on a hook next to the door. The colonel's collection of walking sticks stood underneath in an umbrella stand. I winced at the sight of his favorite with a bronze bulldog's head as the handle. The colonel wouldn't be needing that again.

When I clasped the leash onto MacArthur's collar, he burst out into his yard as though he was overdue for a morning walk.

Francie locked up and hid the key. "Should . . . should we go in and look around?"

I wrapped an arm around her. "There's nothing to look for anymore, Francie. I'm sorry."

We returned to my house, where Francie all but collapsed into her seat at the dining table. While Mom encouraged her to eat something, I took MacArthur into the kitchen and fed the dogs and Mochie a snack.

Nina toddled into the kitchen. "Your mom says to put on another pot of coffee." She leaned over to pat MacArthur. "This is just terrible. Do you really think it's connected to the murders? Maybe he, you know, got frisky with the tart and it was too much for him."

I glanced at the kitchen door to be sure no one would overhear. "Mochie found this in the dining room." I pulled the napkin from my pocket, dropped the cylindrical vial into a clear plastic bag, and sealed it shut.

Nina frowned as she examined it. "They sold these last year at the Christmas Bazaar. You can put perfume inside. They weren't cheap but they're not worth burglarizing a house for." Her eyes widened. "You think the killer brought the poison in this!"

"It would have been easy to carry in a pocket. I can't think of any other reason it would be in my dining room."

Nina held it up to the light. "This must be what the intruder wanted. Either he knew he dropped it on Thanksgiving or he got home that night and realized he'd lost it."

But why ransack Vicki and Andrew's house? Unless he thought one of them or Natasha or Mars found it," I mused. "When he didn't locate it at their house, he came here."

"Could any of them know who the killer is and be blackmailing him? Andrew always needs money. Or what if the killer thought the colonel had the little vial, broke into his house, and scared him so badly he had a heart attack last night?"

My phone rang and I answered reluctantly, unwilling to receive any more bad news.

"It's your husband." I handed the phone to Nina.

She groaned and said, "Be right there," before hanging up. "I forgot all about lunch with the monster-in-law before they leave."

"They?" I asked.

"She's going home, my husband is off on another business trip, and someone adopted Duke yesterday. I have to hand him over on Monday. Soon I'll have an empty house."

Nina left while I brewed more coffee. MacArthur waggled his hind end at me as though he was sure I must have more treats. I fed him another dog biscuit because I felt terrible for him. Of course, Daisy ate another as well, and I gave Mochie a tiny bite of bacon. MacArthur didn't appear particularly upset about being at my house. Later in the day when he couldn't go home, he'd probably grow uneasy and miss the colonel.

"Empty house." Nina's words echoed in my mind. Her house would be empty, as would the colonel's. If the killer thought my house would be empty, he might come back to search for the little vial.

Carrying the carafe of coffee, I returned to the gloomy group around my dining-room table. MacArthur, Daisy, and Mochie trotted along, no doubt hoping for more treats. If Francie or June had eaten anything, I couldn't tell. Even Bernie moved food around his plate without interest.

"Dad," said Hannah, "did you get a picture of the pink tablecloths that were bunched up in swags with coordinating bows?"

I couldn't believe Hannah could be so unfeeling. Didn't she ever think of anything except that ridiculous wedding?

Dad shrugged. "If you told me to take one, I probably did."

Her voice devoid of enthusiasm, Mom said, "Sophie printed thumbnails last night. They're in the kitchen."

Francie jumped up. "I'm sorry, I have to go." She didn't bother with her coat and fled out the front door.

Mom wrapped her hand over Dad's. "June, would you like to walk with us? Fresh air would do us all good before the rain sets in. We can take MacArthur and Daisy and maybe we can light a candle for the colonel at one of the churches."

Craig leapt at the suggestion. "Excellent. I think I'll go for a run."

A little too eagerly, I thought. Running after eating? That didn't sound right. Unlike the others, I noticed that Craig managed to eat everything on his plate. Ten minutes later, Bernie, Hannah, and I were left to clear the table and store the leftovers. Hannah carried a few dishes to the kitchen but soon settled at the table with the thumbnail photos.

"How could Dad manage to take only two pictures of Craig?" she whined. "And both are so bad. He'll have to take a lot of pictures today because I want some to frame." She bent forward for a closer look. "Soph, do you have a magnifying glass?"

"In the desk in the den, top drawer."

Hannah returned in less than a minute. She studied the photos and quietly said, "Soph, come here a second."

Handing me the magnifier, she pointed a blush-pink fingernail at a tiny picture. "See your work space behind Craig? Move all the way over to the right. Anything strike you as odd?"

TWENTY-SEVEN

From *"Ask Natasha"*:

Dear Natasha,

You always look so elegant and pulled together on your show. I bet you even look gorgeous at home. People who drop by always catch me in my bathrobe or with curlers in my hair. How do you do it?

—Grubby in Grundy

Dear Grubby,

Never linger in your bathrobe. Bathe, do your hair and makeup, and dress first thing in the morning, before you do anything else! Even before that first cup of coffee. Hang a mirror in the kitchen and another in the foyer so you can do a quick check before answering the door. I keep lipstick and a brush in a drawer in my foyer. It only takes a second to freshen up before answering the door.

—Natasha

I passed the magnifying glass over the photo and concentrated. It showed my ingredients clustered on my workspace counter and . . . "Is that an arm?"

"Exactly!" crowed Hannah.

The arm appeared to originate in Wendy's work space behind the curtain that divided our sections. I followed the sweater-clad arm in the other direction and discovered what I thought were tiny fingers on one of my spice jars.

"I'll enlarge it on the computer. I think we might be able to identify the crumb who swapped the salt for sugar and messed with your thyme." Hannah picked up Mochie and disappeared into the den.

As Bernie slid the last plate into the dishwasher, he said, "You've been very kind to put me up, Soph. But I suppose I should be shoving off soon. I'd like to stay through the contest tomorrow if that's okay."

"Are you going back to London?"

"To tell the truth, I thought I'd make some job inquiries around here."

It was my chance to ask about Mrs. Pulchinski. "To stay closer to your girlfriend?"

He snapped his head up in surprise. "Something like that."

Had I alarmed him? Maybe I shouldn't have asked about the girlfriend. But did he plan to brazenly move in with the widow so soon after her husband's death?

"Sophie!" Hannah shouted.

Bernie and I rushed to the den. I didn't really think anything untoward had happened to Hannah, but after all we'd been through lately, I wasn't taking any chances.

Hannah was viewing an enlarged photograph on the computer screen. "I zeroed in so it's a little bit fuzzy, but I think we have a major clue."

The printer whirred as it churned out a page.

"Look here," she said, pointing. "The guy is reaching

with his left hand and you can see his wedding ring with
an etched circular design. Do you recognize the ring?"

I didn't. "Thanks for trying, Hannah."

"Don't give up yet. At least we know it's a man. Those
chunky fingers couldn't possibly belong to a woman. Craig
and I will make a point of checking wedding bands when
the contest resumes tomorrow. I can pretend I'm looking at
them because I don't know what I want for our wedding
bands."

Her offer startled me. She was still focused on the
wedding but this time, it wasn't in a selfish me-me-me
way.

"Thanks, Hannah."

She tilted her head. "You do realize I've been overdo-
ing the wedding bit to distract Mom and Dad. They're so
worried about you. When Craig showed me the newspaper article about the dead PI, we put it together with your
lame explanation about how you found Mochie and realized you were in trouble. I've been trying to lighten the
mood by bringing up the wedding, which is a much
cheerier subject."

I threw my arms around Hannah. "And I thought you
couldn't think of anything but your wedding."

"Aw, c'mon. I know I've been a pill, but Craig and I
have been discussing the murders, too. If there's anything
I can do to help you, I will. We can't quite figure it out,
though."

Sprawling on the unmade sofa bed, Bernie said, "We
should lay a trap for him tomorrow."

"For the killer?" I asked.

"No, for the guy who monkeyed with the ingredients."

Hannah spun toward him in the desk chair. "Great idea!
Sophie can leave her work station and you and Craig and I
can be on the lookout."

Bernie ran with the idea. "You could print little pictures
of the ring. Then June and your parents can help as well."

Emotion welled inside me. I wanted to pull them both into a huge grateful hug but someone called my name.

Bernie sat up. "Is that Francie?"

The three of us returned to the kitchen. Francie sat by the fire like she had this morning, but now she hid her face behind her fingers.

Hannah knelt beside her and asked, "Are you okay? Do you need a doctor?"

I wet a kitchen towel, wrung it out, and offered it to Francie.

She pressed it against her forehead. "I'm never like this, I just can't believe he's dead." Tears squeezed out of her eyes. "I'm so sorry. I only came to pick up my coat."

"Nonsense. You stay with us for a while." Hannah stroked Francie's arm. "You shouldn't be alone right now."

Was it my imagination or did I like my sister a lot better when Craig wasn't around?

The scratching at the kitchen door alerted me to Daisy's return. When I opened it, she and MacArthur bounded inside and wedged their noses in Daisy's water bowl at the same time. Then Mom, Dad, and June entered and clustered around the fireplace. Dad hung up coats while Mom clasped her hands and said, "We've had the best idea. June will be leaving tomorrow after the stuffing contest and we'll be going home the next morning, so we thought we should all get together and go out to dinner tonight."

Francie let out a little cry.

Mom patted Francie's hand. "I wish the colonel were here to come with us, but we think it's a way of honoring him. We should invite everyone who came for Thanksgiving. Sophie, will you call Mars and ask them to come? I'll call Humphrey."

Having dinner again with Mars and Natasha, not to mention Humphrey and Wolf, appealed to me about as much as a root canal. But Mom unknowingly handed me exactly what I needed—an empty house. Except it wouldn't be empty. I would make some kind of last-minute excuse and stay home to spy and see if anyone turned up to retrieve the vial. I embraced her suggestion with enthusiasm.

I could hear Mom giving Francie a little pep talk while I dialed Mars's cell phone number.

He answered on the first ring and asked, "Is Mom okay?"

"She's fine. Right here in front of me. Why? Has something happened?"

He took a minute before answering me. "Sophie, I don't know what to do with her. Natasha is certain that something awful will happen to her if she goes home and stays by herself, and I couldn't live with that. We've been talking about this all morning and I'm afraid . . . Andrew and I don't have any choice, we're going to have to put her in a home where they can watch her."

I bristled at the thought. June would not go to a retirement home until she wanted to go. Even if I had to take her in to live with me. This time Natasha had gone too far. Lowering my voice so June wouldn't overhear, I wandered into the sunroom with the phone. I told Mars about the dinner plans and insisted he come over immediately to discuss June's situation.

When I hung up, I found Mom behind me, listening.

"Is he on his way?" she asked.

I nodded.

"Run upstairs right now and change into that white sweater I gave you last year. And put on some makeup."

"Mom, they want to put June into a home for the aged."

"Because she talks to her sister's ghost?"

"No, because they think she started the fire at Natasha's. Mars is afraid something horrible will happen to her if she lives by herself."

Mom crossed one arm over her abdomen and massaged her chin with the other hand. "Nonsense. We can't have that. I'll have a talk with Mars when he arrives."

The knocker on the front door sounded.

"Too late to change." Mom reached toward me and fluffed my hair. "You couldn't have put on a little lipstick? You ought to keep some in the console in the foyer for these emergencies. Natasha does."

I escaped her and answered the door. It couldn't possibly be Mars yet anyway.

When I opened the door, Wolf stood on the stoop. "Is Mrs. Winston here?"

I presumed he meant June. "She had nothing to do with the colonel's death. I promise you she did not kill him." I stepped outside and closed the door behind me. "I don't know what you've heard but she's a very sweet lady and she's not incompetent."

He drew back, a perplexed look on his face. "Someone murdered the colonel?"

I'd put my foot in it. "I don't know that he was murdered. But whatever happened, June wasn't involved."

"He's dead? When did this occur?"

"Last night. I assumed you knew."

Wolf flipped open his phone.

I motioned for him to come in the house. "You can talk in the living room. I can't guarantee privacy but it's your best bet."

Digging in my pocket for the vial, I followed him and said, "Mochie found . . ."

Wolf held up his forefinger in a gesture that meant "wait a minute," turned away from me, and spoke into his phone.

I didn't want to stick around the living room to eavesdrop, but when I retreated to the dining room, I caught Craig ducking into the foyer. I'd had about enough of his creeping around and spying and was about to tell him off but thought better of it. Maybe the poison vial did belong to him.

Pretending I hadn't seen him, I acted as though I was hiding the vial in the top drawer of the dining room buffet, while actually leaving it safely in my pocket. Hopefully when we were all out to dinner and he thought the house was empty, the killer would feel free to come back to retrieve it. Except I would be waiting.

Mustering courage and a friendly smile, I strode toward the kitchen, feigning surprise when I saw Craig. "Back from your run? Good that you got it in. I think they're calling for rain this afternoon."

I continued to the kitchen. What a horrible day.

Craig followed me, plopped into a fireside chair, and Hannah promptly sat on his lap. Why did she turn into a simpering sexpot around him? *Yuck.*

Mom handed me a lipstick that she must have retrieved from the bathroom upstairs. "Humphrey agreed to meet us at the restaurant. We should invite Wolf, too. Where is he, Sophie?"

"He's in the living room. He didn't know about the colonel."

Francie stiffened. "The detective is here? In the house?" She looked around frantically, jumped up, and lunged toward the kitchen door.

TWENTY-EIGHT

From "The Good Life":

Dear Sophie,

My elderly mother-in-law is moving in with us and we'd like to make her as comfortable as possible. What can we do to make her life in our house easier?

—Worrier in Woodstock

Dear Worrier,

Throw rugs cause a high percentage of falls in the home. Remove them from main walking areas. A grab bar in the bath and shower will make her feel more secure. Round doorknobs and water handles can be difficult for older hands to grasp. Replace them with lever handles for your mother-in-law's comfort.

—Sophie

But just as Francie gripped the door handle, she suddenly went limp. Luckily Bernie leapt to her aid and caught her before she hit the floor. Then Mom rushed in to fan her and everyone spoke at once.

"Should I call an ambulance?" I asked.

Bernie carried Francie to the bench in the bay window and Mom opened a window panel.

Francie's entire body slumped. "No ambulance," she murmured. "I'll be fine."

Daisy and MacArthur kept their distance as if they knew she wasn't well, but Mochie jumped onto the bench and sniffed her.

"Maybe she needs a good, stiff drink," said Dad.

"What's going on?" asked Wolf.

I hadn't noticed him come in.

"I'm afraid the colonel's death has been too much for her." Mom wrapped a comforting arm around Francie, who looked like she might be sick.

And then my mom, never one to be deterred for long from thinking about my love life, or lack thereof, proceeded to invite Wolf to join us for dinner. Wolf paused before he said, "Sure. I think it would be very interesting to see the whole group together again."

Oh, great. Mom had just set up a detective's dream. He'd be scrutinizing us for clues to the killer. But if my plan worked, the killer would be here. Maybe Nina could help me watch for him. And I should corral the dogs in the sunroom—

"Sophie!" Mom interrupted my thoughts. "Mars and Andrew just drove up. June, would you be a dear and brew Francie a strong cup of tea?"

Trust Mom to keep people occupied. She snagged Dad's sleeve and pulled him into the foyer. "Bring June some rum for Francie's tea and make sure June stays in the kitchen."

Promising to return shortly, Wolf strode out the front

door just before Mars and Andrew walked in. June's sons said hello to her before following Mom and me to the sunroom.

"Sophie, please don't start arguing," warned Mars. "We've discussed this issue thoroughly and it's for Mom's own protection. I know you love her, too. But how would you feel if she started a fire and burned to death?"

"You're overreacting because of Natasha," I said. "She's laying a guilt trip on you to achieve what she wants."

"I don't even like Natasha." Andrew flashed a guilty look at Mars. "Well, I don't. I'd argue the sun was purple just so I wouldn't have to agree with her. But the fire at Natasha's house was huge. We're not talking about some little flicker in a pan on the stove. Natasha talked to the folks who run the place we're sending Mom. She won't have access to an oven. Won't have to cook at all. She'll have a nice room and she can take her own furniture."

I had no doubt that Mars would only allow June to live in a lovely facility. I wasn't worried about that at all. "But I don't think she's ready. You're pigeonholing her based on one incident. Besides, we don't even know how the fire started."

"Now listen here," said Mom. "I've spent the last few days in June's company and there's not a reason in the world for you to put her away like she's some kind of inconvenience."

Go Mom! I swelled with pride.

"Inga, I don't want to do this. But don't you understand? She set fire to Natasha's house. She's a danger to herself."

"That's baloney," I said. "Except for the little quirk, she's fine. She hasn't fallen or left water running or started a fire here."

"What quirk?" asked Andrew.

"Andrew," said Mom in her no-nonsense-mother voice, "couldn't you and Vicki take her in?"

Andrew winced. "We don't want her to burn our house. And I don't think she'd like having a babysitter when we're out. But what's this quirk you mentioned?"

Before one of us could answer, someone screamed.

A bloodcurdling scared-to-death scream. Like someone saw a ghost.

A blast of frigid air swept through the house. All four of us jumped up and dashed into the foyer. Francie lay in the doorway, half in and half out. Behind her, June stood frozen, her back to us.

"What happened?" I slid to a stop next to Francie and knelt. Memories of Simon's corpse pounded in my brain as I reached for her wrist. Thankfully, this time I felt a pulse.

Hannah shook my shoulder. "Soph . . ." I ignored her.

"Francie!" I gently patted her cheeks to rouse her.

"*SOPHIE!*" Hannah shouted.

"Not now, Hannah."

She shook my shoulder and pointed outside. I followed the line of her finger and jerked upright. Waves of shock and relief rendered me momentarily speechless. I blinked hard, my brain not quite making sense out of what I saw.

The colonel marched along the sidewalk, tapping his walking stick, and turned up the walk to my house. "MacArthur's missing!" he yelled. "Have you seen him?"

At the sound of the colonel's voice, MacArthur scrambled over Francie's body and raced to the colonel.

Francie's eyelids fluttered and she gasped, "I thought I saw the colonel."

I leaned over her. "You did. He's alive and well."

"What?" She sat up. She trembled and tears flowed down her weather-beaten face. I clasped her hand, not sure which one of us was shaking harder. A little cheer went up and the gloom that had hung over us all day lifted.

The colonel appeared bewildered by the pats on the back and the hugs he received. I clasped him to me as though it would prove he was alive, while Bernie and

Dad helped Francie to her feet. Then Mom herded us all into the kitchen just as a downpour began. On the way I explained to the colonel that we thought he'd died and been carted away by a hearse.

Seated by the fire with MacArthur at his feet, the colonel slapped his knee and laughed. "I wasn't dead, but I was in that hearse."

Dad raised his eyebrows. "Perhaps you'd better explain."

"It was the oddest thing. In the middle of the night, a call girl arrived on my doorstep. I have no idea why."

June's lips pulled tight. She obviously wasn't buying his story.

"The poor child was half frozen so I asked her to step inside while we tried to figure out what had happened. Don't look at me that way, June," he said. "I'm not in the habit of using that kind of service. Besides, she was far too young for me."

"Did you or did you not order a call girl?" demanded June.

"I did not," said the colonel emphatically. His shoulders squared in military fashion. "She called her, uh, office and there was some confusion about the order. I made the poor girl a cup of tea to warm up. But when she left, she twisted her ankle on the sidewalk. Little wonder, you should have seen her shoes."

We had. Those five-inch heels were an accident waiting to happen. His story sounded authentic so far.

"I didn't know quite what to do. A twisted ankle isn't really worth calling an ambulance for. But while she sat on the front walk, your friend, Humphrey, came along. He offered to deliver her to the emergency room. Humphrey and I helped her to his hearse and I thought I'd better go with them. I was afraid she might not have medical insurance and I certainly didn't want her suing me."

June's expression softened. "Did she break her ankle?"

"It's only a sprain, though I understand they can be very painful. A most unsavory boyfriend arrived to pick her up. It was dawn by the time Humphrey brought me home. I went straight to bed and when I awakened, Mac-Arthur had vanished."

"I'm so sorry. We thought you had died and that Mac-Arthur was alone," I said.

"Sophie"—he flashed me an emotional smile—"it's good to know I have such caring neighbors. Thank you for looking out for MacArthur. One mystery solved. But I still don't understand how that young woman got my name. I would never use that sort of business. It's most peculiar."

"She had Sophie's address. If you'd"—June cleared her throat—"placed the order, surely you'd have given the correct address."

"It's almost like someone sent her here on purpose," said Bernie.

I turned very slowly toward Francie, who held a damp cloth to her forehead. She averted her eyes.

Bernie's lips curled into his lopsided grin.

Mom scolded, "Francie, you didn't!"

"I've suffered a huge shock. I don't know what you're talking about." Francie avoided looking at any of us. It was no small feat given that the kitchen was packed.

"Francie?" said the colonel.

"Okay, okay. I ordered the call girl. I wanted to get you back for not being interested in me. You know, a gag. And then I thought I'd killed you."

"You mean he didn't arrange for the tart?" asked June.

"Of course not." Color flooded back to Francie's skin. "He's much too proper for anything like that. I never meant to kill him, just shake him up a little bit. Maybe start some neighborhood rumors to embarrass him."

Funny how life turns out sometimes, I thought. Francie's vengeful little game backfired on her. No wonder she'd been inconsolable. She thought she'd murdered the colonel by sending the tart. I started to giggle and poor Bernie couldn't hold back his amusement any longer. It was contagious. In a flash, everyone, even the colonel and Francine Vanderhoosen, laughed and wiped teary eyes.

When we recovered, the colonel asked, "Just one thing. Did I leave a door unlocked? How did you get MacArthur out of my house?"

The color that had returned to Francie's face turned an ugly shade of red.

"A neighbor knew where you hide the key," I said.

My vague answer wasn't lost on the colonel.

He looked straight at Francie when he murmured, "I see."

Just then the knocker banged on the door again. Daisy barked and we all heard the door open and close. Wolf appeared in the doorway to the kitchen. He raised an eyebrow at the sight of the colonel. "Glad to see you hale and hearty, sir. That explains why we didn't have any record of your demise."

The colonel grinned. "I'm fairly pleased about it myself."

"I didn't expect to find so many of you gathered here," said Wolf. "I came to see Mrs. Winston, but I suspect she won't mind if the rest of you hear what I have to say. The Loudoun County fire chief called me this morning. They know how the blaze at Natasha's home started."

TWENTY-NINE

From "THE GOOD LIFE":

Dear Sophie,

My guests are still hanging around for the weekend after Thanksgiving. I'm itching to start decorating for Christmas, but I don't dare make that kind of mess until my mother-in-law leaves. How do I create a transitional ambiance without a lot of work?

—Eager in Earlysville

Dear Eager,

Think red and amber. It doesn't take a lot to create a cozy winter feel. Look around for wide-mouthed jars in shades of amber and red, drop a votive candle in each and use them on your table or mantel. The amber and red glass will cast a soft romantic glow. Use similar narrow-necked jars and glasses by popping in a single branch of berries or pine and place them among the candles. Just be sure they don't get too close to the flames!

—Sophie

Mars tensed and protectively snaked an arm around his mother's shoulders. They wouldn't arrest June for arson, would they? Even if she did set the fire, I felt sure it was an accident.

"Apparently there were small glasses of candles on the stairs in the foyer," said Wolf. "It seems they had something flammable tied to them." He shook his head in disbelief. "Stairs are no place for candles. One of them caught fire. It ignited a basket of dry pinecones on the stair landing, basically a basket of kindling. The basket rolled down the back stairs into the kitchen and the blaze spread from there."

Andrew and Mars stared at Wolf, speechless. June rushed Wolf. She hugged him like a long-lost friend and Wolf broke into a grin for the first time in days. Pointing a finger at her sons, June said, "There is nothing wrong with your old mother. Just because I have a few wrinkles and I sag in the wrong places doesn't mean I'm ready for the old folks home. And don't you pretend you weren't planning on that. I'm young enough to see a gentleman friend and enjoy myself and that's what I intend to do. Talking to a ghost doesn't mean a person is a looney tune."

She straightened her shoulders and strode from the room.

Simultaneously, Andrew and Wolf said, "Ghost?"

Their question brought Mars to life. "It's nothing. Wolf, would you mind going over to Andrew's house to tell Natasha about the fire? We'll follow you. Mom should come with us." Mars walked across the kitchen toward Wolf, paused, and turned. "Colonel, perhaps you'd care to join us for lunch? Bernie?"

Hannah jumped up. "It's been fun but we have a little shopping to do . . ."

"Good golly, Hannah. Haven't you seen every bridal store yet?" asked Dad.

"Christmas shopping, Dad."

But we'd forgotten all about Francie. She huddled on the bench, forlorn. Everyone else had someplace to go and something to do. Following the colonel wouldn't be fun for her anymore. Actually, I wasn't sure she deserved much sympathy, but I felt sorry for her anyway. She left my house as though each step zapped her strength.

Within half an hour, everyone scattered for the afternoon. I invented an excuse to stay home because I needed a little time to think through my scheme to reveal the killer and bring Nina up to speed on my plan.

I packed my black burglar-chic outfit, shoes and all, in a duffle bag. With all the commotion, I'd forgotten to give Wolf the poison vial. I withdrew it from my pocket and studied it. The rounded ends or gemstones might have yielded good fingerprints if I hadn't inadvertently messed them up. No one could have worn gloves on Thanksgiving without being noticed. No wonder the killer wanted it back so desperately.

I debated letting Wolf in on my plan to identify the murderer but decided against it. He'd say it wasn't accepted police procedure and would surely throw a monkey wrench into my plans. Tonight had to be the night. Everyone else would be accounted for at the restaurant. An opportunity like this wouldn't come along again.

Using masking tape, I attached the plastic bag containing the poison vial to the underside of a drawer in my nightstand. It wasn't the most original hiding place, but it wouldn't be discovered by snoopy Craig right away, either.

Carrying the duffle bag, I dashed through the rain across the street to Nina's. After filling her in about the colonel, I laid out my proposition for the evening. Naturally, she jumped at the opportunity to help.

After much gnashing of teeth that she didn't have a widow's walk on top of her house from which she could spy, we decided her best vantage point would be the dormer window in her attic. From there, she could observe anyone entering through my front door or the kitchen door. Only the sunroom entrance would be out of her field of vision. It was a chance we had to take.

I jogged home, adrenaline coursing through my veins already. I had never been a risk taker, but I didn't feel this was too dangerous. Besides, I would have Mars's Taser with me.

One key factor remained to be set up. I needed a spy at the restaurant. Mom or Dad were the obvious choices, but they'd be worried to death the whole time. But there was one other person who shared our parents' spying genes with me. Hannah. Could she be trusted not to say anything to Craig? If he was the killer and she revealed our plans, I'd be putting myself in danger. On the other hand, I needed a spy whom I could trust. And the one thing I knew for sure was that Hannah wasn't the killer.

As soon as she came home, I corralled her in my bedroom, claiming I needed help with my hair. I closed the door and whispered in case nosy Craig was outside listening. "There is something you can do to help me but you have to promise me you won't say anything to Craig. Not a word."

Hannah grinned and held out her pinkie. I hooked mine into hers and squeezed just like we did when we were kids. "I think Mochie found what the killer has been looking for. It's a small vial that Nina and I think could have contained the poison used on Mars." I pulled the drawer out of the nightstand and showed it to her.

She ripped the baggie off the drawer and held it up to examine it. "Looks handmade. Indian or African, maybe?"

"When you go out to dinner tonight, I'm going to make an excuse and stay behind. Nina will be outside watching the doors and I'll be hiding in the living room."

"Cool. What do you want me to do?"

"I need you to call me and tell me who doesn't show for dinner. That way Nina and I will know in advance who the killer is and who to expect."

"I'm in. We'll communicate through cell phones?"

"That's the plan."

"Better give me yours now for a minute so I can set it on vibrate and it won't ring."

I handed my cell to her. "And not a word to Craig?"

"I pinkie swore, didn't I?" She laughed.

While she fixed my phone, I hunted for an outfit sexy enough to please my mom. I'd forgotten about the white hand-knitted sweater she'd made. It crossed over in the front, creating a deep V-neck. I pulled it on and Hannah gave me a thumbs-up. Then I put hot curlers in my hair and sat down next to her on my bed.

"So you realize that you've been dressing like a coed from the sixties, don't you?" I asked.

Fortunately she laughed.

"You mean my new demure look? Craig says only single pearls for earrings unless we're going to a gala. He hates short skirts, so they're out. And he loves these old-fashioned sweater sets."

"I like the sweater sets, too. But I'm worried about you changing yourself so much to please him."

"So I can't wear fuchsia or dangly earrings anymore. If it makes him happy, I'm willing to do it. But you can wear anything you want. C'mon, I'll do your makeup." Despite my misgivings, I let Hannah smudge my eyes with smoky eyeliner.

"Too bad only the killer will see you looking so good." She giggled. Her words sent a little tremor through me. I didn't want to be foolhardy. But Nina would have my back.

Mom yelped with glee when I emerged from my bedroom. "Mars will have to come to his senses when he sees you tonight."

I took her hands into mine. "It's over with Mars, Mom. You and June have to give up and let us move on with our lives."

She bit her lip and squeezed my hands. "Well, then, I hope Mars notices how gorgeous you are and that he makes Wolf jealous."

I hugged my hopeless romantic of a mother. Nothing would ever change her quest to see her daughters happily married. Even if it meant one of them would be married to weird Craig.

The rain had stopped and darkness had descended on Old Town by the time we gathered in the kitchen. While the others donned their coats, I carefully walked through the house, turning out lights.

"I'm taking Daisy to Nina's to play with Duke while we're out," I announced as we left. Daisy and I ran across the wet street to Nina's while everyone else waited on the sidewalk.

Nina was already wearing her burglar black outfit when she answered the door. "You look great. It's a pity you're not going out," she said, closing the door behind me.

I released Daisy from her leash. "Are you ready?"

"Honey, I've got two pairs of binoculars, my phone, and a thermos of coffee upstairs waiting by the window. Who do you think is going to show up?"

Hot air escaped from my mouth and I sagged like a deflating balloon. "The colonel, Mars, Andrew, and Bernie all hated Simon and were at the hotel that day. The only one who scares me is Craig. If you see him going in the house, call the police immediately."

"Craig? Why would he be the killer?"

"I haven't been able to get anything out of him. But he went back to the scene of the crime the next day and he acts so strange and creepy. He's up to something."

"My money's still on Natasha. Maybe Simon found out about her affair with Clyde and threatened to tell Mars. Besides, it would be so like her to bring poison in a fancy vial."

"I don't know, Nina. I'm still kind of hoping it will be Mrs. Pulchinski."

"Fat chance. Are you ready for act one?"

I had no choice. It was now or never. I took a deep breath of air and nodded.

Nina swung the door open and I ran outside and across the street.

"Nina's husband was taken to the hospital in Chicago," I said, trying to catch my breath. "She's a complete wreck! You go ahead and I'll catch up as soon as I can calm her down a little bit and find out what's going on with her husband."

"Oh, honey," said Mom, "maybe I can help."

"No. We have reservations. Besides, the others will be waiting for you."

"Let's go, Mom. Sophie will come soon, I'm sure." Hannah prodded them along.

I felt guilty as I watched them walk away in the dark. Hannah hooked her arm into Craig's. The colonel walked beside June. Mom consoled Francie, and Bernie brought up the rear with Dad.

When they were out of sight, I hurried back to Nina's. After changing into my black outfit, I patted Daisy and Duke and scurried out of Nina's back door. The alley behind her house was inky and much creepier than I'd expected. The lights from the houses simply didn't reach that far. I ran behind the Wesleys' house, turned right, and dashed up the sidewalk. But when I reached our street, I kept going until I hit the entrance to the alley that ran behind my own house. I stopped to catch my breath.

An occasional car drove by. I shivered, only partly from the cold night air. The other part stemmed from my nerves, which were stretched to capacity. Searching the night for any hint of movement, I knew it was time for the final leg of my return home. I fled through the alley, fumbled with the latch on my gate, finally managed to open it, and slid through. I closed it slowly and without noise. Leaning against it, I watched the back of my house for a couple of minutes but it appeared peaceful. No shadows crossed through the sunroom.

I let myself in through the sunroom door and locked it behind me. Tiptoeing, I collected Mars's Taser from the cabinet in the kitchen where I'd stashed it. Lest anyone see me from the street, I hurried back to the den. Propping the door to the living room ajar so I could see, I picked up my phone to call Nina and let her know I was in place.

The phone was already vibrating.

THIRTY

From "THE GOOD LIFE":

Dear Sophie,

Our church is sponsoring a turkey dinner for the less fortunate and everyone is supposed to make something. I'm hopeless in the kitchen, but when I tried my usual trick of offering to bring rolls from the bakery, they expected me to bake them myself. I got out of that, but what can I make from scratch that I can't goof up?

—Praying in Pulaski

Dear Praying,

Offer to make the cranberry sauce. There's nothing simpler. All you need are cranberries, water, and sugar. The recipe is on the back of every bag of fresh cranberries. Dump all three ingredients together, bring them to a boil, then turn down the heat and let cook for five minutes. Just watch them to be sure they don't bubble over. They won't be ruined if they do, but you'll have a big mess on your hands, so don't walk away from them. The sauce is delicious hot or cold.

—Sophie

"Sophie," whispered Hannah, "I'm so sorry. The killer is your pal, Bernie."

I should have felt fearful or anxious. Instead, sadness enveloped me. "Everyone else is there?"

"Not yet. But Bernie peeled off while we were walking down here. Like he couldn't wait. He muttered something about having to check on a friend and that he'd catch up with us at the restaurant."

A friend? Did he go to alert Mrs. Pulchinski? She could come to search the house while he had an alibi, eating dinner with us and the detective in charge of the case. What a coup. "Is Wolf there?"

"Not yet. Mars and Natasha are here, though."

Had Bernie returned the key he borrowed? What if he hadn't gone to see Mrs. Pulchinski? What if he doubled back and was already in the house? "Call me back when everyone's there," I hissed and hung up.

I had to know about the key. The old floors creaked underneath me when I stood up. I'd never make it to the console in the foyer to check on the key without being heard. Grasping the Taser firmly, I scanned the sunroom and the backyard. When it seemed the coast was clear, I snuck into the dark hallway to the foyer. I couldn't risk turning on a light. I placed the Taser on the console so I could pull the drawer with both hands. It squeaked when I opened it. Unwilling to pull it completely open, I slid my hand in and felt around.

My phone vibrated again. I couldn't answer. It would have to wait.

The key wasn't in the drawer and I couldn't recall Bernie handing it back to me. Wasn't that the night he came home so late? I heard a thunk and jumped. My breathing sounded raspy in the still house. I scuttled back to the den to wait for Bernie. Positioned in a crouch near the door to the living room again, I flipped open the phone and called Nina.

"He's in the house!" she screamed.

She had to mean Bernie. But where was he? "What did you see?"

"Either he used a key or he's really good at picking locks. He went in through the front door. Glanced around a little like he was checking to be sure no one saw him."

"It's Bernie," I whispered.

"Wait . . ."

I could hear rustling sounds and assumed she needed both hands for the binoculars. "There's someone else. He's going in through the kitchen door."

Something soft brushed my knee and I stifled a squeal. Mochie purred loudly at my feet.

"I have to call Hannah!" I hung up and dialed Hannah's number. "Who's missing?"

"Sophie!" she said in a conversational tone. "Are you coming soon? Almost everyone is here now. We're still waiting for Bernie and Humphrey. Vicki isn't here yet, either, but she's coming. Andrew says she promised to bring meringues to her office tomorrow and she's waiting for them to finish baking so she can take them out of the oven."

"Okay, thanks." I flipped the phone shut. Humphrey. I never would have thought it. But if Humphrey was the killer, why was Bernie here? My head throbbed. My hands were clammy. My breath sounded like a winded elephant. I forced myself to breath shallowly. I couldn't. I would pass out.

Okay, Sophie. Slow, deep breaths. Stay alert.

The phone vibrated. I flipped it open, wishing the LED wasn't so darned bright. I covered it with one of Bernie's shirts.

"It's the darndest thing," said Nina. "Now somebody's watching your house from a parked car."

I heard something in the living room. "Hang on, Nina," I whispered. The person was making no effort whatsoever to hide his presence. I leaned forward and peeped. The beam from headlights of a car driving by flashed through the living room for a moment. Long enough for me to see Mochie jump to the top of the grandfather clock.

Where were the two people Nina had seen entering the house? I recognized the squeal of the drawer in the foyer console. Bernie. He must be putting the key back.

Or was the killer looking for the poison vial?

Nina's voice screeched on the phone. I held it to my ear.

"Somebody's running to your house. He's going for the kitchen door. Having trouble opening it."

Three people? How was that possible? Did Hannah say Wolf was there? I couldn't remember. I hoped Wolf was the person in the car because I would need him if there were three killers. I couldn't defend myself against three people with one lousy Taser.

The Taser. I felt around on the floor. No Taser. I must have left it on the console in the foyer. And now I had to face three people. My hands shook at the thought.

Who could they be? I had to call Hannah. This wasn't working the way I'd planned at all.

Mochie mewed and a light flashed in the living room. I snapped the phone shut. I couldn't call Hannah now. I gulped for air. What had Hannah said? Bernie and Humphrey weren't there. Had she mentioned Wolf? *Think, Sophie, think!* Vicki would be on her way as soon as she took meringues out of the oven.

Vicki. Meringues should be left in the oven to cool. They baked on a low heat to dry out and were supposed to stay in the closed oven with the heat off for at least two hours. Especially on a rainy day like this.

Moving as silently as possible, I kneeled by the cracked door. The intruder shone a flashlight in the silver drawer of my buffet.

Footsteps slammed through the house accompanied by hoarse, hacking breaths.

The flashlight turned off.

A single gunshot echoed.

Heavy feet staggered in my direction. It took every ounce of fortitude not to slam the door and run. I was safer if no one knew I was there.

A terrific thud resounded and shook the old house so hard I could feel the tremor under my knees.

"Vicki?" A man's voice, scared and small.

"Nooooo!"

The high-pitched scream melded with the sound of someone running into the living room.

A flashlight flickered on Vicki, who hovered over Andrew sprawled on his back.

But who held the flashlight? Wolf? I squinted to see better, but it didn't help.

"Why is it that you make a mess of everything? You couldn't just come in this house, find the poison bottle, and leave? Why am I always cleaning up after you?"

The man's voice sounded vaguely familiar, but I couldn't place him.

Somebody sniffled. Vicki?

"You're not even supposed to be here! And neither are you, Andrew," she wailed. "I didn't mean to shoot you. I thought you were Sophie or Wolf. And now you're bleeding . . ."

"You poisoned Mars?" Andrew sounded remarkably calm for someone who'd been shot. "But why?"

"You're such a dolt, Andrew," said the other man. "She was supposed to poison Natasha, but, as usual, little Vicki couldn't get the simplest thing right and she poisoned Mars instead. I thought she'd outgrown that, but it's just like when we were kids."

"That's not true," protested Vicki. "I don't mess up everything."

"Really? I suppose you thought it through before you whacked Simon over the head?" He walked to the buffet and shone the flashlight on it. The drawer complained when he jerked it open. "Thanks to you, I'm unemployed. Today is another perfect example. Instead of finding the poison container, you've shot your husband and I'm going to have to clean up after you. Again."

"You . . . you killed Simon? Why did you want to kill Natasha?" Andrew's voice had grown weaker.

Had he already lost too much blood? I wavered. If I went to his aid, they'd kill me. Where was Wolf?

I inched back, praying the floorboards wouldn't creak. Holding the cell phone under my sweater to dim the light, I pressed 911.

The operator answered too loudly. I looked up, afraid I'd given myself away, but Vicki's sobbing must have covered the operator's voice.

Whispering as loud as I dared, I said the address and "shooting."

"I can't hear you. You have to speak up."

I tried again. "Send ambulance."

"I can't hear you," she shouted.

I flipped the phone shut immediately and hoped Nina had the good sense to call the cops.

"Andrew," blubbered Vicki, "I'm so sorry. I never meant for any of this to happen."

The other man continued to jerk open drawers and cabinets. "Now I have to decide what to do with you, Andrew. Clearly you're too stupid to live. Your dear wife has been having an affair with Simon for a year."

"Is that true?" Andrew asked in a whisper.

Amid snuffles and snorts Vicki said, "Can you ever forgive me? In the beginning, Simon was so good to me and I felt like a princess. I never stopped loving you, Andrew. I just wanted . . ."

"She wanted somebody to clean up her messes and take care of her like her big brother always has." The man dropped to the floor and shone the light underneath the furniture. "Instead she married a dufus whom she had to take care of." He sneezed.

"Natasha hired that private investigator," said Vicki, "and found out that Clyde was my brother and that I was seeing Simon. She pressured me to get Simon to give her a TV show on his channel."

Clyde! Simon's driver was Vicki's brother?

"But that day at the stuffing competition"—she paused to blow her nose—"Simon asked Sophie on a date in front of the whole world and then when I went to talk to him on Natasha's behalf, he made fun of me. He . . . he said it was over and that he didn't care if people knew about our affair and it ruined my life. I would have lost everything if he exposed me. My job, you, everything. But he wouldn't have lost anything. Wouldn't even have noticed. He would have gone right on to the next woman without giving me another thought."

Vicki's voice grew cold. "He made jokes and I realized that I meant nothing to him. He thought I'd left the room, but I watched him from the door to the service corridor. The turkey trophy was on a table behind him and I clobbered him with it. All he cared about was money. He used me and threw me away like that girl on his TV show who lost her leg."

"I don't see the stupid poison vial in here anywhere," said Clyde. "Where do you think you lost it?"

The flashlight traveled around the living room. Any second the beam would land on me.

THIRTY-ONE

From *Natasha Online*:

Every house should have an area that serves as a coffee bar. Locate it away from the kitchen work triangle so that coffee drinkers can help themselves without getting underfoot. The coffeemaker, espresso machine, and coffee grinder as well as measuring spoons and filters should be grouped in this area. I always use gold filters. The coffee tastes better and they can be washed and reused for years. If you don't have a drawer or cabinet for the small items, place them in an attractive basket. And don't forget to set out porcelain coffee mugs that match your decor.

"Oh, for pity's sake. Give me that gun before you shoot me, too," said Clyde. "I've never known anyone so incompetent. What are we going to do with Andrew? Too bad he hasn't died yet. I hate to add another bullet wound. It's so unprofessional."

"No!" I screamed, flying to Andrew's side before I thought about it. "He hasn't done anything to hurt either of you. Leave him alone." I looked at Vicki, who still knelt by him. "You can both go right now. You have time to get away. Please, Vicki. Don't let Andrew die."

Andrew wore a leather jacket and I wondered if it was Mars's. I unzipped it, my hands slipping from the blood. I pulled a decorative throw off a plaid chair and felt Andrew's abdomen, trying to find the spot where the bullet entered. When I thought I had it, I pressed the throw against it in what was probably a vain attempt to prevent him from bleeding out.

I bent close. "Andrew, can you hear me?"

His hand gripped my wrist with more strength than I'd expected. I shrieked.

At that moment, a blur leapt from the shadows near the foyer.

Clyde grunted as someone attacked him from behind. The man clung to Clyde's back as he staggered through the living room. Clyde waved the gun wildly and I feared he'd shoot.

The two men slammed into the wall beside the grandfather clock. The chimes dinged softly and a fuzzy missile landed on Clyde's head like a bad toupee.

Clyde screeched and I imagined that Mochie sank his claws into Clyde's scalp to hold on. The gun skittered across the floor as Clyde sneezed and fell.

Relief flooded over me. It had to be Wolf who wrestled with Clyde.

"The gun, Vicki. Get the gun!" yelled Clyde.

She rose to her feet.

I glanced around; where had it gone?

Vicki was quicker than me. She retrieved the gun from the floor near the door to the den where I'd hidden. "Let him go or I'll shoot!" she shouted.

The person who'd attacked Clyde now sat on him with his back to me. I squinted but couldn't make out who it was. It looked like he had Clyde's arms pinned behind him.

"Shoot him, Vicki." Clyde spoke without emotion. So matter-of-fact that I was alarmed by his cold-blooded nature.

She held the gun in both hands and aimed. Behind her, the door to the den opened wide and someone slammed a frying pan over Vicki's head. She crumpled to the floor.

I lunged at the light switch on the wall and surveyed the scene.

Natasha stood in the doorway to the den, staring down at Vicki. Andrew lay on the floor, pale but alive, his eyes wide with terror.

It was Bernie who sat on Clyde's back and said, "Could I trouble you for something to tie him up with?"

I raced to the kitchen for turkey twine and returned to the living room. Bernie continued to sit on Clyde while I tied his wrists and ankles together. For added security, when Bernie rolled off Clyde, I trussed Clyde's wrists to his ankles so he couldn't stand up. Mochie sniffed Clyde's head.

Clyde sneezed again. "Ged it away," he said with a clogged nose. "I'b very allergic."

Bernie called 911 while Natasha helped me truss Vicki.

"Vicki?" called Clyde. "Vick, can you hear be?" he slurred.

Vicki groaned. I had a feeling she would be all right, since she screwed her eyes shut like she wanted this nightmare to go away.

"Huh," said Bernie, "they're already on their way."

"Nina probably called them," I said, pulling the twine tight around Vicki's ankles.

"Don't tell them anything. Don't admit to anything." Clyde wormed along the floor toward Vicki. "I'll take care of you."

Vicki's nostrils flared. "You won't be able to take care of anything when you're in jail for killing that private investigator."

"Shut up!" yelled Clyde.

"You think I'm so dumb. Well, I knew Simon's secrets. I knew he rigged the outcome of his shows. I don't know where Otis found that rope, but Simon wouldn't have paid you to kill Otis if he wasn't desperate."

"That was different. It was business. Otis knew the kind of chance he was taking when he tried to blackmail Simon."

Mochie tentatively patted Clyde's head with a paw.

Clyde sneezed again. "Simon would have been ruined."

Flashing lights strobed the windows. I ran to the front door and opened it. A stream of police officers poured into the living room, followed by Wolf.

He paused for the briefest moment, cupped my cheek with one hand, and sucked in a deep breath. "You're okay."

I followed him into the dining room, where he took in the chaos.

Natasha sagged against me, her head in her hands. "I feel so responsible. I never intended for anything like this to happen. I hired Otis. Sophie"—she lowered her voice to a whisper—"I hired him to research Simon so I could know how to pitch my TV show to him. I want to go to a national audience and Simon could have made that happen. I never thought it would lead to all this mayhem."

I shook Natasha. "Didn't you hear Vicki? Your TV show didn't have anything to do with Simon's death. Simon brought it on himself, I'm sorry to say, by being callous and treating her like dirt."

"But don't you see? If I hadn't hired Otis, he never would have dredged up the information he used against Simon."

"You didn't force Otis to blackmail Simon. Get a grip, Natasha."

She sniffled. "Otis told me about Clyde being Vicki's

brother and gave me a photograph of Clyde. I thought Vicki could help me. I thought she could get Clyde to put in a good word for me, I never imagined that anything like this would happen."

Paramedics rolled Andrew by us on a stretcher.

He reached out to me and croaked, "Vicki?"

She'd cheated on him, shot him, and murdered her lover, yet he still worried about her. "Natasha gave her a good thunk on the head, but I think she'll be fine."

I watched the paramedics carry him out the door. Nina, my family, Craig, Humphrey, the colonel, Francie, June, and Mars stood next to the sidewalk in a line. They called out when they saw me.

"Andrew's been shot!" I yelled.

June and Mars walked beside Andrew as he was rolled to the ambulance.

"Mom!" I called. "Come on in."

"They won't let us," she said. I pointed toward the kitchen door.

On my way there, Natasha said, "Shouldn't we offer all these police officers something to eat?"

Everyone piled into the kitchen, except for June, who remained with Andrew. Mars asked excitedly, "Did you use the Tasers?"

Natasha's eyes met mine. "I left my Taser at home."

"Mine is in the foyer."

Mars shook his head in disbelief. "Mom and I are going to follow the ambulance to the hospital. I'm guessing you'll have to stay here, Nat, to give the cops your story?"

She gave him a kiss and said, "Pick me up on your way home."

We spent the next half hour raiding the refrigerator and freezer. Everyone, even Francie, Nina, and Hannah, pitched in to make pizzas and panini grilled sandwiches.

We set up a buffet in the sunroom for the police officers to help themselves to coffee and food.

An hour later, only Natasha and I remained in the kitchen, baking the last of the chocolate chip cookie dough I kept in the freezer for emergencies.

"I know how Bernie entered the house, and I gather Vicki and Clyde were adept at picking locks, but how did you get in?" I asked.

Natasha didn't flinch. "I used Mars's key."

"Mars gave his keys back to me."

She shot me an incredulous look. "Like you really didn't think he'd make a copy first? You know Mars, always the prepared Boy Scout."

Since we were getting along fairly well for a change, I asked, "When you hired Otis, did you ask him to check me out?"

The surprise on her face seemed genuine. "Why would I do that? I wanted the TV show, Sophie. I thought I was doing what men would do in my position, getting the goods on the man who could make it happen. I never intended to blackmail Simon; I wanted to know more about him personally, to find some common ground that would help me get an edge with him. I already know pretty much everything about you . . ."

So why did Otis have my picture I wondered to myself.

Natasha pulled a tray of cookies from the oven. "I'm sorry I wasn't honest with you about the stalker. That night I ran into you, I realized someone was following me, but I thought it was Andrew. Actually, I thought it was exceptionally nice of you and Nina to warn me."

"Did you tell Wolf that Clyde was Vicki's brother?"

"And admit that I hired Otis? No way. My lawyer scared the pants off of me. I couldn't admit anything. Besides, I didn't know about Vicki's affair with Simon. That would have been different."

I leaned against the dishwasher. "How could we not have known that Clyde was her brother?"

Natasha raised her eyebrows. "Are you kidding? Mars and Andrew hated Simon vehemently. They said such ugly things. I'm sure she was ashamed to admit that her brother worked for Simon. And then when the affair started, well, I guess it wasn't a good idea to say anything then."

"I feel sorry for her."

"She killed Simon!"

"I know." I twisted a dish towel in my hands. "But she worked so hard while Andrew ran through their money with his ridiculous ideas. All the while she had to hide her affair and her brother's identity. She must have been miserable."

In the doorway to the kitchen, Wolf cleared his throat. "Could I have a word with Sophie?"

Natasha nodded and hurried out of the room.

"In case you haven't figured it out, Vicki was your intruder," he said.

"Then who ransacked her house?"

"She did it herself. To throw us off. And it appears that Clyde was Natasha's stalker, waiting for an opportunity to kill her since Vicki hadn't managed to do it. Natasha was the only one who could tie them together and they thought she knew about the affair."

"Then one of them planted the turkey trophy in Natasha's yard?"

"Clyde snagged it at the stuffing contest and passed it along to Vicki to bury at Natasha's party that night. He was pretty sharp." Wolf jammed his hands into his pockets. "I ought to chew you out for doing something so dangerous."

"You should have believed me and trusted me."

Mochie marked Wolf's legs by rubbing against them.

"I didn't know you. Everywhere I went I learned things that were the opposite of what you claimed."

"Like about Humphrey dating me?"

He swallowed hard. "Not true?"

I closed in on him. "Nope."

He looked over my head at the stone wall. "So this is where Faye's ghost resides?"

I grinned. "So I'm told."

He wrapped his arms around me. "I hope she doesn't mind this."

He kissed me tenderly but not nearly long enough.

When I turned around, I would have sworn Faye's eyes glittered in approval.

THIRTY-TWO

After one more lingering kiss, Wolf took off to check on
Andrew at the hospital.

I wanted some answers, though, and no matter how angry it might make Hannah, I planned to get them. I joined
the rest of my clan in the sunroom and helped myself to a
turkey panini.

"Craig," I said, "now that we know that Vicki and
Clyde were behind the killings, what were you doing over
at the Washington Room the morning after Simon was
killed?"

I expected Hannah to scold me, but she frowned and said, "Is that true? You went over there?"

"Of course not." He looked me in the eye. "You must be mistaken."

"Andrew saw you," I insisted.

Craig blinked hard. "I did it for you, Sophie, and for your family. I could see how upset everyone was and, well, sorry, Bernie, but I thought if I dropped a clue it would throw suspicion off Sophie."

"Why are you apologizing to me, then?" asked Bernie.

"I found your key card with the hotel logo on it in the den and sort of dropped it in the Washington Room for the cops to find. It was a stupid idea but I meant well."

If I hadn't pushed him, he wouldn't have admitted it. I was glad Hannah could see him for what he really was.

Instead of being angry, she leaned against him and kissed his cheek. "You did that for us?" she cooed. Give me a break. I'd thought Hannah would finally see Craig's slimy side. Craig smiled at her and it seemed adoring, but when he turned his smile toward me, it looked smug. I consoled myself by thinking the wedding wouldn't be until June. Maybe Hannah would still come to her senses and dump Craig.

"Bernie," I said, "when you came back to the house tonight, where did you hide?"

"In the foyer closet. I heard you come in through the sunroom. You couldn't have been noisier when you opened that drawer. It's a bloody good thing I wasn't the killer. I could have jumped you right then and there."

The knocker on the front door sounded, but Mars didn't wait for anyone to open it. He and June found us in the sunroom.

Everyone talked at once.

Mars held up his hands. "Andrew will be fine. He lost blood, but the bullet has been removed and he'll be okay."

The colonel rose to his feet. "I, for one, am glad it's over and we can get back to normalcy on this block." He glared at Francie. "And there will be no more Peeping Toms."

June saw the colonel to the front door and I did my best to prevent Francie from following them.

"I have to pick up Daisy from Nina's house. How about I walk you home, Francie?" I asked.

Nina brought us our coats and we deftly steered Francie out the sunroom door so we wouldn't interrupt June and the colonel.

Before the door closed, Humphrey slipped his hand into mine. "This has been the best weekend of my life."

That was a frightening thought.

"I'll see you at the stuffing contest tomorrow," he said.

What had my mother started by calling him? I was too tired to deal with him tonight. I snatched my hand back, said good night, and left with Francie and Nina.

When Daisy and I came home, the police had left and everyone had gone up to bed. Only the light in the den still shone.

I walked through the sunroom and tapped on the door to the den. Bernie's clothes were still strewn about and he hadn't pulled out the sofa bed yet.

"I wanted to thank you, Bernie. If you hadn't come back to the house tonight, things might have turned out quite differently."

"Glad to be of help. Don't give it another thought."

"So," I said, "are you moving in with Mrs. Pulchinski tomorrow?"

"Mrs. Pulchinski?" he sputtered. "Blimy! Why would I do that?"

"I thought you were dating her. I saw you with her in a restaurant."

His mouth curled up into that lopsided smile. "I was

being a nosey parker, trying to find out what I could about her husband."

I felt awful. Bernie had been trying to find the killer and I'd suspected him of being the killer.

"If you're not moving in with her, where will you go when you move out?"

"Back to the hotel."

He had saved my life. It was the least I could do to put him up a little longer. "I won't hear of it. Tomorrow we'll move you upstairs to a real bedroom. You're welcome to stay as long as you like."

And if that happened to discourage Humphrey, it would only be a bonus!

I trudged upstairs. After all we'd been through, Natasha and I would be exhausted tomorrow and not on top of our game. Daisy and Mochie jumped onto my bed and nestled together like they were old pals. I changed clothes and gratefully slipped under the comforter.

≈

Monday morning, none of her fans could have guessed that Natasha's life was anything less than perfect. She had no place to call home, had lived in terror of a stalker intent on killing her, and almost lost Mars to poison. Once again, her gleaming hair flowed to her shoulders, her makeup was flawless, and if she had bags under her eyes like I did, she'd managed to camouflage them. I made a mental note to ask her how she did that.

Even though Natasha had been up as late as I had, she'd found the time to decorate her work space with handmade snowflakes. Exactly like real snowflakes, no two were the same and many glittered as they swirled. She signed autographs, smiling and murmuring gracious thanks to her fans.

A reporter shouted, "How did you identify the killer?"

She turned her head slightly, chin up, for his camera-man.

"It was nothing any domestic diva wouldn't have figured out. Everyone knows meringues should remain in the oven after turning it off, especially on a rainy day."

A second reporter asked, "How do you feel about competing with Sophie today?"

Natasha turned in my direction. She winked at me before saying, "Oh, darlin', Sophie's little herb recipe can't begin to compare with my oyster stuffing. And I know that for sure because I've tried hers. Oysters are so much more sophisticated for today's palate. It's not even going to be a close call. You know oysters are aphrodisiacs—"

I put her fighting words out of my mind and looked over at Wendy's work space. She must have been on a bathroom break because her husband, Marvin, edged slowly inside.

I slid the incriminating photograph of the hand on my thyme bottle out of a manila envelope. Pulling the curtain aside, I caught Marvin with his hand on Wendy's thyme.

"Drop the thyme, buster," I growled.

He jumped back but recovered his composure quickly. "This . . . this is my wife's."

I flipped the photo of his hand in front of him. His pudgy face registered shock.

"Why'd you do it, Marvin?"

"That's nothing but a picture of a hand. I don't know what you're talking about."

"May I see your left hand?"

"His attempt at glibness faded and he reluctantly held up his hand. The wedding ring on his finger matched the one in the photo. "Have you seen her?" he asked.

"Wendy? Sure."

"Isn't she beautiful? So much warmer and more charming than *her*." He pointed to Natasha. "Wendy's everything to me. If she wins, our lives will change. I won't be good enough for her anymore."

"So you sabotaged her?"

"I just switched a few things around. Then I didn't want it to be so obvious that she was the only one, so I monkeyed with your ingredients, too." He seemed truly contrite when he muttered, "Sorry."

His worried eyes caught something behind me and he stiffened. I turned to see Wendy trundling toward us, her broad face without a hint of makeup, revealing freckles and hot red cheeks. Any hint of a waist had long disappeared.

I seized Marvin's hand. "You will never do this again. Promise me."

The skin under his chin wobbled when he shook his head. "Never. I promise."

Wendy joined him inside her work space. "That Natasha makes me so darned mad. She had the nerve to tell the press that my wild rice stuffing should be eliminated because I used a can of commercial soup in it. There's nothing about that in the rules. She's such a snob. Maybe she'd have been happier if I picked the mushrooms myself? What hogwash. If she keeps it up, she might just get an earful of my opinion of her slimy oysters. Why does she think she's the queen diva? How do you put up with her?"

I sensed a new Natasha rival in the making and suppressed a smile. "She just does that for the press. You'll note they're all over at her station. Look at it this way—she did you a favor because she just got you a little publicity."

"It doesn't upset you?"

I couldn't lie to her. "Sometimes." She didn't need to know how much Natasha aggravated me. Even though I felt generous toward Natasha right now, I suspected that would fade with time as Natasha got on her high horse again.

Wendy asked Marvin, "Did you protect my ingredients? Did any suspicious people stop by to tamper with them? Like Natasha, for instance?"

The color drained from his face and he looked to me.

"No one stopped by," I said. "You're very lucky to have a husband who is so crazy about you, Wendy."

She smiled and planted a kiss on his cheek. "I think I'll keep him."

I wished her luck and let the curtain drop. I could only hope that I had scared Marvin into helping Wendy instead of ruining her chances.

"Sophie?"

I turned and found Mr. Coswell, my editor, standing on the other side of my counter. He shook my hand. "I came by to offer my support to our newest star. Your advice has been a hit. My wife even quotes you."

I thanked him for his kind words. "I've been a little busy, but I plan to work on that website this week."

"Not to worry. I would have been here on Wednesday, but I was quite shaken when Otis was murdered. I'd known him for years. He met me, well, he met me at the grocery store, the same day I ran into you there. He'd just given me his report about you and when he was leaving, he was killed. But you know more about that than I do."

I blinked at him, wondering if I'd heard right. "You hired Otis Pulchinski to check me out?"

"We have to check on everyone. It was nothing personal. You wouldn't believe the false credentials people claim. He gave you a very good report."

"I guess you didn't tell the cops you hired him to find out about me?"

"Good heavens, no. The way things are these days, everything we do in personnel is confidential." He lowered his voice, "Besides, Defective Kenner never gives me any information when I need it for an article in the paper."

Defective Kenner? Was that what locals called the stiff, unfriendly guy?

Coswell grinned. "If he wanted to know why I met with Otis at the grocery store, he would have to subpoena that information. Besides, it wouldn't have helped the cops to know Otis was impressed by your devotion to your dog. He really liked that you and your husband share custody. Said he was going to leave a homeless kitten on your doorstep because he knew you'd give it a good home." He snorted. "Poor Otis. The cops said Clyde must have followed him and lured him behind the store."

The loudspeaker crackled. "Contestants, your time begins . . . *now*!"

I waved to Coswell, preheated the oven, and started chopping celery.

Aromas of thyme, sage, and bacon filled the air in the ballroom. With all the ovens going, our work spaces turned into saunas. I was thrilled when four hours had passed and we lined up for the announcement of the results.

I should have been nervous, but this moment signaled the end of all the tension I'd been under. The killer was in custody and the stuffing competition was behind me.

"And in third place, we proudly present this medal to local celebrity chef Pierre LaPlumme."

"Zut alors," he muttered as he walked up to accept his medal.

"In second place, for her Crusty Country Bread, Bacon, and Herb Stuffing, Sophie Winston."

A hoot went up from the crowd. My family and Mars's applauded. Humphrey, Bernie, and Wolf stood front and center with Nina, cheering. I looked over at Natasha. They'd managed to find a duplicate of the original turkey trophy. Somehow, I didn't think either one of us wanted it.

"And the winner of the TV special and the magazine cover is Wendy Schultz!"

Wendy glowed.

Marvin screamed.

I hoped he'd remember his promise. Wendy accepted the turkey trophy with unrestrained glee and said, "I am so flattered to have won over these distinguished cooks." She looked straight at Natasha when she said, "This proves that plain old good cooking is never too ordinary. It doesn't have be exotic to taste good and be a winner."

THIRTY-THREE

From *"Ask Natasha"*:

Dear Natasha,

Everyone on my street decorates their houses for Christmas beautifully, except for one little old lady who does nothing. She's a bit ornery and slammed her door in my face last year when I brought her a fruitcake. How can we convince her to put a wreath on her door and some lights in her windows?"

—Christmas-Crazy in Christiansburg

Dear Christmas-Crazy,

Plan a decorating block party. Ask the city if you can block your street to traffic for one day. Set up a table outside with hot cider in a crockpot and serve homemade doughnuts. Perfume the air by roasting chestnuts. When the whole block gets together to decorate your street, she won't be able to turn away the wreath you make especially for her or the lights that neighbors string on her home. She'll be thrilled to be part of the holiday festivities.

—Natasha

"Sophie! It's the worst . . . the worst possible nightmare!"

I tightened the sash on my bathrobe and ran outside to see what was upsetting Nina. Wrapped in her silk bathrobe, she stood on Francie's lawn. Francie, dressed in an enormous down bathrobe that doubled her girth, held the leash of a golden retriever. They faced the end of the block. A large truck bearing the arched logo of Alexandria Fine Antiques blocked the road in front of the Wesleys' house. The front door stood open and men carried furniture up the stairs. Natasha supervised the process.

"I can't believe it. With all the houses in this town, she had to move into that one," said Nina.

"She better not start trying to tell us what to do," growled Francie. "I'm not putting one of her tacky wreaths on my door. And I'm not planting topiary in urns, either."

I grinned at Francie. "Is that Duke?"

"Yeah, I adopted him. What with all the Peeping Toms and murders, a single woman needs a dog."

"Francie," I teased, "you were the Peeping Tom."

She looked annoyed. "Not all the time."

"Sophie!" Mom called to me from the sidewalk. Dad wedged around her and carried suitcases to their car.

I trotted over to her.

"We're ready to go, sweetie. But I have wonderful news. Hannah and Craig had such fun that they've decided to be married here. We'll check out places for the wedding when we come back for Christmas in a few weeks."

"I thought we were going to your house for Christmas."

"That's all changed now. Oh, and June has promised to stay with us, too. It'll be a big reunion."

Oh, swell.

I walked Mom to the car and hugged my parents and Hannah. As much as I loved them, it would be good to get back to normal, even for a few weeks. I skipped the hug for Craig, though, stepped back, and waved to them.

As they drove away, Mom stuck her head and arm out of the window and shouted to me, "And I want to see the invitations and menu this time. Natasha's serving goose!"

RECIPES &
COOKING TIPS

First Murder Bourbon Pecan Pie

3 tablespoons butter
½ teaspoon instant coffee (Sophie uses Sanka.)
1 tablespoon unsweetened cocoa powder
3 tablespoons bourbon (Airline-size bottle holds
    about 4 tablespoons.)
2 eggs
½ cup dark brown sugar
¾ cup dark corn syrup
½ teaspoon salt
1 teaspoon vanilla
2 cups roughly chopped pecans
1 unbaked 9-inch pie shell

Preheat the oven to 300 degrees. Microwave the butter in a cup for about 30 seconds and set aside to cool. In another cup, stir together the instant coffee, cocoa powder, and bourbon until the coffee crystals and cocoa powder are dissolved.

In a mixer, beat the 2 eggs. Add the brown sugar and the cooled butter and beat. Add the corn syrup, the salt, and the vanilla. Beat to combine all the ingredients. Mix in the pecans. Pour into the pie shell and bake 55 to 60 minutes.

SERVE WITH WHIPPED CREAM:

Pour 1 pint whipping cream into mixer and beat until it begins to take shape. Add 3 to 4 tablespoons powdered sugar and ½ teaspoon vanilla. Beat until soft peaks form. Don't overbeat!

SOPHIE'S HINT:

If your piecrust doesn't have a beautiful crust around the edge, pipe part of the whipped cream on the edge to cover it!

Brining Basics

Brine your turkey in a large roasting pot, clean bucket, or food-safe plastic container large enough for the bird to be covered with water.

About 32 hours before cooking the turkey, remove the giblets and place the bird in the container. Cover with salted water made of ¾ cup of kosher salt per gallon. Add ¼ cup sugar to the brine.

Place the container in the refrigerator for 8 hours. (The turkey must be kept refrigerated during the brining process.)

Remove the turkey and discard the water. Rinse the turkey and place on a roasting rack *uncovered* in your refrigerator for about 24 hours before cooking.

NOTE:

Do not brine a kosher turkey or one that has been injected with any solution or is labeled self-basting.

Crusty Country Bread, Bacon, and Herb Stuffing

> *1 pound crusty country-style bread*
> *1 pound bacon (Sophie prefers bacon without added preservatives.)*
> *½ stick of butter (4 tablespoons)*
> *3 chopped onions*
> *3 stalks of celery, chopped*
> *1 apple, peeled and chopped*
> *1½ tablespoons dried sage*
> *1 tablespoon dried thyme*
> *½ tablespoon dried rosemary*
> *2 cups chicken broth*
> *salt*
> *pepper*

Slice the bread and toast in the oven at 325 degrees until dry. Chop into 1-inch chunks. Cook the bacon in a large pan until crisp. Remove the bacon and pour out all but a couple of tablespoons of bacon fat. Add the ½ stick of butter to the pan along with the onions, celery, apple, and herbs. Cook until soft. Remove from heat and mix with bread chunks, crumbled bacon, and chicken broth. Salt and pepper to taste.

At this point, the stuffing can be spooned into a baking dish and stored, covered, for up to 24 hours. Be sure you use a refrigerator-to-oven-safe baking dish.

Bake for one hour at 325 degrees and serve.

Chesapeake Cornbread Stuffing

CHESAPEAKE CORNBREAD
> 2 eggs
> 2 tablespoons Chesapeake Bay Spice
> ¼ cup sugar
> 1 cup self-rising yellow cornmeal
> ½ cup self-rising flour
> 2 tablespoons olive oil
> ¾ cup buttermilk

Preheat the oven to 350 degrees. Butter a 9-by-9-inch pan well.

In a large mixing bowl, lightly whisk the eggs. Add the Chesapeake Bay Spice and the sugar and whisk again to mix thoroughly. Add the rest of the ingredients and whisk lightly or stir until well mixed. Pour into greased pan and bake for 20 to 25 minutes.

CHESAPEAKE CORNBREAD STUFFING
> ½ stick butter (4 tablespoons)
> 2 cups chopped onions
> 1 cup finely chopped celery
> 3 tablespoons sage
> 1 tablespoon thyme
> 1 Granny Smith apple, cut into small pieces
> ½ cup pecans (Best if toasted but that's optional.)
> 2 tablespoons Chesapeake Bay Spice
> 1 9-by-9 pan of Chesapeake Cornbread
> 4 slices of toasted white bread (Emma uses Pepperidge Farm Hearty White.)
> 2 cups chicken broth (Use vegetable broth for vegetarian version.)

Melt the butter in a large skillet. Add onion, celery, sage, and thyme and cook until the onion and celery begin to soften, stirring occasionally. Add Granny Smith apple. When the onion, celery, and apple are soft, add the toasted pecans and Chesapeake Bay Spice, mixing thoroughly. Remove from heat.

Crumble the Chesapeake Cornbread into a very large bowl. Cut or crumble the toasted white bread and add to the bowl. Mix in the contents of the skillet. Add two cups of chicken broth and mix so that all the contents are coated and slightly moist. (For a fun variation, add cooked crab meat or chopped cooked shrimp.)

Pour into a casserole dish or a loaf pan. (If you're cooking a day ahead of time, at this point it can be covered and refrigerated overnight. Be sure to use bakeware that can go from the refrigerator to the oven if you do this!) Bake at 350 degrees for about an hour.

Cranberry Mushroom Wild Rice Stuffing

> *1 4-ounce box all-natural wild rice*
> *2 cups chicken broth (Use vegetable broth for*
> *vegetarian version.)*
> *1 teaspoon sage*
> *1 tablespoon butter*
> *2 tablespoons olive oil*
> *1 carrot*
> *1 cup diced onions*
> *1 cup minced celery*
> *1½ tablespoons sage*
> *1 tablespoon thyme*
> *1 16-oz package white mushrooms (Washed,*
> *stems discarded.)*

½ stick (4 tablespoons) unsalted butter
2 cloves garlic, minced
1 can condensed cream of mushroom soup
1 bag Craisins

Cook the wild rice according to the directions on the box but substitute chicken broth for the amount of water in the instructions on the box and add the teaspoon of sage and tablespoon of butter.

If using a low-salt broth, you may need to add a small amount of salt to the broth when it's cooking. The wild rice will take approximately 1 hour to cook. Taste to be sure it is soft. When done, take off the heat, pour into a sieve, and set the rice aside. Discard the cooked liquid that remains.

Heat 2 tablespoons of olive oil in a large skillet over medium heat. After peeling the carrot, use the peeler to make thin slices, then chop until it looks like confetti. Add the onions, celery, carrot, sage, and thyme to the olive oil and cook, stirring occasionally, until the onions and celery are soft. Meanwhile, dice the mushroom caps. Add the butter, mushrooms, and garlic to the skillet. Mix thoroughly and cook until the mushrooms are tender. Add 1 can of condensed cream of mushroom soup. Mix thoroughly. Remove from heat and mix in the Craisins. Spoon into a casserole or loaf pan.

(If you are cooking ahead, at this point, you can cover the stuffing and refrigerate until the next day. But be sure to use a baking dish that can go from the refrigerator to the oven.)

Bake in a casserole or loaf pan at 350 degrees for about an hour.